Sir Alexander Cunningham

Report of a tour in Bihar and Bengal in 1879-80

From Patna to Sunargaon

Sir Alexander Cunningham

Report of a tour in Bihar and Bengal in 1879-80
From Patna to Sunargaon

ISBN/EAN: 9783742840141

Manufactured in Europe, USA, Canada, Australia, Japa

Cover: Foto ©Andreas Hilbeck / pixelio.de

Manufactured and distributed by brebook publishing software
(www.brebook.com)

Sir Alexander Cunningham

Report of a tour in Bihar and Bengal in 1879-80

𝕬𝖗𝖈𝖍𝖆𝖔𝖑𝖔𝖌𝖎𝖈𝖆𝖑 𝕾𝖚𝖗𝖇𝖊𝖞 𝖔𝖋 𝕴𝖓𝖉𝖎𝖆.

REPORT

OF

A TOUR IN BIHAR AND BENGAL

IN

1879-80

FROM PATNA TO SUNARGAON.

BY

ALEXANDER CUNNINGHAM, C.S.I., C.I E.,

MAJOR-GENERAL, ROYAL ENGINEERS [BENGAL RETIRED],
DIRECTOR-GENERAL OF THE ARCHÆOLOGICAL SURVEY OF INDIA.

VOLUME XV.

"What is aimed at is an accurate description, illustrated by plans, measurements, drawings, or photographs, and by copies of inscriptions, of such remains as most deserve notice, with the history of them so far as it may be traceable, and a record of the traditions that are preserved regarding them."—LORD CANNING.

"What the learned world demand of us in India is to be quite certain of our data, to place the monumental record before them exactly as it now exists, and to interpret it faithfully and literally."—JAMES PRINSEP.

CALCUTTA:

OFFICE OF THE SUPERINTENDENT OF GOVERNMENT PRINTING.
1882.

CALCUTTA :

PRINTED BY THE SUPERINTENDENT OF GOVERNMENT PRINTING,

166, DHURRUMTOLLAH STREET.

PREFACE.

THE present volume gives the results of a Tour which I made in the cold season of 1879-80 in Bihár and Northern Bengal. I first visited Mahábodhi, or Buddha Gaya, where I had the good fortune to pick up two dated inscriptions, one of which is of considerable importance in fixing the date of the accession of Dharma Pála, the second Prince of the Pála dynasty of Bengal. I had already placed the date of his accession in A.D. 830,[1] but the present inscription affords the means of fixing it absolutely to the following year 831 A.D. The inscription is thus recorded : *S. 26*—"*Bhádrapada badi 5 Saturday.*" The mention of the week day shows that the 26th of Dharma Pála must have fallen in A.D. 856, and his first year in A.D. 831, and not in 830. I am the more particular in mentioning the above fact, as Babu Rajendra Lál has asserted publicly that his discovery of the Lakhshmana Sena era of Bengal has *upset* my date of the Pála kings of Bengal.[2] But, in addition to the above proof of the accuracy of my chronology, I can now refer to a second inscription of Madana Pála Deva, which is dated in "*S. 9 (Navame) Aswina badi 11 Friday,*" or A.D. 1144; so that the first year of his reign was A.D. 1136, or only one year later than the date previously given by me.

The two colossal statues of Yakshas, which are given in Plate II, are of considerable interest on account of their

---

See Archæological Survey, Vol. I, p. 181; and for a translation of the inscription, see Bengal Asiatic Society's Proceedings for November 1880, p. 80.
[2] Proceedings of Bengal Asiatic Society for April 1878.

antiquity, as they are certainly not later than the beginning of the Christian era.

The rock sculptures of Jâhngira and the rock-cut temple of Kahalgaon are also very interesting, the latter more especially on account of its peculiar style, which differs widely in style from the highly decorated shrines of the mediæval period.

Some interesting discoveries of an early date were made at Dharâwat, to the north of the Barâbar hills. Taking these discoveries in conjunction with the name of the *Kunwa* hill in which they were made, I think there can be no doubt that the Dharâwat ruins are the remains of the monastery of *Gunamati*, which Hwen Thsang visited on his way from Pâtaliputra to Gaya. This identification is rendered absolutely certain by the very exact correspondence of the Barâbar Hill, and the Kauwa Dol Peak, with the lofty mountains from whence Buddha viewed Magadha, and the Silâbhadra monastery above which towered a lofty peak shaped like a stûpa.

I have given a long and detailed account of the Muhammadan buildings at Gaur and Hazrat Pandua, the two western capitals of Bengal. The Plans of all the Tombs and Masjids will form a useful addition to Ravenshaw's illustrated work on Gaur. His Photographs give striking and well-chosen views of all the principal buildings, but they require the assistance of Plans to show their extent and general disposition. I have also given several new inscriptions, including one of Jalâluddin Masâud Jâni, one of the early Governors of Bengal. The Sketches of carved bricks in Plates XVII and XXVI will give a very good idea of the style of ornamentation used in all the great public buildings of Bengal during the Muhammadan period. I believe, however, that, as we now see it, the effect of this style must be somewhat different from what it was in its original state. The whole surface is now of one uniform colour of red brick; but from the fragments of glazed tiles which I have picked up at the foot of the walls of several buildings, I conclude that most of the ornaments of the principal Tombs and Masjids were relieved by backgrounds of glazed tiles of various colours, but chiefly of azure blue.

Much ingenuity also was displayed in the arrangement and shapes of the letters of the inscriptions. This will be seen at once by comparing the elegant record of Sikandar's reign, which was prepared by *Zarin-dast*, or the " golden-handed " writer (Plate XXVIII) with the formal arrangement of the club-headed letters of Masáud Jáni's time (Plate XXI), the barb-headed letters of Yusuf Sháh's time, and the railing-like letters of Bárbak Sháh's time.

One of my objects in visiting Northern Bengal was to seek for the site of the ancient capital called Paundra Varddhana by Hwen Thsang. Of the name I could find no trace, but I was fortunate enough to discover the site of the ancient city in Mahásthán on the Karatoya River. The proof of the identification rests partly on the agreement of the distance and bearing from the neighbourhood of Rájmahal, and partly on the immediate vicinity of Bhásu Bihár, which corresponds exactly with Hwen Thsang's account of the Buddhist monas-tery of *Po-shi-po* (i.e., *Bhásu* or *Bhaswa*), 4 miles to the west of the capital.

Eastern Bengal is most remarkable for the great changes which have taken place in the courses of its principal rivers, the Ganges and the Brahmaputra. In former days the whole district of Bikrampur was to the south of the Ganges, which, under the name of Kirttinása, or the "fame destroyer," now flows far to the south in an entirely new channel. Before this change the two great cities of Dhakka and Sunárgaon were close to the Ganges. The former is still a large city, owing to its being the head-quarters of the civil administra-tion of the province; but its commercial importance is fast giving way before the rising prosperity of the neighbouring town of Náráyanganj, on the Lakhia River. Sunárgaon, which was formerly the capital of Eastern Bengal, is now a mere village hidden in the midst of a dense jungul, and only accessible from a small creek, which was once the bed of the Megna River. Such buildings as still remain are described in this report.

A. CUNNINGHAM.

CONTENTS.

PLATES.

ARCHÆOLOGICAL SURVEY OF INDIA.

REPORT OF A TOUR IN BIHAR AND BENGAL IN 1879-80, FROM PATNA TO SUNARGAON.

I.—PATNA.

IN a former report I gave a long account of the existing remains at Panch Pahâri on the south side of the city of Patna, all of which are Buddhist. I can now add the dis-covery of two colossal Buddhist statues in the grounds of the Asiatic Society's Museum at Calcutta, where they had been hidden amongst the foliage for the last forty years. Three statues were discovered by Dr. Tytler outside the city of Patna, of which two only were sent to Calcutta by the Doctor's brother. When I saw the two statues in the new Indian Museum in Calcutta, I then remembered that a broken statue of a similar kind was still standing at Agam Kûa, just outside the city of Patna, adorned with a new head and a pair of roughly marked breasts, so as to do duty for the great goddess *Mâta-Mâi*. As I luckily had a rough sketch of this figure in my note-book, I was able to compare it on the spot with the two tall figures in the museum, and this comparison at once showed that the broken figure at Agam Kûa corresponded in attitude, in the position of hands and in every particular of dress, with the two colossi which had been sent from Patna by Dr. Tytler's brother. The Agam Kûa is a very large and very old brick well, just outside the city of Patna, and to the north of the Buddhist ruins of Panch Pahâri. The broken figure is said to have been found in this well, and it seems probable therefore that the two statues were also found either at or near the same place.

The two figures in Calcutta are made of grey sandstone, which has been highly polished like all the edict pillars and statues of the time of Asoka. One of them has lost its head, and both are mutilated in the arms; but from a comparison of the two I think that every part of their dress, as well as their action, can be made out with certainty. Each figure is standing straight to the front, clad in long robes from neck to foot, the full height of the statue being 6 feet 2 inches. The robe is without sleeves, and the bare arm of one figure still retains its original glossy polish. The sculptor has here shown his close observation of the human form by his skilful delineation of all the dimpled depressions of the bent elbow. The one remaining face is weather-worn, three of the arms are gone, and both bodies are covered with drapery; but the easy attitude and the calm and dignified repose of the figures are still conspicuous, and claim for them a high place amongst the best specimens of early Indian art.

The robe appears to be only a loose sort of dressing-gown without sleeves, fastened round the waist by a broad belt or girdle tied in a bow, with a long loop and two tasseled ends hanging down in front. It was apparently tied round the neck by a cord, with its ends hanging down behind. At the back the robe reaches the ground, but it is slightly raised in front to show the bare feet. The right hand carried a *chauri*, and the left hand rests on the girdle. The arm is ornamented with an armlet of a fleur-de-lis pattern, such as is worn by the figures in the Bharhut sculptures. A broad scarf crosses the left shoulder to the right hip, hanging down in a loop in front of the breasts, and in a long train behind. The folds of the scarf are marked by deep parallel lines, between which, at the back of the shoulder of each figure, there is a short inscription. At first I thought that the statues might be of the age of Asoka; but the forms of the letters show that they must be of later date, somewhere about the beginning of the Christian era.

The *chauris* carried in the hands of these statues show that they were only attendant figures; but the inscriptions further tell us that they were both *Yakshas*. Their names

have not yet been read satisfactorily, as some of the letters
are doubtful owing to the deeply cut parallel folds of the
scarves on which they are engraved. Both inscriptions are
given in the accompanying plate; that of the headless
statue marked A may be read as *Yakhe Sanatananda*, or
perhaps *Bharata*. The other marked B may be read as
Yakhe Achusatigika, or perhaps *Sanigika*. The parallel lines
of the scarf, like the lines of music, render the reading of
several letters very doubtful, as they interfere with both head-
strokes and foot-strokes, so that *t* and *v* and the attached
vowels *a* and *e* cannot always be distinguished. In the word
Yakhe the vowel *e* is fortunately placed in a sloping direction
upwards. On the third statue, at Agam Kūa, outside Patna,
the scarf at the back has peeled off, and the inscription is
therefore lost. All these figures were complete statues cut
in the round.[1]

The only other remains that require notice are the stone
seats or stools which are found at all ancient Buddhist sites.
There are a considerable number of these scattered about
Panch Pahári, and in a field to the west of the village there is
a small pile of them. They are here worshipped as *Goreya*,
or spirits—a name derived from the Persian *goristán*, or burial-
ground. I have selected a few specimens in the accompanying plate to show the shape and style of these curious articles.
From their numbers I am inclined to think that they must have
been the seats of the monks. They are eminently Buddhist-
ical, as they are found only at Buddhist sites, and are ornamented with Buddhist symbols. They vary from 5 to 6½ inches
in height and breadth, and from 12 to 16 inches in length.
All the Patna specimens are flat-topped; but many others
that I have seen are slightly hollowed on the top, as if to
make the seat easier. But wherever they are found, from
Taxila to Palibothra, they are of the same general pattern,
and are ornamented with the same symbols.

---

[1] See Plate II for sketches of these two statues made by my Assistant,
Mr. H. B. W. Garrick. The statues themselves were first brought to notice by
Mr. J. D. Beglar, who recognized their importance.

2.—KURKIHÂR.

I first visited Kurkihâr in the end of 1861, and my account of the ruins will be found in the first volume of my
Reports[1]. I then identified the site with the *Kukuta-pâda-
giri,* or "Hill of the Cock's Foot," which is described by the
two Chinese pilgrims FaHian and HwenThsang. I was then
informed that the true name of *Kurkihâr* was *Kurak-Vihâr,*
which I took to be only a contracted form of *Kukkuta-pâda
Vihâra,* as the Sanskrit *kukkuta* is now represented by the
Hindi forms *kukkar* and *kurak.* Mr. Beal has accused me
of confounding the "*Vihâr* of the Cock's Foot," which was
just outside the city of Pâtaliputra, or Patna, with the "*Hill*
of the Cock's Foot," which, according to Hwen Thsang, was
16 miles to the east of Gyaa[2]. But it is Mr. Beal himself who
has made a mistake, as I particularly mention in my report
(Vol. I, page 16) that "there was a monastery also of the
same name (Kukkuta-pâda Vihâra), but this was *close to*
Pâtaliputra, or Patna." The name of *Kurkihâr* I took to be
only a shortened form of *Kurak Vihâr,* which must certainly
have referred to a monastery. In fact no Buddhist establishment could have existed without a monastery, and I presume
that the monastery of Kurkihâr was known as the *Kukkuta-
pâda-giri Vihâra,* or "Vihâr of the Cock's Foot Hill," while
the monastery at Pâtaliputra was simply the "Kukkuta-pâda
Vihâra, or Vihâr of the Cock's Foot."

I paid a second visit to Kurkihâr in the end of 1879,
chiefly with the object of exploring the *hill* to the north of
the town, as it was the scene of some of Mahâ-kâsyapa's
miracles, and eventually of his nirvâna, or death.

FaHian's account is as follows[3] :—"The great *Chia-yeh*
(Kâsyapa) is at present in this mountain. He split the moun-

---

[1] Archæological Survey of India, Vol. I, pp. 14-16.

[2] Beal's Fahian, C. XXXIII, p. 132, note. FaHian himself has made a mistake in placing the Cock's Foot Hill at only 3 *li*, or half a mile, to the south of Pâtaliputra. Mr. Beal would correct this to 3 *yojanas,* or 21 miles. But as the actual
distance is over 50 miles, I would suggest 300 *li*, or 50 miles, as the true reading.

[3] Translation of Fahian's Travels by Herbert A. Giles, p. 83.

tain to get in. The place where he entered will barely admit
a man. Going down to a great distance there is a niche in
which stands a full length image of Chia-yeh. Outside the
niche is the place where he used to wash his hands, and the
people of the district, if they have the headache, use the earth
(from that spot) for plasters, and are at once cured. Therefore, since that time there have been Lo-hans on this mountain, and when the devotees of the neighbouring countries
come yearly to make their offerings to Chia-yeh, the Lo-hans
appear by night to the steadfast ones, converse with them, and
resolve their doubts; they then suddenly vanish. On this
mountain there are quantities of trees; also a great many lions,
tigers, and wolves; so that travellers have to be cautious."

Hwen Thsang describes the hill as lofty and scarped,
with three bold peaks that spring into the air[1]. These peaks
I have already identified with the three peaks of the *Murali*
mountain, which stands 3 miles to the north-north-east of
the town of Kurkihár. According to the pilgrim, "twenty
years after he had received Buddha's instructions, Kâsyapa
ascended the Kukkuta-pâda mountain on the north side, and
walked along towards the south-west, where he was stopped
by a scarped face. He struck the rock with his staff, and
cleft it in two, and then marched boldly into the heart of the
mountain. On reaching the middle peak, he took up Buddha's
Chivara (dress). The three peaks approached and retired
(or closed and opened) according to his mere wish. When
Maitreya visited this mountain, Kâsyapa presented him with
the Chivara of Buddha, and after performing some miracles,
entered into nirvâna."

On the top of the mountain there was a stûpa. This is
most probably represented by a square basement which still
exists on the highest or middle peak of the Murali hill,
surrounded by quantities of broken bricks. Numbers of
bricks are also lying on the slope, and at the foot of the hill
to the north. There is only one small figure on the top of
the hill, 1 foot 11 inches in height, of a female, either Mâyâ

---

[1] Julien's Hwen Thsang, Vol. III, p. 1.

Devi or Dharma. There are also two small granite pillars. But the space is very confined, being not more than 50 paces across. The bricks are of two sizes: 17 by 10 by 3 inches, and 12 by 10 by 3 inches.

The monastery of the "Cock's Foot Hill" is now represented by a high mound, about 120 feet square, to the north of the village. This mound is called Sugatghar, or "Buddha's house," Sugat being one of the well-known titles of Buddha. But the most extensive remains lie to the south of the village, where they form a mass about 600 feet square. Here numerous Buddhist statues and other remains were dug up by Major Kittoe and myself, and at a later date by Mr. Broadley. Several of these I have described in my former Report (Vol. I, page 15). But numbers of figures still remain to attest the former importance of the Buddhist establishment of *Kukkuta-páda-giri.* I have a record in my note-book of 37 figures, now collected together at and near the temple of Bágheswari. I found also ten inscriptions of about A.D. 800 to 1000, of which one was set up by two Sakya mendicants from *Kánchi* (Kánchi-vasika) or Conjeveram.

Kurkihár is 6 miles to the north-east of Punáwa, 3 miles to the north-east of Wazirgang, and 16 miles to the east of Gaya.

3.—PARBATI.

On leaving *Indrasila guha,* or "Indra's cave," which I have already identified with Giryek, Hwen Thsang says that he travelled for 150 or 160 *li* to the north-east to the Kapotika *Sangháráma,* or "Pigeon Monastery," close to which on the south there was a steep isolated hill covered with holy buildings. Now there is clearly some error in the distance, as a journey of from 25 to 27 miles would have taken the pilgrim into the old bed of the Ganges, now called the Halohar River, and at least 12 miles away from the nearest hills of Shekhpura. I proposed, therefore, to read 50 to 60 *li,* a distance which would suit exactly either for the hill of Bihár or for that of Párbati; but as the former is almost due north, while the latter is as nearly as possible north-east

of Giryek, I am now satisfied that Pàrbati was the place
actually visited by the pilgrim. The name does not belong to
the hill, but to the village, and as it is pronounced Pàrbati, I
think it must be a slight alteration only of the original name of
Párâvata, a "Pigeon." But as the place is also called *Ghar
Párávat*, or the "Pigeon's House," I think there can be no
doubt whatever that it is the "Pigeon Monastery" of Hwen
Thsang.

I think also that it may be identified with the small rocky
isolated hill of the earlier pilgrim Fa Hian. It appears to
me almost certain that the pilgrim has jumbled two places
together, and has described the little isolated hill and the
hill of Indra's cave as if they were only one hill. The distance of each from Patna is about the same, and as the
temple of Avalokiteswara, on a hill close to the Pigeon
Monastery, was a very famous one, the pilgrim would no
doubt have visited it on his way to Indra's cave.

The village of Pàrbati is just 10 miles to the north-east
of Giryek, and 11 miles to the south-east of Bihàr. The foot
of the hill is washed by the Sakri River on the west. On three
sides it rises precipitously, but in the middle of the north
side it shelves down towards the village by gentle stages.
It is a small rocky hill as described by Fa Hian, being only
1,750 feet in length from east to west by 1,000 feet in breadth.
But the whole surface is literally covered with ruins, the
remains of the "multitude of vihàras and temples" seen by
Hwen Thsang. In another place he describes the hill as
isolated and precipitous, with its surface laid out in terraces,
and covered with a great number of holy temples. Now this
is a very exact description of the hill even at the present day,
as the level terraces still remain quite distinct. Its position
to the south of the village also agrees exactly with Hwen
Thsang's description, whereas the Bihàr Hill, which Mr.
Broadley identifies with the Pigeon Monastery Hill, is due
west from the town of Bihàr.

The principal remains on the hill are marked in the accompanying map with the letters A. to H. Most of them
have been noticed by Mr. Beglar, to whose account of earlier

explorations I will hereafter refer. From all that I could learn on the spot, it would appear that the ruined buildings on the hill were used as a quarry by the local road officers to furnish materials for the road which has only been partly made between Gaya and Lakhi-Sarai. The mound on the plain below, to the west of the village, has always been used as a quarry by the villagers, and it was being excavated for bricks at the time of my visit. This mound, marked G in the map, I take to be the ruins of the " Pigeon Monastery," which gave its name to the village. It is upwards of 400 feet square, and from 10 to 12 feet in height. On the east side an excavation was being made to furnish bricks for two new houses. I examined all that had just been exhumed, amongst which I found several wedge-shaped bricks, which could only have belonged to a stûpa of some size. As the spot where these were dug up is on the east side of the mound, their discovery offers another proof of the correctness of the identification of Pârbati with the site of the Pigeon Monastery, as Hwen Thsang places the stûpa to the east of the monastery. The story of the fowler and his starving family, for whose benefit Buddha changed himself into a pigeon, is told by Hwen Thsang. When the man went to return thanks to Buddha for the opportune relief, he was duly converted, and repenting of his faults became a new man and eventually obtained the dignity of *Arhat*. The stûpa was built by Asoka in commemoration of the event [1].

Exactly on the middle of the hill to the south stood the famous temple of Avalokiteswara with an image of the Bodhisatwa in sandal-wood. He bore a lotus in his hand, and over his head was a figure of Buddha. The pilgrim tells a wonderful story of a king of Ceylon, who, when bathing in the sea, saw as if in a mirror not a reflection of his own body, but the statue of Avalokiteswara standing on the top of a small hill surrounded with palm trees in the kingdom of Magadha. Accordingly he proceeded to seek for the statue, and after he had paid his devotions to the statue on the hill of the Pigeon Monastery, he built a vihâra on the spot.

[1] Julien's Hwen Thsang, Vol. III, p. 62.

Other kings afterwards followed his example, until the whole hill was covered with temples.[1] A glance at the map will show that the position marked A, which is in the very centre of the hill, must be the site of this temple. That this was the holiest spot on the hill is proved by the fact that it is now occupied by the dargâh of Hâji Chandar or Chând Saudâgar, the Musalmân cuckoo having as usual occupied the Hindu nest. The dargâh stands on a small eminence in the midst of a level terrace and is built of Hindu materials. Here Mr. Beglar traced rows of cells as of a monastery, which are traditionally said to be the remains of the palace of Bâwan Suba.[2] As the legend of Bâwan Suba has been given by Mr. Beglar, I need not repeat it here.

On the highest part of the hill, 500 feet to the south-west of A, there are the ruins of a brick building which now form a high peak marked B. This was excavated by one of the road officers, who found nothing but ashes. As it stands now it is only a confused mass of broken bricks.

One hundred and fifty feet to the west of B there is another conical-looking peak marked C. This was excavated by Mr. Beglar, who found it to be the remains of a stûpa from 15 to 18 feet in diameter. It had been previously dug into by one of the people of the place, who found in it " some coral beads and a few coins." On examining the outside I found that it had been coated with plaster 9 inches in thickness.

On another high mound marked D, 300 feet to the south of A, I made a complete exploration of the upper part, where I found the basement of a building 18½ feet square outside, with walls 2½ feet thick, made of bricks set in lime mortar. On this basement I found the stumps of 16 granite pillars, which I think may have formed the verandah of the court-yard of some square building. The walls are too thin for those of a temple; but it is quite possible that pillars may have formed a verandah round a small temple 10 or 12 feet square. But whatever the building may have been, it was very

---

[1] Julien's Hwen Thsang, Vol. III, p. 62.
[2] Archæological Survey of India, Vol. VIII. p. 109.

highly ornamented with flowered and beaded mouldings in
stucco. Here I found a portion of a lac seal, showing the
upper part of a tall temple, with streamers hanging from the
pinnacle.[1]   Several fragments of terra-cotta were also found,
of which one bears three small stûpas on its border. But the
most valuable discovery was a rude shapeless piece of hard
unbaked clay bearing four impressions of a monastic seal.
Apparently the impressions were merely trials on a lump of
moist clay, as all the unbaked clay seals that I have hitherto found have been of regular shape. The inscription on the
seals is on two lines of well-shaped letters of the Gupta period, surmounted by five horizontal lines, rising in a pyramidal
form.   It is just possible that they may represent the step-like
terraces of the hill rising one above the other. The inscription has not yet been read satisfactorily, owing to its bad
state of preservation. The word *sanghasa* at the end is, however, quite distinct, so that there can be no doubt that the
seal belonged to one of the Buddhist *sanghas* of Pârbati.
To my eye the letters appear to be[2]

Rodaksha Sanghasa.

Two hundred feet to the south of C, near the edge of the
cliffs, there is a cave marked E, 18 feet long, 8 feet broad, and
6 feet high.   There is no cutting; but I suspect that a small
natural opening may have been enlarged by the removal of
several stones.

On the eastern slope of the hill, just 500 feet to the east of
the dargâh, there is a rocky ridge marked F, on which is set
up a four-armed statue called Mahâ Mai.

4.—APHSAR.

From the Pigeon Monastery Hwen Thsang travelled
40 *li* to the south-east to a monastery containing about 50
monks, near which there was a great stûpa, built on the site
where Buddha had preached for seven days in favour of the

---

[1] See Plate ☷ fig. 4.

[2] See Plate ☷ figs. 1 and 2, for the two sides of this piece of clay with the
seal impressions.

god Brahmá.[1] In the position indicated there are no remains.
of any kind.   It seems probable therefore that we should read
4 *li* instead of 40, which would take us to the high conica-
mound of Aphsar, where there are both Buddhist and Brahmanical remains. Mr. Beglar notes that there are only a
" very few Buddhist statues;" but Mr. Broadley had been there
before, and had *recovered* five figures—a euphemism for *removed*. There is a very fine statue of a boar, with the Rishis
nestling in his bristles, and I have no doubt that Aphsar was
an important Brahmanical site, and only an unimportant Buddhist settlement, as might indeed be inferred from Hwen
Thsang's omission to mention its name.

It was at Aphsar that Kittoe discovered a very important
and almost perfect inscription of the later Gupta dynasty.
The stone itself has been lost, but a translation of the record
was published by Babu Rajendra Lála from a Deva-nágari
transcript which Kittoe had kindly sent to me many years before. Since then Mr. Beglar has discovered in the box of
inscriptions in the Asiatic Society's Library a very fine impression of the inscription made by Kittoe himself, from which
I am able to make an important correction in Kittoe's reading of the name of *Hashka* Gupta, which is clearly and un-
mistakeably *Harsha* Gupta.

5.—SHAHPUR.

Three miles to the north-east of Párbati there is a small
village named Sháhpur. It is situated on a mound, and possesses several pieces of sculpture in basalt, which are collected together under a tree. One of these is a four-armed
Vishnu, holding the *Chakra*, or discus. Another is a standing female, holding out a child in her right hand, and having
a staff in front marked with the *trisul* of Siva. A third is a
standing figure of the Sun, 2 feet 10 inches in height, holding
a lotus in each of his two hands. On each side is a small
standing figure, that on the right being armed with a club.
On the pedestal there is a very important dated inscription of

---

[1] Julien's Hwen Thsang, Vol. III, p. 64.

Aditya Sena Deva, one of the early kings of Magadha, who preceded the Pâla dynasty. The record is in four lines, of which the upper one is engraved on the lotus leaves of the pedestal. Some parts are unfortunately indistinct ; but the greater part is legible, and I hope soon to see a translation of it by Babu Rajendra Lâla, in whose hands I have placed it. In the meantime I may give the opening part of the record according to my own reading :—

Aum-Samvat 55 Mârgge Sudi 1 ; asyin—
Divasa Mâsa Samvatsarânda purvvayam
Sri Aditya Sena Deva râjye (vala) Sri Mahâgrahâra
Sâdhu, valâdhikrita Saladakshena Dedharmayam, &c.

"In the year 55, on the 1st of Mârgga Sudi, on that said day month and year, during the reign of Aditya Sevna Deva, this statue was presented to the great Agrahâra by Parikshita (?) for the benefit of his father and mother, and the increase of his own merit."

The date is puzzling. It can scarcely be the regnal year of Aditya Sena ; and I can only conjecture that as Magadha was certainly tributary to Kanauj during the time of Harsha Vardhana, it is possible that the year may be reckoned from the establishment of the Harsha Kâl in A.D. 607. The date would thus be $606 + 55 = 661$ A.D.

Pandit Bhagwân Lâl Indraji, however, reads the date as S. 88 of the same era. But I confess that I prefer my own reading of 55, as I look upon the figures as two Bengali fives, which indeed one might expect to find in Magadha on the confines of Bengal.

6.—SHEKHPURA.

From the great stûpa to the south-east of the Pigeon Monastery, Hwen Thsang proceeded to the north-east for 70 *li*, or nearly 12 miles, when he arrived at a large and populous village to the south of the Ganges, which possessed many Brahmanical temples ornamented with fine sculptures[1].

[1] Julien's Hwen Thsang, Vol. III, p. 64. The expression "to the south of the Ganges" does not mean actually standing on the south bank, but only that the place was on the south side of the river, and not far from it. The same expression is used again in describing a hill on the western frontier of Harana Parvata

There was also a great stûpa built on the spot where Buddha
had preached for one night. Both distance and direction
point to the vicinity of Shekhpura, a position which is confirmed by the subsequent easterly route of the pilgrim
"through forests and gorges of mountains." At Murâdpur,
3 miles to the north of Shekhpura, there is a single isolated
hill; and at Brindâban and Barâr, a few miles to the south-
west and south-east, there are two other isolated hills; but
from none of these would the pilgrim's subsequent route have
taken him through gorges of mountains, nor even through
forests on that dreary and treeless plain of rice fields. I feel
sure therefore, that the large Brahmanical village visited by
Hwen Thsang must have been situated in the pretty and well-
wooded oasis of Shekhpura. The remains here are all Brahmanical, of which the principal is a fine tank called Mathokar
Tâl. On its bank there is a *dargâh*, which is referred to a
Mathokar Khân. But as the site is said to have been originally occupied by a temple of Kâli, and as the tank is still
called Kâli-mathokar, I conclude that the name is only a
contraction of *Mathpokhar*, or the Temple-tank, the full
name having been *Kâli-math-pokhar*, or the "Kâli-temple-
tank." Thus Budha-pokhar has everywhere become Budho-
khar.

7.—RAJJANA.

From the large and populous Brahmanical village with its
sculptured temples of the gods, the pilgrim travelled for
100 *li*, or nearly 17 miles, to the east, through forests and
hills to a monastery in the village of *Lo-in-ni-lo*. The bearing and distance would have brought him to the bank of the
Kiyul River near the railway station of Lakhi-Sarai. Nearly
2 miles to the north-west of the station is the large village
of Rajjâna or Rajjaona, with numerous remains, both Buddhist
and Brahmanical. That this is the true position is proved by

(Mongir), Vol. II, p. 70. As this hill was certainly in the Kharakpur group of
mountains, of which the nearest is from 4 to 5 miles from the river, it is clear that
the expression "to the south of the Ganges" does not mean actually standing on
its bank.

the pilgrim's subsequent journey of 200 *li*, or 33 miles, to the east which brought him to Mongir. Now the distance by the Quarter-Master General's route-book from Bálguzar, just 1 mile to the north of Rajjána, to Mongir is 30½ miles, and the direction a little to the north of east. The route also for the whole distance skirts the Kharakpur Hills, which agrees with Hwen Thsang's description of his journey through " forests and gorges of high mountains." Lastly, the great lake which the pilgrim mentions as being 2 or 3 *li*, or less than half a mile to the north of the stúpa, is now represented by the Bálguzar Jhíl, which lies midway between Rajjána and Bálguzar. This lake the pilgrim describes as about 30 *li*, or 5 miles, in circuit, which is just about double the size of the Bálguzar Jhíl in the dry season. But during the floods it becomes a vast lake, which most probably far exceeds the dimensions given by the pilgrim.

Rajjána is a large village surrounded by numerous mounds. It was one of the *Mahals* of Sirkar Mongir in the time of Akbar, the name of "*Rowhenny*" in Gladwin's " Ain-Akbari" being no doubt a misreading for Ráojani. Although the ruins of Rajjána have furnished several miles of brick ballast to the railway, yet the supply seems to be inexhaustible, as the remains extended over several miles along the western bank of the Kiyul River. As these remains have already been described in another report, I will confine my present notice to the Buddhist mounds on the north, as they serve to strengthen my argument for the identification of Rajjána with the *Lo-in-ni-lo* of Hwen Thsang.

On the most northerly mound to the east of the village, there are two Buddhist statues in black basalt. One is the ascetic Buddha sitting under the Bodhi tree ; the other is the Bodhisatwa Padmapáni, or Avalokiteswara, as Hwen Thsang always calls him. From the square form of the mound I take it to be the remains of a monastery. Touching it on the west side, there is a second mound, which is probably the remains of the great stúpa mentioned by the pilgrim. It is to the north of this monument that he places the great lake at a distance of from 2 to 3 *li*, or less than half a mile. Now

this is the very position of the Bâlguzar Jhil, which I have
already noticed. I conclude, therefore, with some confidence,
that Rajjâna is the true representative of the *Lo-in-ni-lo* of
Hwen Thsang. Its position, midway between the Pigeon
Monastery of Parbati and Mongir, coincides most precisely
with the distances given by the pilgrim, while his description
of hills in his route, both as he approached and as he left the
place, agrees with the actual position of the Shekhpura Hills
to the west, and the Kharakpur Hills to the east.

8.—MONGIR.

The hill of Mongir is said to have been named *Mudgalapuri* and *Mudgalâsrama*, after the Rishi Mudgala who had
taken up his residence on it. But before his time the hill bore
the name of *Kashta-harana Parvata*, as it overlooked the
famous bathing place on the Ganges called *Kashta-harana
Ghât*, or the "pain-expelling bathing place," because all people
afflicted with either grief or bodily pain were at once cured by
bathing there. This is illustrated by the following story of
Râma :—

When Râma returned from Lanka after killing Râwan, he was unable to sleep at night, so he consulted his preceptor Vasishtha, who told
him that as he was a Kshatriya and had killed the Brahman Râwan, he
must expiate his sin before he could obtain sleep ; and that he should
visit the Rishi Mudgala, who would instruct him how to obtain expia-
tion. So Râma, with his three brothers, and Sita, and Hanumân, all
presented themselves before the Rishi Mudgala, to whom they offered
presents of fruits, &c. The Rishi accepted all save Sita's offering,
whose chastity he doubted since she had remained so long in Râwan's
palace in Lanka, so she agreed to undergo the ordeal by fire. For three
days she sat in the midst of the flames unharmed, and on the fourth day
the Rishi himself invited her to come out of the fire, and accepted her
offering. Thence the pit of fire in which she had sat for three days,
became a spring of hot water, and was accordingly named after her, the
Sitâ Kund, or "Sitâ's well."

This story of Râma is told in a different way by Buchanan,
but with the same result[1]. According to his information,

[1] Eastern India, Vol. II, p. 43.

"Râma after having killed Râwan, king of Langka, was haunted by the constant appearance of that prince, who, although a Râkshas or devil, was a very holy Brahman, and on account of his piety was served by the gods as his menial servants. Râma, in order to expiate the crime of such an atrocious act, was desired to travel as a penitent until he met all the gods and obtained a pardon. In order to procure this meeting he and his wife and brothers came to *Kashta-harani*, where they knew all the gods would be assembled to bathe. Here he obtained a remission of his sins, and he is said to have left the mark of his foot at the place.

Now, this name of *Harana-Parvata* is clearly the original of Hwen Thsang's *I-lan-na-Po-fa-to*, which Julien has rendered by Hiranya Parvata or the "Hill of Gold." The name of Mudgalagiri is not mentioned by the pilgrim, but it seems nearly certain that he must have heard of it, as he relates how the householder, *Sruta-vinsati-koti*, whose stûpa was close to the Harana Parvata, was converted by the famous disciple of Buddha *Mudgalaputra*. [1]

The highest point of the hill is known by the name of *Karna-chuḍa*, or *Karna-chaura*, that is, either *Karna's top-knot*, or "Karna's seat[2]." These names are accounted for by the following legend of Raja Karna, who is said to be a different person from the well-known hero of the Mahâbhârata, although the story of his liberality proves that he has been confounded with him. Karna of Mudgalapuri was a contemporary of Vikrama, and an ardent worshipper of the goddess Chandi Devi. Every day he bestowed one maund and a quarter of gold on the Brahmans, and every night he visited the shrine of the goddess, where he cast himself into a vessel of boiling *ghi*, and his flesh was devoured by the *Joginis*. Pleased with his devotion, the goddess brought the fleshless skeleton to life by sprinkling water over it, and the resuscitated Karna on rising up found the *ghi* vessel filled with one maund and a quarter of gold. This he bestowed on the Brahmans, and again appearing before the goddess cast himself into the

[1] Julien's Hwen Thsang, Vol. II, p. 67.
[2] Chaura is a contracted form of Chaubutra.

vessel of boiling *ghi*, and was again restored to life by Chandi Devi. At last the fame of his continued liberality reached Vikrama, who came to Mongir and became his servant. By close watching Vikrama at last discovered the secret of the daily supply of gold, and having one night preceded Karna to the shrine of the goddess, he threw himself into the vessel of boiling *ghi*, and being afterwards restored to life, he cast himself into the vessel a second time, and a third time. His devotion pleased Chandi Devi so much that she told him to ask a boon, and, on his claiming the secret of making gold, she gave him the *Páras*, or Philosopher's stone.

When Karna visited the place shortly afterwards, both the goddess and the vessel of *ghi* had disappeared. He then began to sell his property to make his customary gift to the Brahmans until at last he had nothing left. When Vikrama asked him the cause of his dejection, Karna told him the whole story, and Vikrama at once gave him the Páras stone. Then Karna thought to himself "this must be Vikrama," as there is no one else who would be so generous, so he fell down at his feet and honoured him.

A somewhat different version of this legend is given by Buchanan :[1] "At Vikrama-Chandi, near the town, is a hole in a rock sacred to Chandi, the Gráma Devata of the place, and covered by a small building of brick. This goddess was courted by two of the most powerful sovereigns of India, Vikrama and Karna, who are here considered as having been contemporary. Karna, in order to procure the favour of this goddess, hit upon the happy expedient of tormenting himself by a daily immersion of his body in boiling butter, and by this means he every day procured one and a quarter maunds of gold, which he distributed to the poor. Vikrama, jealous of such favour shown to a neighbouring king, came in disguise, and entering the service of Karna, found out the manner in which his rival worshipped. He then determined to excel him, which he accordingly did ; by slicing his skin in various places, and having offered his blood to the goddess, he gave himself

---

[1] Buchanan's Eastern India, Vol. II, pp. 44-45.

exquisite torment by filling the gashes with salt and spices, after all which he went into the bath of his rival. Such a gallant worship obtained the decided favour of the goddess, who has ever since been called Vikrama Chandi."

In the Sanskrit inscriptions of the Pâla Rajas, the place is called *Mudga-giri*. As Mudga is the Sanskrit name of the well-known pulse called Mung, the present name of Mongir, or more properly *Munggir*, is only a simple contraction of the Sanskrit name. I have a strong suspicion, however, that the original name may have been connected with the Mons or Mundas, who occupied this part of the country before the advent of the Aryans. This seems the more probable from the fact that the river of the Kharakpur Hills which joins the Ganges a few miles below the fort of Mongir is called *Mun* or *Mon*. It is, however, not impossible that this name may have been derived from the Sanskrit *Muni*, as the hill is said to have been the residence of the *Muni Mudgala*, and is therefore known as *Muni-parvata*, as well as *Mudgala-giri*.

9.—BHIMBAND.

On the western frontier of Harana Parvata (Mongir) Hwen Thsang places a double-peaked hill of great height, where Buddha had overcome the Yaksha Vakula[1]. On the top of the hill was the ancient house of the demon, and at its south-eastern foot was the cave in which Buddha had dwelt for three months. In front of the cave there was a stûpa and a stone on which Buddha had sat, and which still bore traces of his body. Close by there was a second stone on which Buddha used to place his water vessel, and which still bore the mark of a flower of eight leaves, 1 inch in depth. At a short distance to the south-east there were marks of the demon's feet, about 18 inches long, 7 or 8 inches broad, and 2 inches deep. Here there was a stone statue of Buddha seated, 6 or 7 feet in height. To the west was the place where Buddha used to walk for exercise. Here also on the north were Buddha's foot-marks, near which there was

[1] Julien's Hwen Thsang, Vol. III, pp. 70-71.

a stûpa. To the west of this spot there were six or seven hot springs, the water of which was extremely hot.

This place I would identify with the hill of Mahâdeva and the hot springs of Bhimbând, which are situated only 11 miles from the Kiyul River, on the western frontier of the Mongir district. The hill of Mahâdeva has two peaks, and is isolated from the main range ; and the hot springs of Bhimband which are on its northern side flow into the Mon River. The spot is thus described by Buchanan[1] : "About 15 or 16 miles south from Rishikund are the hot springs of Bhimbând by far the finest in the district. They issue from the bottom of a small detached hill on its east side and a little distance from the Mon River, which receives their water, and which rises from another detached hill a little way farther south. The hill from which the hot springs issue is situated east from the great irregular central mass of the Mongir Hills, and is named Mahâdeva. It consists, so far as can be seen, of quartz or silicious hornstone. The hot water issues from four different places, at some distance from each other ; and at each place it springs from many crevices of the rock, and from between various loose stones with which the ground is covered. Each of these four sources is by far more consider-able than the Sitakunda, and many air bubbles accompany the water, which is limpid and tasteless."

There were formerly several ruins at this spot, but the whole of the cut stones have been carried off to Kharakpur. There were also some figures called *Panch Kumâr*, or the "five Princes," but these have also disappeared. Nothing in fact now remains save the two peaked isolated hills and the hot springs, which are the hottest in the district, thus agreeing with Hwen Thsang's description of them as being "extremely hot."

10.—SINGI RIKHI.

The temple of Singi Rikhi, or Sringi Rishi, is situated on a high hill in the Kharakpur Range, 20 miles to the south-

---

[1] Eastern India, Vol. II, p. 198. See Appendix for another account of Bhim-bând.

west of Mongir, and 10 miles to the west-north-west of Bhim-band. The place is rather difficult of access, and is not mentioned by Buchanan; his Rishi Kund being a hot spring at the foot of the hills due south from Mongir, and only 6 or 7 miles from the Sita Kund. At the temple of Singi Rikhi there are several figures, both Buddhist and Brahmanical, and two inscriptions, of which one is certainly Buddhist.

The Buddhist record is engraved under a line of several figures, the chief one being Buddha himself, who, seated before a kind of altar, is addressing two kneeling figures offering garlands. Behind Buddha are two of his disciples, also seated, and beyond them are a horse and an elephant. The inscription consists of one long line containing the Buddhist creed, with the name of the donor below. The letters are tolerably clear, but they offer no known name. They seem to read *Savatha dcdharma*, " the pious gift of *Savatha*."

The second inscription is in three lines, the upper one being taken up with the date in words, or Samvat 35 on the 13th of Jyeshto sudi. I read it as follows :—[1]

1—Samvatsara pancha trinsatime Jyeshta sudi trayordasyâm
2—Ida bhavatu sugam stapite udhayâchali pâshive
3—Madhu bhunekâtam ja ta punya mâta pita.

11—JÂHNGIRA.

Wherever the Ganges changes its easterly and southerly course, and makes a sudden bend to the north, that place is esteemed peculiarly holy and named *Uttara bâhinî*, or the " northern reach." The best known of these places are Mongir, Jâhngira, and Kahalgaon, but the most holy and by far the most frequented is Jâhngira. Here the course of the river is changed by two rocky hills; one called Jâhngira, standing in the middle of the water, and the other called Bâls-karan, forming a bluff head-land at the bend of the stream. The former derives its name from Jahnu Rishi, who had established his cell or *Asram* in a cleft of the rocks. Hence the rock itself was called *Jâhnavigriha*, or " Jahnu's

[1] See Plate XI, N. 6.

house," which was gradually shortened to *Jáhngira*, just as *Rájagriha* has now become *Rájgír*. As the river rushing against the rock disturbed the saint's devotions, he angrily drank up its waters; but afterwards, at the intercession of the sage Bhagiratha, he relented, and allowed the stream to issue from his ear. Hence the Ganges received the name of Jáhnavi, or the daughter of Jahnu. Originally it is said there was only the cell of Jahnu Rishi on the rock; but in the Muhammadan times a Sádhu named Hamáma Bhárathi settled there, and being driven away by the Musalmans, went to Delhi and appealed to the Emperor, who gave orders that he should be reinstated. A *farmán* is said to have been granted to him engraved on copper, but I could not see the plate, as the owner was conveniently absent, and a similar excuse was afterwards made to my Assistant, Mr. Beglar, during a much longer stay. Everybody has heard of the *farmán*, but only one man named Gajádhar Pandit professed to have seen it. According to the common belief, the Emperor was Jahángir, after whom the rock was named Jahán-gira. But one of my informants proved too much by spelling the name *Jahánnabi-gira*, which is clearly only a Persianized form of the Hindu *Jáhnavi-gira*. In refutation of this story I may also note that the masjid on the Bálskaran Promontory, which is said to have been built *after* the Muhammadans had been obliged to give up the rock, is a building of the Pathán style, and apparently of much older date than the time of Jahángir. Buchanan, however, who calls the Sádhu Harináth, says that he was the 13th mahant in regular succession from the founder, and as no young man can hope to aspire to the dignity, the establishment of the present temple " could not have been in a remote period." I am willing to accept the thirteen mahants, but as the succession of these dignitaries is not liable to be tempered by assassinations, their tenure of office is usually a long one, averaging from twenty to thirty years, as in the case of the mahants of Bodh Gaya. Twelve predecessors at an average of twenty-five years each would place the settlement of the first just 300 years before 1800, or in A.D. 1500, or a full century before the reign of Jahângir. This date would also agree with the Pathân style of the mosque.

There is a lingam temple on the top of the rock called *Gebinath* and *Ajgebiñath*, which is said to mean formed by " nature." Formerly it was called *Anâdnâth*, and one inform- ant even said it was the lingam of *Jâhngira Muni*, the Rishi who drank up the Ganges. The pile of granite rocks rises up boldly from the water to a height of 70 or 80 feet in gigantic masses, only slightly separated from each other by narrow fissures and surrounded at the base by huge blocks rounded by the weather. Many of the blocks undermined by the river have slipped from their original places, as proved by the sloping positions of some of the sculptures. This is especially noticeable with the standing figure of the Ganges, which is now as much as 38° out of the perpendicular. There is only one safe landing-place on the south side, from which a steep flight of rough steps leads to the top. In the rainy season, when the river is swollen, the waters sweep with such an impetuous rush round the rocky island as to make it almost inaccessible, and the mahant and his disciples some- times remain for two or three weeks without any communica- tion with the shore.

Many of the larger blocks and more prominent masses are covered with bold sculptures in high relief. These have been briefly noticed by Bâbu Rajendra Lâla, who states that most of them are Brahmanical, including representations of—

" Ganesa,[1] Hanumân, Krishna, Râdha, Vâmana, Ananta sleeping on a snake and other Pauranic divinities. But there are a few which are decidedly of Buddhist and Jain origin. The Buddhist figures, mostly Buddha in the meditative posture, occupy more centrical positions than the Hindu ones, and appear to be more worn away than the latter ; both circumstances affording conclusive evidence of the place having been originally a Buddhist sanctuary which the Brahmans have appropriated to themselves since the downfall of Buddhism. A Jain temple still exists on one side of the rock, to which a few pilgrims occasionally come to offer their adoration of Pâraswanâtha, the 23rd teacher of the sect."

---

[1] Bengal Asiatic Society's Journal, 1864, Vol. 33, p. 360.

As far as my examination went, the sculptures are pretty evenly divided between Saiva and Vaishnava figures. I noticed several groups of Hara Gauri and numerous lingams, and at least one figure of Siva alone. I recognised seven out of the ten Avatârs of Vishnu, the Vâman, Narasinha, Parasurâma, Varâha, Buddha, Râmachandra, and Kâlki, while Krishna and Râdha were seen by Buchanan. I noticed also several figures of Sûrya, but perhaps the most interesting of all is a figure of the Ganges on her crocodile. Both Sûrya and Gangâ will be seen in Plate XII. Prominent in Plate XI are the Avatârs of Parasurâma and the elephant-headed Ganesa, with two lingams above. Under the principal figure of Sûrya there is a perfect inscription of two lines in well-formed characters of the early Gupta period, which I read as follows:—

Aum! Deya dharmmayam Chihadanttasya
punyam tad bhavatu mâta pitrorasmâkanchâ.
"Salutation! The pious gift of Chihadantta.
May it be to the benefit of our father and mother and of ourselves."

Only two figures of Buddha were observed, one small, sitting, and one large, standing. But one of these may have been the Brahmanical Avatâra of Buddha, judging from the company in which it was found.

About two hundred yards below the Jâhngira Rock there is a bluff rocky headland named Bâiskaran, about 100 feet in height, jutting boldly into the river, which must once have been crowned by some Hindu temple. The river face of the bluff point is made still more steep in the upper part by retaining walls of brick which carry the broad platform on which the Muhammadans have placed their Jâmi Masjid. On many of the larger masses of rock near the base there are sculptures of the same style and age as those of the Jâhngira Rock. The most prominent sculpture is that of a female lying on a bed with her head resting on her left hand, and her right hand holding a bunch of flowers, which a monkey is snatching away.

To the left are two small panels with sculptures and several large heads in niches. Under one of these is written

Kumârasya, "of Kumâra," in beautifully formed Gupta characters. To the left is a large panel containing two male
figures, with an antelope between them. One of the figures
has four arms. Still further to the left there is a pair of feet
with an inscription in boldly cut Gupta letters, reading *Rudra-
Mahâla,* which I take to be a contraction of *Rudra-Mahâlaya,*
or "Siva, the supreme lord." I do not, however, remember
ever having seen a *Rudrapada* before. Under another figure
there is a short inscription of two lines of Gupta characters
reading *Dedharmmayam Vahakasya,* or "the pious gift of
Vahaka."

From this account of the sculptures on the Jâhngira and
Bâiskaran Rocks it is clear that both sites were in the possession of Brahmans and not of Buddhists, and that the flourishing period of their occupancy was during the third century
A.D., under the early Gupta kings. The great bathing *ghât*
is on the bank of the river just above the Bâiskaran promontory, and immediately opposite the Jâhngira Rock. Three
great *melâs* are held here during the year, on the full moons
of Vaisâkh, Kârtik, and Mâgh, or April, October, and February,
and smaller melâs at every eclipse. I was present during the
assembly of the people on the full moon of Mâgh, near the
end of February 1879. For three whole days the people
were arriving from all quarters, in a continuous stream all day
long, and for two days afterwards all the roads were thronged
with people carrying away vessels of water of the Ganges
from Jâhngira Ghât. Most of these people were going to
the famous shrine of Baijnâth at Deogarh in the Birbhûm
district. I estimated the number of pilgrims at from forty to
fifty thousand.

Between the bathing ghât and the Railway station lies
the flourishing mart of Sultângunj, for nearly a mile in length,
parallel to the river. Close to the Railway station there is a
large brick mound, from 10 to 30 feet in height, which furnished brick ballast for many miles of the line. On the
highest point Mr. Harris, the Railway Engineer, built a house,
and as the excavations for ballast disclosed several walls, a
great part of the mound was carefully explored by him, of

which a portion still remains open. The only account of his
excavations is a notice by Bâbu Rajendra Lâla[1]; but as no
plan is given, I find it rather difficult to follow his description,
I will therefore give his own account in full, instead of at-
tempting to make an abstract of it—

" The space between the mart and railway station forms a quadrangle of 1,200 feet by 800. It seems never to have been under much
cultivation, and is covered by the debris of old buildings, the foundations of which have lately been excavated for ballast for the railway.
The trenches opened along the line of the foundations are not continuous, and in several places have been filled up, but from what
remains, I am disposed to believe that the place was at one time
divided into court-yards, having lines of small cells or cloisters on all
four sides. This idea has been strengthened by the discovery of a
series of six chambers in a line at the south-western corner of the
quadrangle. These chambers form a part of the western side of a
large court-yard, on the north of which Mr. Harris, Resident Engineer,
East Indian Railway, under whose superintendence the excavations
under notice have been carried on, has brought to light the foundations of two similar chambers. The southern and the eastern façades
yet remain unexplored. But the accumulation of rubbish on those
sides, rising to the height of 10 to 20 feet, clearly indicates that the
chambers corresponding to those on the west and north are to be met
with under it.

" At the middle of this long ridge of rubbish Mr. Harris has found
the foundation and the side pillars of a large gateway, which was
evidently one of the principal entrances to the quadrangle. Similar
gateways probably once existed on the other three sides, but their
vestiges are no longer traceable.

" The accumulation of rubbish at the south-east corner is greater
than anywhere else, and on it is situated the bungalow of the Resident Engineer. It would be well if a shaft could be run through
this mound, as it is here that relics of importance are most likely
to be met with.

" The chambers excavated at the south-western side are not all
of the same dimensions. They measure within the walls from 12' x 10'
6" to 14' x 12'. The depth from the top of the plinth to the lowest
part of the foundation (the only portion now *in situ*) is 13 feet. This
depth was found full of earth and rubbish, but divided at intervals of
3 or 4 feet by three distinct floors formed of concrete and stucco.

[1] Bengal Asiatic Society's Journal, Vol. XXXIII, p. 361.

The lowest shows no trace of plaster. The upper floors had openings or hatchways through which people descended to the bottom, and used the different stories as cellars or store-rooms. No valuable property or remains of corn or other goods have however been traced in these cellars, as most probably they had been removed before the monastery fell into the hands of the destroyer.

"The interior of the walls had never been plastered, but the front facing the court-yard has a thick coating of sand and stucco, such as are to be seen in modern Indian houses.

"Beyond the western wall of the chambers there is the foundation of another and a broad one, which formed the boundary wall of the quadrangle. It runs due north and south and is joined by one which runs along the ridge on the southern side. Similar boundary walls, no doubt, once existed on the north and east, but their traces have long since been effaced.

"In front of the chambers there are to be seen the remains of a hall or verandah, which formerly formed the most important part of the building on this side of the quadrangle. Its floor is on a level with the highest floor of the chambers, and seems to have been made of concrete and stucco, and painted over in fresco of a light ochrous colour. How it was enclosed in front has not been made out. Probably there was a range of square pillars, forming a verandah or pillared hall resembling a modern Bengal *dalan* or the *choultry* of Southern India. The floor of the court-yard has not yet been laid bare, but, judging from the position of a water-course formed of scooped flags of granite which runs under the floor of the hall and through one of the partition walls of the chambers to a drain beyond the boundary wall of the quadrangle, and which was evidently intended to carry off its drainage, I am induced to believe that it stood about 3 feet lower than the hall. Similar water-pipes of granite have been met with at Buddha Gaya, Sârnâth, and elsewhere.

"Of the relics which have been collected by Mr. Harris in course of his excavation at this place, the most important appears to be a colossal figure of Buddha, which was lying on a side of the hall described above. It had evidently been knocked down by some iconoclast before the destruction of the hall, and removed several feet away from its pedestal. The latter too had been tilted over, but not much removed from the centre of the hall, which was its original position. It was formed of a slab of granite 6' 11" x 3' 9," the thickness being 9½ inches. The statue was secured to this stone by two bolts, the remains of which are still visible. The statue is of copper and seems to have suffered no injury from the hands of the destroyer, except the mutilation of the left foot across the ankle."

The copper statue is a standing figure of Buddha, 7 feet 3 inches in height, his left hand holding his robe, and his right raised in the attitude of teaching. Along with the colossal statue were found two small basalt statues of Buddha, the teacher, 1 foot 10½ inches and 1 foot 5 inches in height, each with the Buddhist creed carved on the pedestal in Gupta characters. The same creed was also engraved on the back of the smaller figures. Bâbu Rajendra Lâla gives a list of various things found during the excavations, out of which the following appear to be the only remains of any particular interest :—

No. I.—A mutilated terra-cotta figure similar to the above.

" No. 22.—*Miniature terra-cotta chaityas,* containing within the seals of the Buddhist creed, some having seals stamped on the bottom.

" No. 23.—*Ditto,* having the figure of nine chaityas stamped on its sides and of seals at the base.

" No. 24.—Several of the above *seals* detached.

" No. 32.—Handles of terra-cotta basso-relievo figures, red-glazed.

" No. 33.—*Head of Vishnu* in baked clay, seasoned with paddy and glazed in red, with the seven-headed cobra over-head (the only Hindu relic met with).

" No. 34.—*Well-formed heads of Surki* cement plastered with stucco, one with a particularly beautiful profile.

" No. 40.—*Fragment of white stucco* coloured red in fresco from the floor under the great copper statue.

" As the Bâbu justly remarks, all these articles leave no doubt as to the building in which they were found. The quadrangle was evidently a large Buddhist monastery or vihâra, such as at one time existed at Sârnâth, Sânchi, Buddha Gaya, Mânikyala, and other places of note, and at its four corners had four chapels for the use of the resident monks. Two of these, which abutted on the mart, have already disappeared, and of the other two that on the south-west has yielded the relics noted above, and the last remains under the railway bungalow, a most promising field for the antiquary who could devote a week or two to its exploration. Of the history of this vihara nothing is now traceable. From its extent and the style of its construction it is evident that at one time it was a place of great repute, and the resort of innumerable pilgrims. But its glory set a long while ago, and even the name of the place where it stood is now lost in obscurity. The present appellation (Sultanganj) is quite modern, not more than two or three centuries old, and is due to a prince of the house of

Akbar. Fa Hian makes no mention of it, and Hwen Thsang talks of the ruins of several large monasteries in the neighbourhood of Bhagalpur, but gives us no clue to the one under notice. It is to be presumed therefore that it had been ruined and forsaken, or at least had fallen into decay, before the advent of the latter Chinese traveller. The inscriptions on the minor figures, in the Gupta character of the third and fourth century, show that the vihara, with its chief *lares* and *penates*, had been established a considerable period before that time, probably at the beginning of the Christian era, or even earlier, for Champa (modern Bhagalpur) was a place of great antiquity, and the Buddhists took possession of it very early as capital of Eastern India, and established many viharas and chaityas in and about it."[1]

A drawing of the copper statue of Buddha accompanies the Bâbu's account of the excavations. It is clearly of the same style as the Gupta Buddhist statues which I dug up at Sârnâth, Benares, in 1835-36, thus agreeing as to age with that already deduced from the inscriptions in the Gupta characters.

After Mr. Harris's departure, his house was pulled down, and the mound then remained untouched until my visit in February 1879. A mere glance showed that it was most probably the remains of a stûpa, which was turned to certainty by a few hours' excavation, which showed that it was a solid mass of brick-work laid in regular course. The top was found to be 48 feet by 43 feet, with a height of 28 feet above the floor of the monastery excavated by Mr. Harris. I began sinking a shaft down the centre, which I was obliged to make over to Mr. Beglar after it had reached a depth of 6 feet, owing to an accident which severely sprained my knee, and kept me confined to a recumbent position for upwards of a month. The excavation was successfully carried out by Mr. Beglar down to the water level, just above which he found the relic chamber of the stûpa.

The cupola or dome of the stûpa must have been not less than 90 feet in diameter, as the octagonal plinth on which it stood had a side of 39 feet, and a diameter of 94·146 feet. Near the bottom of this mass there was a small brick stûpa, only 8 feet in diameter, standing in the midst of a square com-

[1] Bengal Asiatic Society's Journal, 1864, p. 369.

partment, the intervening space being filled with earth. In this small stúpa there was a common round earthenware vessel, or *ghara*, standing with the mouth upwards. In this were deposited the "Seven Precious Things" of the Buddhists, namely, 1, Gold ; 2, Silver; 3, Crystal ; 4, Sapphire ; 5, Ruby; 6, Emerald ; 7, Jacinth or Zircon. All these things are shown in the accompanying plate.

1.—*Gold* was represented by a small ornament, something like a *fleur-de-lis* in shape, but very thin, and weighing 7 grains. There was also a thin piece of very pale gold, weighing only 4¼ grains.

2.—The *Silver* consisted of a thin plate, 2⅞ inches long by 1¼ inch broad, weighing, with the chloride incrustation, 180 grains. There were also two small silver coins which will be noticed hereafter.

3.—The *Crystal* was a mere broken fragment.

4.—The *Sapphire* was an uncut oval, three-eighths of an inch in length and one-quarter of an inch broad. It is of a very light greyish blue, and is of no value.

5.—The *Ruby* is about half the size of the sapphire, of a very pale pink colour, and of no value.

6.—The *Emerald* is of the same size as the ruby, a pale green beryl, of no value.

7.—The *Jacinth* or Zircon consists of three small flat pieces, little more than one-eighth of an inch in breadth. They are of a deep red colour and of no value.

On removing the brick on which stood the earthen vessel, there was found a cavity one-brick deep, 9 inches long and 6 inches broad, containing a piece of bone 1⅛ inch long by ⅝ inch broad, imbedded in some fine red clay. This was only a few inches above the water level. Here then was the veritable relic for the enshrinement of which this great stúpa was erected. With it there was no writing or inscription of any kind. I turned therefore to the two little coins, which were thickly coated with verdigris, and had consequently been taken for copper coins. On cleaning them I found one to be a silver coin of *Maha Kshatrapa Swámi Rudra Sena*, the son of M. Ksh. Satya, or Surya, Sena. The

other was a coin of *Chandra Gupta Vikramâditya*, or Chandra
Gupta II.

From these coins we may deduce the date of the stûpa
to have been about A.D. 250. I have a dated coin of this
Saurâshtran satrap with the date of 310 odd, the unit being
doubtful. If we reckon the year 310 in the Vikramâditya
Samvat, the date of the satrap will be 310—57=253 A.D.
Now, applying my initial point of the Gupta era in A.D. 167
to the two dated inscriptions of Chandra Gupta in S. 82 and
93, we get the years 248 and 259 A.D. for the period of
Chandra Gupta II. This agreement of date is strongly supported by the fact that this satrap was the very last of whom
we have yet obtained any coins, while the province of
Saurâshtra was certainly conquered by Chandra Gupta. The
one would thus appear to have been the immediate successor
of the other in Saurâshtra, and this inference is now rendered
almost certain by the discovery of their coins in the same
stûpa, which may be taken as an evidence that they were
both contemporary with the building of the stûpa.

Now much the same date had already been inferred by
Bâbu Rajendra Lâla from the striking similarity of the style of
sculpture to that of the statues of the Gupta period, which
I had exhumed at Sârnâth, Benares. To these examples I
can now add a stucco head of Buddha which was found by
Mr. Beglar in excavating around the stûpa. This is a very
close copy of the Sârnâth style of Buddhist sculpture[1]. A
photograph of this head will be found in the accompanying
plate, in which I have given three other fragments to show
the general style of the stucco work of the period. I conclude
that the whole of the exterior of the stûpa was thickly plastered, and divided into compartments by pilasters, each compartment being filled with a figure of Buddha with various
attendant figures.

On the west side of Sultânganj there is a second mound,
both larger and loftier than that near the Railway station.
It is called Karnagarh, and is said to be the remains of a fort

[1] See Plate XIII, fig. A.

built by Raja Karna. Of this king nothing certain is known. His name is also connected with Mongir and Champânagar, near Bhâgalpur. He should therefore be one of the old kings of Anga, of which Champânagar was the capital. It is certain that he cannot be the famous elder half-brother of the Pândavas.

12—BHAGALPUR.

I paid a visit to Bhâgalpur for the purpose of learning something about the long subterranean passage at Mâyâganj, on the bank of the Ganges, 2½ miles to the east of Bhâgalpur. It is thus described by Buchanan :—

"The place of most remarkable antiquity according to the pundit of the mission is a cave and subterraneous gallery overhanging the Ganges at Mâyâganj, a little east from the town. He alleges that this was the abode of Kasyap Muni, the son of Kasyap, who was made by Brahma at the creation of man. They say that it was the residence of a hermit, who lived about 150 or 200 years ago, that is some time before they remember, but that until the English Government the small hills around were covered with thickets, among which no one ventured, as they sheltered thieves and wild beasts. The cave, in fact, is very small and unfit for the father of such a progeny as Kasyap possessed. It had been dug in a dry hard clay containing calcareous concretions. The roof is low, for the pillar by which it is supported is not 6 feet high. Two narrow subterraneous galleries lead from this cave, and are said to terminate, in small chambers, at a considerable distance. About 15 years ago one of these was opened, and in it was found the skeleton of a man who, from the position of the bones, Mr. Glas, the surgeon of the station then present, supposes to have died in the spot. These circumstances would rather seem to point out the cave as the retreat of a robber than as that of a hermit, although it is not unlikely but that the same person may have united both professions."[1]

As Buchanan wrote in 1811, the exploration of the cave must have taken place in 1811—15=1796 A.D. according to his informants. In the Indian Museum in London I found the following memorandum attached to seven silver punch-marked coins : "Out of a number found by Mr. Grant about

[1] Eastern India, Vol. II, p. 31, by Buchanan.

40 years ago, in a subterranean passage in Bhâgalpur," and "found at the end of the passage with some human bones." Of these seven coins, which I examined carefully, two are round and five square, but I saw nothing that was peculiar about them. They bear the usual figures of the sun, bull, elephant, chaitya symbol, tree, soldier with shield, and a dog such as is found on some of the Mathura specimens.

In Buchanan's account, the person who examined the bones is named Dr. Glas, while Colonel Mackenzie calls the explorer Mr. Grant. The explanation of the difference in the names is very simple. Mr. James Grant was the Collector of Bhâgalpur at the same time that Dr. Glas was Civil Surgeon, and they most probably explored the cave together.

The two accounts agree in the main facts of the exploration of a long subterranean gallery and the finding of some human bones. The discovery of the coins is mentioned by Mackenzie only, but as he was a zealous coin-collector, he was just the person to hear of the discovery, and to get some of the coins if obtainable. The bones may have been, as the Doctor supposed, of comparatively late date, but the antiquity of the coins is undoubted, and I see no reason to doubt that these subterranean places must have existed for several centuries before the Christian era.

The entrance is now fitted with a door, which had become so tightly jammed at the time of my visit that I was unable to go inside. I could see that there was a small entrance hall from which two galleries branched off, one to the right and the other to the left. Both of these were narrow and dark, and could only be explored with torches. One of my servants examined the left hand gallery for a considerable distance with a guide and torch, without finding any change either in its course or in its size. According to the belief of the people, the left hand gallery communicates with Kahalgaon, 10 miles distant on the east, while the right hand gallery communicates with Jâhngira, 16 miles distant on the west. This excavation is no doubt very old, as proved by the punch-marked silver coins found in it, which were current

in North India for several centuries before the Christian era.
A similarly remote age is claimed by Hwen Thsang for a long
gallery at this very place, regarding which he gives the
following legend :—[1]

"According to tradition *before the birth of Buddha*, there was a
herdsman who tended several hundreds of cattle in the neighbourhood of Champa (or Bhagalpur). One day a bull having separated
from the herd roamed into the forest. The herdsman feared that he
was lost, but in the evening the bull returned radiant with beauty.
Even his lowing was remarkable. The rest of the cattle were seized
with fear and would not go near him. This continued for some time
until the herdsman determined to follow the bull in his wanderings.
The bull entered a cleft in the rocks and the herdsman followed for 4
or 5 *li*, about 4,000 feet, when the gallery suddenly opened into a pretty
wood filled with fruit trees and flowers. It was altogether a dazzling
and charming scene. Then the bull went aside and cropped the
shining leaves of a sweet-smelling plant unknown to men. The fruits
on the trees were yellow as gold, of most exquisite scent and large
size. The herdsman plucked one, and though he longed to taste it he
was afraid to lift it to his mouth. Soon after the bull started on his
return, and the herdsman followed him. On reaching the cleft in the
rock he saw a frightful looking demon who snatched the fruit from
him and kept it. On his return he consulted a doctor, who advised
him to visit the place again, and to be sure to eat the fruit.

"Two days afterwards the herdsman again followed the bull and
entered the cavern. On returning he plucked a fruit and hid it in
his clothes, but just when he was about to leave the cave the same
demon came to take the fruit. The herdsman at once thrust it into
his mouth, when the demon seized him by the throat, and he was
obliged to swallow it whole. No sooner had it reached his stomach
than his body began to swell to an enormous size, and although his
head was outside his body remained jammed in the cleft of the rock.
Some days afterwards his relatives found him in this position and
were frightened to see the change in his body. As he was still able
to speak, he told them how it had all happened. Then they brought
a great number of men, but were not able to release him, and so he
remained in that painful position."

On hearing this, the king of the land went to see the
place himself, and fearing that some misfortune would befal

[1] Julien's Hwen Thsang, Vol. I, p. 179.

him he sent a great number of workmen to cut away the rock, and release the herdsman, but they were quite unable to move him.

Afterwards he became gradually changed into stone, but still preserved his human form. In later times, a certain king thinking that it must possess some medicinal properties, tried to chisel away a small portion; but the workmen after ten days' labour were not able to get even a pinch of dust. The stone still existed in the time of Hwen Thsang.

Now, though there are no rocks at the mouth of the Máyáganj cave at the present day, yet the story of the long gallery can only apply to this cave, as there is no other now known at Bhágalpur. However, as rocks crop up in many places in this neighbourhood, it is quite possible that there may once have been some rocks at the mouth of the Máyá-ganj cave.

13—KAHALGAON.

On leaving Champa, the Chinese pilgrim travelled eastward for 140 or 150 *li*, about 24 miles, to an isolated hill surrounded by the waters of the Ganges, near its southern bank. Its bluff peaks were of great height, and on the summit there was a Brahmanical temple. There were tanks of pure water and groves filled with flowers and rare trees, and on every side there were rock-cut caves, the abodes of famous and learned men. "Whoever visits this place forgets to return[1]." Both bearing and distance point to the rocky hill of Kahalgaon (Kolgong of the maps), which is just 23 miles to the east of Bhágalpur.

There are three separate rocky islets at Kahalgaon, the upper one being to the south, as the river here takes a bend to the north. At present the Ganges has almost deserted these rocks, which are surrounded by a considerable extent of good rich land, all under cultivation. The old channel, however, still exists, and is known as the *Marganga*, or "dead

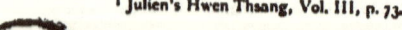

[1] Julien's Hwen Thsang, Vol. III, p. 73.

Ganges." In 1837 this was the main channel of the river, which I ascended in a steamer with some difficulty.

On the summit of the rocks there is a level terrace, on which there was once a large brick temple with white sandstone pilasters and doorway, of which the door jambs are still standing. There are also heaps of broken bricks of large size, 11 inches broad by 2½ inches thick, with a probable length of 15 or 16 inches, with numbers of smaller bricks only 7½ inches square and 1¾ inch thick, besides a few carved bricks. These are no doubt the ruins of the temple seen by Hwen Thsang. The story of its ruin is not known, but it may be guessed with some certainty from the presence of the tomb of Shekh Mári Sháh.

A little below the summit there is a small rock-cut temple of a very peculiar style[1]. In plan it is a square of nearly 12 feet side, with a slight extension of the front on each side. In elevation it has two gable ends, something like the Teli Mandir at Gwalior. Between the gables the roof looks like the imitation of the horse-shoe vault of the great Buddhist caves. The chamber is very small, only 4 feet deep by 1 foot 10 inches in breadth, and 2½ in height. I conclude therefore that it held only a lingam, but no trace of the enshrined object was found on clearing out the cell. In front the entrance of the cell has a round head with a breadth of 2½ feet, a depth of 1½ foot, and a height of only 3½ feet. The people have no name for the temple, which seems to point to a very early date of its desecration by the Muhammadans.

Hwen Thsang's remark, that "people who visited the place forgot to leave it," is susceptible of a very different explanation from what he intended. In later times Kahalgaon has been noted as a favourite haunt of the "River Thugs," and as dead men tell no tales there can be no doubt that all their victims who visited Kahalgaon FORGOT to leave it, at least they did not leave it alive, as their bodies were always thrown into the river. So notorious was the name of Kahalgaon as the haunt of thugs that its name became proverbial.

---

[1] See Plate XV for plan and view of this curious temple.

The following verse records the popular opinion regarding
Kahalgaon :—

> *Bhágalpur ka Bhagaliya,*
> *Aur Kahalgaon ka Thug,*
> *Patna ka Dewáliya,*
> *Tinon nám sad.*

"The Swindler of Bhâgalpur,
The Kahalgaon Footpad,
And Bankrupt of Patna, are
Three names very bad."

14.—PATHARGHATTA.

At Patharghatta there is an isolated pile of granite rocks
like those of Jâhngira and Kahalgaon, but the place derives
its name from the "Rocky Ghât," where the road passes over
the end of the long hill called Chaurâsi-mûrti, or the "Eighty-
four Statues." This ghât is situated just 8 miles to the north-
north-east of Kahalgaon, where the river resumes its easterly
course. There are a few sculptures on the isolated hill, but
they are of no interest. One of them Buchanan thought
might represent Krishna and Râdha[1]. In the great hill to the
east there are several caves as well as numerous sculptures in
very high relief, and from 2 to 3 feet in height. Two caves
to the north have regular doorways with cut mouldings. A
third cave to the south, called *Pátálpuri*, is reputed to be of
such great length that no one has ever yet been to the end
of it ; and a story is told of a certain Râja, named Jay Singh,
who, with eighty maunds of oil (6,400 lbs. weight) and several
hundred men, penetrated a very long distance, but was obliged
to return because the oil began to fail.

The "Eighty-four Images" are sculptured on a rock high
up the hill, which is now very difficult of access on account of
the thick jungle. The figures face the river and are supposed
to represent eighty-four *munis*, or sages, and they are accordingly called the *Chaurâsi-muni*, just as often as the *Chaurâsi-
mûrti*. Buchanan, however, describes them as representing
the adventures of Krishna and Râma, and this opinion is no

---

[1] Eastern India, by Buchanan, Vol. II, p. 64.

doubt partly correct, as there are figures of the *Vámana* and
Narsingha avatáras, and of a Gopi churning milk. In another place there are two men wrestling, with a woman looking on in astonishment, as expressed by her fore-finger and
thumb placed in her mouth. But the most curious of these
sculptures is a seated figure with the left leg raised, and surrounded by a crowd of human heads, ten on each side, which
are apparently looking at him. At the shrine of the Butesar-
náth lingam there are a number of figures lying, amongst
which were observed a seated female with a seven-headed
snake canopy, and a seated Buddha, now called Bhairon.

15.—KANKJOL.

Kánkjol or *Kákjol* is an old town, which was once the
head-quarters of an extensive province, including the whole
of the present district of Rájmahal, and a large tract of
country which is now on the east of the Ganges, but which
in former days was on its west bank. Even at the present
day this tract is still recorded as belonging to Kánkjol; and
I was, therefore, not surprised to hear the zamindars of
Ináyatpur and the surrounding villages to the east of the
Ganges say that their lands were in Kánkjol. The simple
explanation is that the Ganges has changed its course. At
the time of the Muhammadan occupation it flowed under the
walls of Gaur, in the channel of the present Bhágirathi River.
Part of the Trans-Gangetic Kánkjol is in the Puraniya district bounded by Akbarpur, and part in the Málda district
bounded by Málda proper.

Kánkjol is situated on a jutting point of the old high
bank of the Ganges, just 16 miles to the south of Rájmahal,
and the same distance to the south-west of Gaur. The
province in which it is situated was called *Rárh* or *Rádha,*
by the Hindus, but whether Kánkjol was the capital or not
I have been unable to ascertain. According to Hwen Thsang's
distance from Champa or Bhágalpur, the capital should
rather be looked for in the neighbourhood of Rájmahal. On
leaving Champa, the pilgrim travelled 400 *li,* or 67 miles to
the east to *Kie-chu-u-khi-lo,* which M. Julien renders by
Kajughira. In his Index he gives the Chinese syllables

differently, as *Kie-chu-uo-k'i-lo*, or *Kajingara*. I confess that
I am not satisfied with the reading adopted by Julien, which
appears to ignore the middle syllable altogether. I have
always had a suspicion that the last two syllables, *Kie-lo*,
might perhaps represent the Indian *gali*, or pass, as in the
names of *Teliya-gali* and *Sikra-gali*, both in the neighbourhood of Râjmahal. The Chinese syllables might then be
Kachwagali or *Kachûa-gali*. But there is no trace of such
a name in this province. Unfortunately we do not know the
old name of Râjmahal, its former name of *Agmahal* being
of Muhammadan origin. It seems probable, therefore, that
the Chinese syllables may represent the ancient Hindu name
of Râjmahal.

I have a theory, however, which if true would most satisfactorily explain this difficult name, and I here give it for
what it is worth. In this part of India there are two kinds
of sugarcane, the pale-yellow, or *Pundra*, and the dark-
purple or black, called *Kâjali* and *Kajoli*, from *Kajjala* or
Kajwala, "lamp-black." The former gave its name to the
province of *Paundra-desa* to the east of the Ganges, the
latter to *Kajolaka,* or the province to the west of the Ganges.
By transposing the last two Chinese syllables, the name
of Kajolaka will represent the Chinese name very closely.
By a similar transposition also of the last two syllables of
the vulgar name *Kie-shing-kie-lo*, we get *Kusaraka*, or the
country of the *Kusar*, which is the common Bengali name
for the sugarcane. As the two names of *Kajolaka* and
Kusaraka are regularly formed, just like those of *Nepâlaka*,
Palâsaka, Pundraka, &c., it seems quite possible that they
may have been applied to this country as I have suggested.

An old name for this province was *Audumbara*, which,
according to Tudar Mall's rent-roll, was a Sirkar, comprising
the *Mahals* of Agmahal, Kânkjol, Kunwar, Partâb, and
Molesar[1]. The same name is also used by Abûl Fazl in the
Ain Akbari[2]. But in spite of all these changes the old name

---

[1] Blochmann in Bengal Asiatic Society's Journal, Vol. XLII, p. 223.
[2] See Gladwin's Ain Akbari, Vol. II, p. 178, where it is erroneously given as Gungjook.

of Kânkjol or Kâkjol has clung to the district down to the present day. I think therefore that it has at least as good a claim as Râjmahal to represent the capital, more especially as it is not more than 70 miles from Bhâgalpur by the direct route through the hills, thus agreeing with the distance assigned by Hwen Thsang.

The pilgrim describes a curious high tower on the bank of the Ganges, and on the northern frontier of the province, which was built partly of stone and partly of brick. When I first read this passage I thought that the tower must have been like that of Dhâmek near Sârnâth, of which the lower half is of stone and the upper half of brick. But when I saw the walls and towers of Teliyagarhi, or Teliya-gali, which are built in alternate courses of stones and bricks, they at once recalled Hwen Thsang's description, and I have no doubt that this has been the common style of building in this part of the country from time immemorial. The pilgrim does not say what was the nature of the tower; but from his description I gather that it must have been a Buddhist building, as its four faces were ornamented with panels filled with figures of Saints, *Buddhas*, and Devas. From the mixture of brick and stone in the building, and its position on the northern frontier of the district, and on the south bank of the Ganges, I am led to think that this tower was most probably situated at Teliya-garhi itself. The place was certainly an old military post, as it completely commanded one of the three passes leading into Bengal. But it must also have been a place of some consequence, as it possessed a considerable number of large statues, both Buddhist and Brahmanical. Most of these were removed to a great house at Kahalgaon, built on the top of the hill facing the rocks; but since the establishment of the Railway close by many of them have disappeared, no one knows where.

16—GAUR.

The great city of *Gauda* or *Gaur*, the capital of Balâl Sen and his descendants, and their successors the Muhammadan Governors and kings of Bengal, is not mentioned at all by Hwen Thsang. In his time, as I will show hereafter, the capital of the country to the north of the Ganges was Mahásthán on the Tista River, and the country itself was called *Paundra*. This name is quite unknown to the people of the present day, who call their country *Barendra*. That this was the common name of the province in former days we learn from two different authorities Táranáth, and Min-hájus Siráj. According to the former, *Varendra* was conquered by Devapála, the second of the Pála Princes of Magadha, about A.D. 850, while, according to the latter, who was at Lakhnauti in A.D. 1243, the name of the province in which Lakhnauti or Gaur was situated was *Barbanda* or *Baranda*. At the same time we know that the Gaudas were a tribe, and that the Pála Rajas took the title of *Gaureswara*. It seems certain therefore that the western part of the province at least must have been called *Gauḍa* or *Gaur*. But from a passage in the Rája Tarangini, it would appear that the whole province was sometimes called Gauḍa, as Jayapida, Rája of Kashmir, from A.D. 782 to 813, is said to have married the Princess Kalyáni, the daughter of Jayanta, king of Gauḍa, of which the capital was Paundra Varddhana[1]. As mention is also made of the "five kings of Gauda" who were all vanquished by Jayapida, it seems probable that each small district had its own king. But whether this was the case or not, we learn from Jayapida's story that so late as the end of the eighth century A.D. Paundra Varddhana was still the capital of the country to the north of the Ganges, as it had been a century and a half earlier in the time of Hwen Thsang. We learn also at the same time that the country of Varendra had not yet fallen into the hands of the Pála Rájas of Bengal.

In my last report I gave a chronological list of the Pála Rájas, in which I assigned the year A.D. 815 to Gopála, the founder of the dynasty.[2] As in that report I have given

[1] Raja Tarangini, Vol. IV, pp. 420, 421, 466, 467.

[2] Babu Rajendra Lal wildly suggests that the temple of Sankara Gaureswara in Kashmir was probably built by order of one of these Sena Rajas I in defiance of Kalhan Pandit's statement that it was erected by Sankara Varmma, Raja of Kashmir, a statement which is proved by the companion temple of Sugandheswara built by his Queen, Sugandha.

my reasons for doing so at full length, I need not repeat them ; but I may say here that I am still quite confident that the date of the establishment of the Pâla dynasty lies somewhere in the first half of the ninth century. Though there are many places named after these Princes in the country to the north of the Ganges, such as Gopâlpur, Dharmpâlgarh, Mahipâlpur, &c., to attest their sovereignty, yet it is nearly certain that their principal place of abode, if not their actual capital, was Bihâr in Magadha. There is no doubt, however, that their successors, the Sena Râjas, lived in the province of Gauda or Barendra, as the building of the city of Gaur is attributed to Balâl Sen, whose name still lives in *Balâl bâri* to the north of the city, while he and his successors all took the title of *Sankara Gaureswara*, or the " fortunate lord of Gaura."

The name of *Gauḍa* or *Gauṛ* is, 'I believe, derived from Guḍa or Guṛ, the common name of molasses, or raw sugar, for which this province has always been famous. In former days when the Ganges flowed past the city, Gaur was the great mart where all the sugar of the northern districts was collected for exportation. But since the city was deserted by the Ganges, the sugar is now brought to the flourishing town of Rahanpur, at the junction of the Purnabhâba and Mâhânadi River, where it is transferred from carts to boats, to be carried down the Mahânadi and Ganges to Calcutta and other places. The extent of the trade carried on at this important mart may be judged by the fact that during the single day and night which I spent there, no less than 2,800 carts, with several thousands of bullocks and men, arrived at Rahanpur, laden with rice, sugar, and betel-nuts.

The ruins of Gaur have already been described by the late Mr. J. H. Ravenshaw in a costly volume, excellently illustrated by forty-four of his own photographs, and by twenty-five plates of inscriptions. Of these inscriptions, no less than fourteen were given by me for Mr. Ravenshaw's use, with an offer of plans of the buildings described in his work. The untimely death of the author in 1874 delayed the publication of the book until 1878 ; and as my plans of the buildings were not required for it, I take the opportunity of a second visit to Gaur, in December 1879, to make them public, along with a few notes and several new inscriptions. One of these inscriptions is the oldest Muhammadan record yet found in Bengal.

The site of Gaur, on a narrow strip of land between the Ganges and the Mahánadi Rivers, would appear to have been selected chiefly for the convenience of water-communication with all parts of the country. Its position is shown in the accompanying map, where the Bhâgirathi River represents the old course of the Ganges. There are no Hindu remains of any kind to point out the landmarks of the ancient city ; but perhaps the native names of *Phulwâri* and *Pâtâl Chandi,* which are still applied to two of the gates, may be taken as evidence of previous Hindu occupation. The old city of the Sena Râjas would thus be confined within the square of 2 miles each side, or 4 square miles of area, extending from the Phulwâri Gate on the north to the *Pâtâl Chandi* Gate on the south, and from the Ganges on the west to the great rice swamps of the Mahanadi on the east. Within these limits also are found other Hindu names, such as *Ganga-asnân,* or the "Bathing *Ghât"* at the north-west corner, on the bank of the Bhâgirathi, or old Ganges; and the *Lohagadh,* or "Red Embankment," on the south, with the divisions of Dharmpur, Biâspur, and Râmchandarpur inside. The temples and gardens of course would have been in the suburbs outside. Thus, *Degaon,* 1 mile to the south of the *Lohagadh,* would have been the site of a temple, while the old fort of Phulbâri on the Bhâgirathi, 1½ mile farther to the south, would have been the Râja's Palace. This demarcation of the old Hindu city seems the more probable from the fact that both Degaon and Phulbâri are included within a long rampart connecting the Phulbâri fort with the Lohagadh rampart. This would extend the length of the city 4 miles, with a mean breadth of about 1½ mile. As the Balâlbâri lies nearly 4 miles to the north of the Phulwâri Darwâzah, and is completely cut off from it by low swampy ground, it never could have formed part of the city. Balâlbâri or Bâgh-bâri, as it is also called, is an irregular square about 1 mile each side. The enclosure is surrounded by a gigantic embankment, 50 feet broad at top and 150 feet broad at base, with a height of 20 feet. On each side, that is, on the inside as well as on the outside, it has a deep ditch 75 feet wide. There are no remains of buildings inside ; but there are several causeways crossing at right angles, which were probably the roads of the place. A plan of the enclosure will be seen in the accompanying map several miles to the north of the city.

The village of Kamala-bâri, rather more than 1 mile to the north of the city rampart and just beyond the great Sâgar Dighi lake, no doubt formed one of the suburbs of the city, as it still possesses a shrine dedicated to the goddess *Gaureswari Devi*, the special patron of Gaur. Buchanan says that the spot is called *Dwârrâsini*, and that an annual *méla*, or fair, is held there in the month of Jyeshta[1]. My informants knew nothing of Dwârrâsini, but assigned the fair to the full moon of Jyeshta, in the month of June.

At *Gangâsnân*, or the " Bathing Ghât" on the old Ganges, close to the north-west corner of the city, there is no temple, but only a long flight of steps leading down to the river. An annual fair is held here on the full moon of Paush, which in 1879 was on the 19th December.

An annual fair is also held at Râmkhel, 1 mile to the south of the Phulbâri Fort. The place must therefore have been one of the southern suburbs of the city.

Towards the end of the Hindu rule, Gaur received the name of *Lakshmanavati* or *Lakhnauti*, from its last king, *Lakshmaniya*, and it is under this name that it is first mentioned by the Muhammadans. *Lakhan* is the common spoken form of *Lakshana*, which is often used for Lakshmana.

The earliest description that we possess of Lakhnauti is by the Muhammadan historian, Minhâj, who actually lived in the city for some years after A.D. 1243. According to him, Bakhtiyâr Khalji, the conqueror of Bengal, after having destroyed Nadiya, where Râja Lakhmaniya then resided,

[1] Eastern India, Vol. II.

established the seat of his government at Lakhnauti in A.D.
1198. Bakhtiyár was assassinated in 1202, and was succeeded by a number of other governors, more or less dependent
on Delhi, until A.D. 1286, when, on the death of the Emperor
Balban, his son Náser-ud-din Bughra became independent
King of Bengal.

Shortly after the death of Kutb-ud-din Aibek, the governor,
Husám-ud-din Iwaz assumed royal state with the title of
Ghiás-ud-din. He lived at Lakhnauti, where he built a fort,
most probably on the site of the Muhammadan citadel, 2
miles to the south of Phulbári. He also constructed two
great causeways, or raised roads connecting the city with
Deokot on the north and with Lakhnor to the west, a total
length of ten days' journey. These embanked roads still
exist, and form two of the principal lines of communication in the country. The position of Lakhnor is doubtful;
but I most emphatically dissent from all those who look for
it in the Birbhúm district, or in fact anywhere beyond the
hills. The total length of the road was only ten days' journey;
and as Deokot is 54 miles from Gaur, with two unbridged
rivers in the way, the Mahánadi and the Purnabhába, the
journey to that place would have occupied five or six days,
there would thus remain only four or five days' journey
to Lakhnor, of which the crossing of the Ganges would
occupy one. The position of Lakhnor should, therefore, be
looked on the edge of the high ground forming the western
limits of the bed of the Ganges, as there would be no necessity for any embankment beyond the low ground. I think
it not improbable that *Kánkjol* is the place intended, and
that *Lakhnor* is only a corrupt reading of the Persian character forming the name of Kánkjol. I have travelled over
several portions of Ghiás-ud-din's road from Gaur to Deokot.
In many places it has been entirely swept away; but for the
greater part of the way the embankment is still in very good
order, being from 80 to 100 feet in breadth, and from 4 to 5
feet in height. During the rule of Ghiás-ud-din, Bengal was
several times invaded by the armies of Delhi, but without
success, until, in A.D. 1227, the Emperor Iltitmish sent his

eldest son, Nâser-ud-din Mahmud, who captured Lakhnauti and put Ghiâs-ud-din to death.

The oldest inscribed record of Muhammadan rule in Bengal is a short inscription of three lines from Gaur, now in the Indian Museum in Calcutta. It describes the building of a well (*ul-ber*) during the reign of Shamsuddin Iltitmish by Kutlugh Khân in A.H. 630. The following is the translation of this short record, the original of which will be found in the accompanying Plate[1] :—

"* * * this well (was made) in the time of the fortunate King of Kings, Shams-ud-dunya wa-ud-din, Iltitmish, the Sultan, the helper of the Khalif, during (the ?) of the late Kutlugh Khân, the sword-master, in the year 633 [A.D. 1235-36.]"

The earliest inscription of any Bengal governor yet found is one of Izzud-din Tughral, who ruled from A.H. 631 to 642. It is dated in A.H. 640 or A.D. 1242. It was obtained by Mr. Broadley at Bihâr. After him came Timur Khan, who died in 644, and Ikhtiyâr-ud-din Tughril, who proclaimed himself king and perished in Kâmrûp[2]. The date of his death is not given; but Minhâj fixes the date of his successor in A.H. 656, which I take to be a mistake for 646, as the inscription of Jalâl-ud-din Masâud Jâni, which I obtained at Gangârâmpur, is dated in A.H. 647. A copy of this important inscription is given in the accompanying Plate[3]. Gangârâmpur is a small village to the south of Mâlda. The inscription, 7 feet 7½ inches long by 1 foot 2½ inches broad, is let into the back wall of a small masjid on the bank of the river, half a mile to the east of the village.

[1] See Plate XX, No. 1.

[2] Blochmann's Geography and History of Bengal in Journal Bengal Asiatic Society, Vol. XLII, p. 246.

[3] This Gangârâmpur must not be confounded with the place of the same name near Deokot, which is a small village without any remains. All the inscriptions which Blochmann refers to Gangârâmpur belong to Deokot, but as the Police station was then at Gangârâmpur, the Civil Officer who furnished the copies to Blochmann called the place by the name of the Police Station in which it is situated. In the same inconvenient fashion the Mangalbâri Pillar has been always described as the Buddal Pillar, although it stands several miles from that place.

From the death of Balban in A.D. 1284, Bengal was ruled by its own kings who resided at Gaur and were quite independent of Delhi. In A.D. 1326, Bahádur Sháh was conquered by Muhammad Tughlak, and Bengal again became a dependency of Delhi, although a branch still held out in the Eastern Provinces, of which Sunárgaon was the capital. At length in A.D. 1339 Háji Iliás brought the whole country under his rule, and afterwards successfully resisted two powerful invasions made by Firoz Sháh of Delhi in person. He was the first king to change the seat of Government, as at the time of Firoz Shah's invasion he appears to have been residing in Pandua, and afterwards made his successful stand against the invader at Ekdála, a great earthen fort surrounded by marshes. His son, Sikandar, made Pandua the Government residence, and it is even now commonly called Hazrat Pandua, " the residence Pandua," to distinguish it from the other Pandua near Hughli. The throne remained with his family until about A.H. 812, when Rája Kans set up a puppet king named Bayázid, in whose name he ruled. The Rája's son, Jalál-ud-din Muhammad, who had become a Muhammadan, succeeded him and held his court at Pandua, where his tomb now forms one of the most picturesque attractions of this deserted place.

In A.H. 846, or A.D. 1442, the seat of Government was again transferred to Gaur by Mahmud I., who claimed to be a descendent of Iliás Sháh. He is said to have reigned 27 years, which should probably be altered to 17 years, from 846 to 863, as the earliest date yet found on his coins is A.H. 846. One of this date, in my possession, gives the Mint name of *Hazrat Khalifábád*. From this time down to the conquest of the country by Sher Sháh, the kings of Bengal continued to reside at Gaur, and all the buildings now standing there were erected during the century of their rule.

The ruins of the Muhammadan city of Gaur extend for a length of 11 miles along the east bank of the Bhágirathi River, from the Phulwári Gate to the suburb of Firozábád on the south. The city proper within the ramparts, from the Phulwári Gate to the Kotwáli Gate on the south, is 8 miles

long, or just twice the length of what I suppose to be the old
Hindu city, the whole of the extension being at the southern
end. At this end are, all the great Muhammadan buildings,
the Minár, the Sona, the Thántipára, the Lattan, the Kadam
Rasul, and the Gunmant Masjids, as well as the Dákhil and
Kotwáli Gates. All these Muhammadan names seem to
point out the position of the Moslem city, just as the Hindu
names of the Phulwári and Chánd Gates and of the *Gangá-
snán,* or " Bathing Ghát," point out the site of the Hindu city.

Owing to the unfortunately low site of the city, it was
found necessary to embank it all round at a very early date.
Thus, not only are the Hindu and Muhammadan cities completely surrounded by earthen ramparts, but all the roads,
both inside and outside, are raised causeways, while the banks
of both the Ganges and the Mahánadi on the city side are
protected by broad ramparts extending for many miles in
length. Thus the causeway on the eastern bank of the
Bhágirathi, or old Ganges, extends the whole way from the
Kalindri River near Gangárámpur to Kansát on the Ganges
below the junction of the Bhágirathi, a distance of 25 miles.
Similarly, the causeway on the west bank of the Mahánadi
extends for nearly 20 miles from Málda to Rahanpur. But
in spite of all these costly precautions, the city of Gaur was
always liable to inundation during the heavy floods, while the
great marsh of *Chatta-bhatta* on the east, covering an area
of about 25 square miles, was never dry[1]. So long as the
Ganges continued to flow under the walls of the city, and
even after its desertion, so long as the Bhágirathi retained a
good flow of water, it is probable that Gaur may have been
fairly healthy. But when the Bhágirathi dwindled away to a
mere rivulet, and the filth of the city was no longer swept
away, its continued accumulation within the ramparts at last
bred a most deadly pestilence, which in A.H. 983, or A.D.
1575, carried off no less than fourteen of Akbar's principal

---

[1] I take this name from the Ain Akbari by Gladwin, Vol. II, p. 8. Abul Fazl
also says " that if the dams break during the periodical rains the city is laid
under water."

officers, including the celebrated Munim Khân, the Governor of the province[1].

Since then Gaur has been gradually deserted until towards the end of the last century, when it had become, as Creighton describes it, "an inhabited waste covered with great forest trees and thick jungle swarming with tigers, leopards and thorns, and wild boars, and full of swamps teeming with mosquitoes and crocodiles." When I first knew it, upwards of forty years ago, annual tiger-shooting parties used to assemble in the ruins of Gaur, and on one occasion I remember that a long piece of the skeleton of a python was found, measuring nearly 9 inches in diameter. Even in 1871 Gaur was in a very jungly state, and several of the ruins could only be approached with difficulty, owing to the dense canebrakes which were too green to burn, and too thickly covered with long sharp thorns to be forced by elephants. At that time the place fully merited Ravenshaw's description of being "concealed in deep jungle." On this point Ravenshaw spoke from actual experience, as he had to cut away the jungle which surrounded the old buildings before he could take his photographs of them. But in December 1879 the whole scene was changed, the greater part of the jungle had been cleared away, and all the lowlands above the water-level were covered with crops of *urad* and *sarsan* [veches and mustard.] The mounds are still covered with jungle, as they are mostly composed of brick ruins which are not worth cultivating. The cause of all this change is due to the Government having offered the lands almost rent-free at the low price of 4 annas a *bigah* for a fixed period. The offer was eagerly taken up by the people, and nearly the whole of the available land is now under cultivation. The effect of this clearance may be judged by a glance at Ravenshaw's views of the Lattan Masjid, which is seen completely surrounded by thick jungle several feet in height. All this has now been cleared away; and at the time of my last visit the masjid was surrounded only by a light fence marking the boundaries of the fields.

---

[1] Blochmann's Ain Akbari, Vol. I, p. 482.

In describing the Muhammadan buildings of Gaur, it is not possible to preserve a strictly chronological arrangement, as most of them have lost their inscriptions, and their dates are consequently more or less uncertain. The Kadam Rasul and the Little Golden Masjids still have their inscribed tablets *in situ;* but the fine lofty minâr, the Great Golden Mosque, the Thântipârâ and Lattan Mosques, and all the gateways and bridges, present only the empty panels from which the inscribed slabs have been removed. The dates hitherto accepted depend chiefly on the statements of Creighton and Franklin that certain existing inscriptions were found *near* particular buildings. If they had taken the measurement of each of these inscribed slabs and compared it with the size of the panel of the building near which it was found, they would have seen at once whether the inscription belonged to the adjacent building or not. But this precaution having been neglected at the time, and no measurements having been given of any of the published inscriptions, I find it almost impossible to fix the site of any one of them. I have myself taken the measure of every one of the vacant inscription panels that I have come across, but they are very few, and, with one or two possible exceptions to be noticed hereafter, the sizes of the vacant panels have afforded no clue to the identification of any of the published inscriptions.

Of the early Muhammadan governors of Bengal, and of their successors, the Balbaniya Kings, not a single trace now remains in the capital in which they lived. There are no remains assigned to them, and not even a ruined mound preserves the memory of their names. Iliás and his son Sikandar and their successors, Raja Kans and his son Jalâlud-din Muhammad, lived usually at Hazrat Pandua, and not a single inscription of any of them has yet been found in Gaur. But with Mahmud I., who claimed descent from Iliás, and his successors, there are both buildings and inscriptions still existing to attest their continued residence in the old capital.

In the following account of the architectural remains of Gaur I have divided them into three groups descriptive of

their position, in the citadel, the city, or the suburbs. The
first group comprises the several gateways of the citadel,
the gigantic Bâis-gazi wall, the mosque of Kadam Rasul,
and a few other remains. The second group includes all the
remains inside the city ramparts, namely, the bridge of
Mahmud I., the old minár, the various mosques known as
Chámkati, Thántipara, Lattan, and Gunmant, with the Great
Golden Mosque in the north, and the Kotwáli Gate in the
south. The third group comprises all the remains outside
the city, in the northern suburb of Sadulláhpur, and in the
southern suburb of Firozpur. In the former stands the tombs
of Sheikh Akhi Siráj and the Janjaniya Masjid ; in the latter
are the Little Golden Mosque and the tombs of Niáma-
tullah and his family.

17.—THE CITADEL OF GÂUR.

The citadel of Lakhnauti is situated on the bank of the
old Ganges, in the southern half of the city, just midway
between the Phulbári Fort and the Kotwáli Gate. It is very
nearly 1 mile in length from north to south, by half a mile
in width at its broadest part opposite the Eastern Gate, but
not more than a quarter of a mile wide at its northern and
southern ends. It is entirely surrounded by a great earthen
rampart, upwards of 30 feet in height and about 190
feet thick at the base, with round towers at all the angles,
and a deep ditch on the outside, about 200 feet wide when
full. The rampart is everywhere covered with large forest
trees, and the ditch is filled with weeds and crocodiles. The
age of the citadel is unknown ; but as there is nothing now
remaining in it of an early date, it seems probable that it was
the work of Mahmud I. and his successors.

The citadel has two great gateways, one on the north
called the *Dákhal Darwása,* a corruption of *Dákhil,* or
" entrance," and the other on the east, which has no special
name. The *Dákhil* Gate is also known as the *Salámi
Darwása,* or " Saluting Gate," because this being the prin-

cipal entrance salutes were fired from the adjoining rampart
Its towers have been much injured by trees springing from
the points of the brick-work, but even in its ruined state it is
one of the finest and most picturesque buildings now remaining in Gaur.[1] It is also one of the largest, being 113
feet 2 inches in length by 73 feet 4 inches in breadth,
with a height nearly 60 feet. Creighton's view, taken from
the outside, makes the sides of the towers much too sloping,
as may be seen by comparing it with Ravenshaw's inside view.
The building consists of a central passage 14 feet wide and
113¼ feet long, with a guard-room on each side 74½ feet
long by 9¼ feet broad. The walls, which are 9¾ feet thick,
are pierced by three doorways on each side of the passage,
with one outer doorway on the inner side of the rampart.
The piers between the doorways are made of brick faced
with stone up to the spring of the arches, but all the rest of
the building is made of brick. At each of the four corners
there is a twelve-sided tower, five storeys in height, crowned
by a dome. The faces of the tower are panelled and ornamented with the usual chains and bells in relief. Creighton
makes the height of the towers 53 feet, but this measurement did not include the domes, which were all ruined
before his time. The walls on both sides of the archway
were ornamented in a similar manner with panels filled
with chains and bells. The outer arch was 34 feet in height,
above which the battlemented wall rose 15 feet, making a
total height of 48 feet. The date of the building is not recorded, but I will show hereafter good grounds for assign-
ing its erection to Mahmud I. Creighton attributes it to his
son Bârbak, who died in A.H. 863.

The *Eastern Gate* of the citadel is a much smaller building, only 25 feet square inside, and is supposed to be of later
date, having been erected, as Buchanan was informed, by
Shujâh, the brother of Aurangzeb. The walls are 8 feet
8 inches thick. A great part of it has been plastered over,

---

[1] See Creighton's Plate II, Ravenshaw's Plate IX, p. 16. There is also a very
good view of this gateway in Daniell's large work. A plan of the gate will be
found in the accompanying Plate, No. XIV.

but the fluted parts at the corners, which are without plaster, seemed to me to be of an earlier age. Very probably the plaster was part of some repairs made when Shujáh took up his residence in Gaur, nearly a century after its desertion in Akbar's reign. In Mr. King's brief notice of the Gaur buildings, it is called the *Lakkha chhippi* Gate. I take this name to refer to the numerous patterns of glazed tiles on the buildings as *chhipi* is the name given to cotton printers, and *Lakkha* is a *lakh*, or one hundred thousand. There is an inscription of the time of Husen Sháh, which records the building of one of the Fort Gates in A.H. 918, which, I think, can only refer to this gate. The following is Blockmann's translation[1] :—

" This gate of the fort was built during the reign of the exalted and liberal king Alauddunya wa-ud-din Abul Muzaffar Husen Sháh, the king, son of Sayid Ashraful Husaini. May God perpetuate his kingdom and his rule ! In the year 918 [A.D. 1512]."

From the northern gate a raised road led to the palace in the southern half of the citadel passing through two intermediate gates called the *Chánd Darwása* and the *Nim Darwása*. As the latter stands exactly half-way between the entrance gate and the palace wall, it is most probable that its name was derived from its position as the " Half-way Gate." When they were built, these gates must have marked certain divisions of the court-yard of the palace; but they are now standing alone and apparently purposeless. A view of the Chánd Gate is given by Creighton in Plate III. Its whole style is similar to that of the Dákhil Gate, with which it also agrees in the height of its arches and battlements. Creighton assigns its date to A.H. 871, or A.D. 1466, from an inscription which he found close by. As this records the building of one of the two inner gates, the date is certain, and from the expression of " middle gateway " I conclude that it refers to the *Nim Darwása*, or " Half-way Gate." The text and translation of the inscription, as given by Francklin,

[1] Journal of Bengal Asiatic Society.

are quoted by Mr. Grote in his notes on Ravenshaw's Gaur[1], from which I make the following extract :—

" The Prince, scattering the seeds of beneficence and diffusing the waters of gladness ; the Sultân, protector of the universe, pillar of religion, the illustrious Bârbak Shâh, son of the most esteemed Sayyid, exemplary to the nations, Sultân Mahmud Shâh model of justice, equally renowned with the princes of the two Irâks, of Syria and Arabia, yielding to none of the princes of the earth in generosity and liberality, without an equal, a Prince whose habitation resembles Paradise, whose palace is the refuge of the unfortunate.

" Behold a reservoir of water flowing under the palace, resembling the waters of paradise whose streams afford consolation to the afflicted.

" Within the abode is soul-refreshing rest, delightful as the fragrance of the sweet basil.

" A gateway also adjoining to the reservoir was erected by the same prince. It is the middle gateway leading to the interior of the royal palace, in the year of the Hijrah 871, in the commencement of the auspicious reign.

" For ever let us pray to the Almighty for the prosperity of this monarch, so long as the feathered tribe shall warble forth their notes in this garden.

" In the reign of the Sultan, asylum of the world, pillar of the universe and of religion, the victorious Monarch, Sultân Bârbak Shâh, whose power and dominion may God perpetuate· (A.H. 871, A.D. 1466)."

This extract shows that Bârbak also made a " canal" or water-course (*nahr*) flowing under the palace ; and as no other works besides the " Half-way Gate " and the " canal " are claimed for him in this long inscription, I infer that the citadel had already been completed by his father, and that the Dâkhil Gate must therefore be assigned to Mahmud Shâh I. The difference is only a few years, as the father was certainly reigning in A.H. 863.

The palace itself is gone, nothing but fields of ruins now remaining to mark its site. But a great part of the gigantic wall which surrounded the court-yard, which is 200 feet in length and 900 feet in breadth, is still standing on the north-east side, and is popularly known as the *Báis Gazi*, or

[1] Ravenshaw's Gaur, p. 19, *note*.

" Twenty-two ell " wall. As the wall is 42 feet in height, the
gas of Gaur must have been the common one of 24 *tassus*, or
" thumb-breadths," or nearly 23 inches. The wall is a solid
mass of brick-work, 15 feet thick at the base, and 8 feet
10 inches at the top under the cornice. At every twelve
courses, measuring 2 feet 1⅜ inches in height, the thickness
is diminished by stepping the next twelve courses inwards on
both sides. I measured the thickness in a broken gap about
18 feet below the top, where it was exactly 11 feet 6 inches.
The receding steps are well shown in Ravenshaw's photograph, Plate X.

Outside the palace to the north is the site of Husen
Shâh's tomb. This was still standing in Creighton's time,
see his Plate VIII, but it has now disappeared, as well as
the tomb of his son Nusrat, and a masjid which stood a little
further to the north. The inscription of Husen A.H. 909,
mentioned by Creighton, probably belonged to this mosque.

Kadam Rasul Masjid.

Close to the eastern gateway of the citadel stands the
Kadam Rasul Masjid, or " mosque of the Prophet's foot-
mark." It is one of the latest buildings at Gaur, and is
the only one that is kept in tolerable repair. It consists of a
single room, 25 feet 2 inches long by 15 feet broad, with a
verandah on three sides, 9 feet 2 inches in width. As the
walls are 5 feet thick, the whole building outside measures
63 feet 3 inches by 49 feet 10 inches. Franklin describes it
as being only 35 feet in length, but this is the measurement
of the centre room with its two walls, and does not include
the verandah at each end[1]. The front of the mosque is in-
correctly given with a straight parapet in Creighton's Plate,
No. XI, whereas it is slightly curved in the Bengali fashion,
as may be seen in Ravenshaw's photograph, Plate XII. In
front there are three arched openings supported on massive
stone pillars. The walls are of brick, very highly ornamented,

[1] Ravenshaw's Gaur, p. 22, *note*.

the whole face being divided into panels by bands of mould-
ing. The building has been repeatedly white-washed, and
the carved brick flowers are disfigured by patches of whitewash still sticking in all the sunken parts. At each corner
there is an octagonal tower of 1 foot 5 inches face. This is
crowned by a single stone pillar or minaret, whose diameter is
only 1 foot 5 inches, equal to one face of the tower. Three
of these minarets have fallen, and the top piece of the fourth
is now lying on the ground at the foot of the tower.

Over the centre of the middle arch outside there is an
inscription in three lines, recording the building of the mosque
by Nusrat Shâh in A.H. 937, or A.D. 1530[1]. The letters
are well formed and the inscription is complete. The following is Blochmann's translation of it[2]:

"God Almighty says: 'He who brings the good deed will be re-
warded tenfold' (Qoran, Chap. VI., p. 161). This pure dais and its
stone, on which is the footprint of the Prophet—May God bless him—
were put up by the great generous king, the son of a king, *Nâsir-ud-
dunyâ waddin Abul Musaffar Nusrat Shâh,* the king, son of Sayyid
Ashraful Husaini,—May God perpetuate his kingdom and rule, and
elevate his condition and dignity! In the year 937 A.H. (A.D. 1530-
31)."

The mosque stands in a small court, with a doorway on
the *south* side (not *north*, as stated by Ravenshaw[3]), over
which there is an inscription of Yusuf Shâh, dated in A.H.
885, which certainly cannot have any connection with the
Kadam Rasul itself. I will refer to this inscription hereafter.

The Jail or Prison.

I made a plan of this building, which is certainly mis-
called a prison, as it consists of a single room, 42 feet square,
covered with a dome. The walls are 14 feet 9½ inches thick
and highly ornamented with a carved Bengali parapet.
Externally the building is a square of 71 feet 7 inches with

[1] Ravenshaw's Gaur, No. 23, Plate 57, from my impression.
[2] Journal Bengal Asiatic Society, Vol. XLI, p. 338.
[3] Ravenshaw's Gaur, p. 22.

towers at the corners 10 feet in diameter. I think it may be the same building that is shown in Creighton's No. X Plate, which he calls "a small gateway covered with a dome," and refers to the year A.H. 909 on the authority of an inscription found near the spot. But the building is in the style of an earlier date, and is in fact almost a facsimile of the tomb of Jalál-ud-din Muhammad at Hazrat Pandua. Both are square buildings with towers at the corners and curved battlements. Each is covered by a single large dome; each has four doors, the eastern door-way being wider than the others. Their dimensions also are much the same, as will be seen by the following comparison :—

	Interior.	Walls.		Outside.
	Ft.	Ft.	In.	Ft.
Pandua Tomb	48½ × 48½	13	0	74½ × 74½
Gaur Tomb	42 × 42	14	9½	71½ × 71½

From all these points of similarity in size and style, I am inclined to assign this tomb to Mahmud I. himself, the immediate successor of Jalál-ud-din's son. It was probably also the burial-place of the different members of Mahmud's family, of his sons Bárbak and Fateh, and his grandson Yusuf. In Mr. King's too brief notice of the architectural remains at Gaur, this building is called the *Chor-khána*, or "Thieves' House," that is, the Prison, and also the *Chikka Masjid*, or "Bats' Mosque," from its being filled with these stinking animals[1].

Outside the citadel on the east are the great Minár, or Muazzin's Tower, and the Chámkatti Masjid. On the south-east are the Thántipára and Lattan Masjids: on the south is the Gunmant Masjid; and on the north the Great Golden Mosque, or Bara Sona Masjid. The remaining buildings, situated in the suburbs outside the city, may be divided into two groups; those of the southern suburb of Firozpur, and those of the northern suburb of Sadullahpur. In this order I will now describe them.

[1] Bengal Asiatic Society's Journal, Proceedings, 1875, Vol. XLIV, p. 94.

18—THE CITY OF GAUR.

Bridge of Five Arches.

The earliest inscription that has yet come to light in Gaur itself is a short record of Mahmud I., dated in A. H. 862. This was found by myself on the sloping bank of the high road at the south end of the bridge between the Lattan Masjid and the Kotwáli Gate. From its small size, only 18 by 12 inches, one might guess that it belonged to the bridge; but this is made quite certain by the substance of the inscription itself, which records the building of a bridge. This is the Bridge of Five Arches which is shown in Creighton's Plate, No. XV.

The bridge consists of five pointed arches, the middle one being 11 feet 6 inches span, the next one on each side 10 feet 3½ inches, and the end arches 9 feet 1 inch. The piers also lessen in the same manner, the two middle ones being 10 feet 6 inches thick, and the other two only 9 feet 3 inches. The road-way is 27½ feet broad and 275 feet long. There are several more bridges of the same description.

The following translation of this inscription is by Blochman[1] :—

The building of this bridge took place in the time of the Just King, Nasir-ud-dunyá wa-ud-din Abul Muzaffar Mahmud Shah, the king, on the 5th day of Safar—May God allow the month to end with success and victory !—A.H., 862 (23rd December 1457)."

The Minár, or Muassin's Tower.

This fine old tower is generally known as the *Firozah Minár*, and the *Chirágh Minár*. Buchanan first gave the name of *Pirása*, which I take to be only a corruption of Firozah, or, as it is often pronounced, *Pirosah*. Creighton was fortunately ignorant of *Pir-Asa*, and referred the tower to Firoz Sháh Habshi. I do not, however, feel at all certain that its name has any connection with a King Firoz, but rather

[1] See Plate VI, No. 3. for a copy of the original. For text and translation, see Bengal Asiatic Society's Journal, Vol. XLIV, p. 289.

that *Firozah Minár* means simply the "Blue Tower," from
the turquoise-coloured glaze with which it was faced[1]. Its
style of architecture is similar to that of the towers of the
Dâkhil Gate, which I have assigned to Mahmud I. It is
divided in the same five storeys (above the plinth at the foot
of the door); it has the same 12 sides, and its height bears
the same proportion to its diameter as in the towers of the
Dâkhil Gateway. I think, therefore, that it must be at least
as old as the time of Mahmud I.

Franklin found a broken inscription at the Gomâlti Indigo
Factory, which, on the strength of the title of *Saifuddin*, he
thought might have belonged to Saifuddin Firoz, the builder
of the tower. That this broken inscription belonged to the
minâr is, I think, highly probable from the fact mentioned by
Franklin that the letters are 9 inches in height. Now the
vacant panel from which the inscription was removed measures
3 feet 11 inches in length by 11 inches in height, which
would exactly suit an inscription with a single line of letters 9
inches in height. Unfortunately the inscription ends abruptly
with the title of the King Saif-ud-dunyâ wa-ud-din, leaving us
in doubt whether it should be assigned to Saif-ud-din Hamzah, who reigned from A.H. 800 to 804, or to Saif-ud-din
Firoz, who reigned from 893 to 896. Certainly the name of
Firozah Minâr, if derived from a king, would settle the doubt
in favour of the later prince Saif-ud-din Firoz. But the older
style of the building is against this assignment, and as the
view of its early date is supported by the strong authority of
Mr. Fergusson, I think it more probable that the inscription
belongs to the earlier prince Saif-ud-din Hamzah[2]. In favour
of this view also I can point to the legends of the respective
coins of the two Princes on which Hamzah takes the title of
Abul Mujâhid, as in the broken inscription, while Firoz takes
the title of Abul Muzaffar.

The minâr stands on the northern edge of a large mound,
350 feet long from north to south by 255 feet broad. On the

[1] Francklin notices this "blue and white tiling;" see Ravenshaw's Gaur, p. 28,
note by Mr. Grote.
[2] See History of Indian Architecture, p. 550.

east there is a fine tank, which was no doubt made for the purpose of obtaining earth for filling in the raised platform of the building which once stood on the mound. The walls have all been cleared away, but I picked up numerous pieces of carved bricks and many fragments of glazed tiles. Now the door of the minâr is on the south-south-west side pointing towards the middle of the mound, just where must have been the central doorway of a masjid. On no other supposition can I explain the variation in the position of the minâr doorway from one of the cardinal points. I have no doubt myself that the minâr is a *Mâzinah,* or tower attached to a masjid, from the top of which the *Muazzin* called the *izan,* summoning the faithful to prayers.

The facing of the lower part of the tower for 10 feet in height, between the ground and the door-sill, has been removed long ago. There is nothing to show its shape, but I suppose it to have been a circular or octagonal plinth, not less than 28 or 30 feet in diameter. From the foot of the door the tower rises in three storeys of 12 sides, separated by bands of ornament. Above this point, in the fourth and fifth storeys, it becomes round and less and less in diameter, the last storey being an open room covered by a dome. The top of the dome is now broken; but in Creighton's time it was still in fair order, as may be seen in his Plate No. I. Each of the 12 sides is exactly 4 feet 10 inches in breadth, which gives a diameter of 19½ feet. Franklin makes the circumference 62 feet, which would give a diameter of 19¾ feet[1]. The height, as well as I could ascertain it, was equal to 4¼ diameters, or between 82¾ and 84 feet. The slab of blue stone, forming the door-sill, must have been taken from a Hindu temple, as it is covered with figures apparently representing a boar hunt. There is a spiral staircase inside of 73 steps, leading to the room in the topmost storey, where the Muazzin's lamp in former days no doubt originated the common name of *Chirâgh Minâr,* or " Lamp Tower."

---

[1] In Ravenshaw's Gaur, p. 28, Francklin's measurement is quoted as 32 feet, which is clearly a misprint for 62. Creighton makes it 21 feet in diameter.

The Chámkatti Masjid.

The pretty masjid given by Creighton in Plate XV is not noticed by Ravenshaw, most probably because the greater part of the front has now fallen down. This mosque is said to have received its present name from certain devotees, who, in religious frenzy, used to gash themselves with knives and were therefore called *Chamkatti*, or "skin-cutters." It is built on the same ground plan as the famous Lattan Masjid, but is much smaller. It stands on the side of the high road, at a short distance to the east of the citadel. The building consists of a single room 23 feet 8 inches square, with a large veranda on the east or entrance side, 9 feet 11 inches broad, and an octagonal tower at each corner. The walls are of brick. The whole building is therefore 50 feet 4 inches long by 33 feet 8 inches broad. There are three doorways in front, and one at each end of the verandah, and three doorways on each side of the main room except the west, where there is the usual prayer niche. The faces of the walls are divided into panels, ornamented with the usual chains and bells, and bordered with glazed tiles in various patterns. The lines of battlements are slightly curved in the Bengali fashion, and the whole is covered with a single dome. Its inscription slab is gone, but the panel in which it was fixed is 4½ feet long, which measurement may hereafter perhaps lead to its identification. I think, however, it may be the identical inscription of A.H. 880 preserved by Francklin, which he says was copied from a mosque "called Mahájan Tolá, adjoining the Lattan Masjid, and of the same kind of architecture." Now this description can apply only to the Chám-katti Masjid, which stands in the very middle of Mahájan Tola, at about half a mile from Lattan Masjid, with which it corresponds most exactly, both in ground plan, and in style of architecture. The following is a translation of the inscription copied by Francklin[1] :—

"This mosque was erected by the most illustrious monarch, the sun of religion and of the world, Sultán Yusuf Sháh, son of Bárbak

---

[1] See note by Mr. Grote quoted in Ravenshaw's Gaur, p. 30.

Shah Sultàn, son of Mahmud Shàh Sultàn—whose dominion may God perpetuate! Erected on the first day of the month Muharam, A.H. 880 (A.D. 1475)."

The Thàntipàra Masjid.

Pàra means a " ward," or division, of the city, and Thàntipàra is the " weaver's ward," so that this is not the name of the masjid, but only of the quarter of the city in which it was situated. A sketch of this mosque is given by Creighton in Plate XII, in whose time the central part of the front wall was still standing. " From an inscription found near " Creighton gives its date as A.H. 885. Now this I believe to be the true date of the building for the following reason. The Thàntipàra Mosque had two inscriptions, one on the outside measuring 5 feet ½ inch by 1 foot 8 inches, and the other inside measuring 2 feet 9 inches by 1 foot 6 inches. The former I take to be the record quoted by Creighton, while the latter must be the small slab which is now fixed over the doorway of the court-yard of the Kadam Rasul Mosque, to which it cannot possibly belong. Now this inscription is also dated in A.H. 885, and its dimensions agree perfectly with those of the vacant panel inside the Thàntipàra Masjid. The slab measures 2 feet 4 inches by 13 inches, or just 5 inches less than the broken panel both in length and in breadth. As this would allow a border of one brick thick all round the slab, which was the usual way of fixing the inscriptions, I think there can be little doubt that it must have belonged to the Thàntipàra Masjid.

This mosque is an oblong brick building of two aisles, divided by 4 stone pillars down the middle. It is 78 feet by 31 feet inside, and 91 by 44 feet outside, with an octagonal tower at each corner. The walls are 6½ feet thick, with five arched openings in front and two at each end. The outer faces are ornamented with large panels with projecting flowered borders, each panel being decorated with a pointed arch, under which is the usual bell-shaped ornament suspended from a long chain. The towers also are ornamented in the

The Cha...

The pretty masjid given b... noticed by Ravenshaw, most p... part of the front has now fallen a... to have received its present name h... in religious frenzy, used to gash then... were therefore called *Chamkatti*, or... built on the same ground plan as the... jid, but is much smaller. It stands on... road, at a short distance to the east of... building consists of a single room or... with a large veranda on the east... the walls are of brick, and an octagonal... 11 inches broad, and... feet... inches... three doorways in front, and one at each end of the main... and three doorways on the east side of the... the west, where there is the usual prayer... usual chains and bells, and... feet 8 inches... ornamen... out... walls are divided into panels... glazed... in Bengali fashion. The lines of battlements are... lik... dome... Its inscription slab is gone, but the... it was fixed... feet long, which... measurement... perhaps lead to its identification of... I think, how... architecture... he copied from... mosque... an Tod, adjoining the Latitan Masjid, and of... Chamkatti Masjid, which stands... very nearly... correspond most exactly... both in... translation of... copied by Franklin. The following stands in Latitan Masjid...

... religious zeal of the world, Sultan Yusuf Shah...

See note by Mr. Cust quoted in Ravenshaw's Gaur...

Shah Sultán. sen of Mahmud Shâh ⁓⁓⁓⁓ ⁓
God perpetuate⁓ Erected on the first ⁓⁓ ⁓ ⁓⁓ ⁓⁓
A.H. 880 (A.D. 1475⁓

The Thántipára ⁓⁓⁓

Pára means a "ward," or ⁓⁓⁓⁓ ⁓ ⁓⁓ ⁓⁓ ⁓⁓ ⁓
tipára is the "weaver's ward," ⁓⁓⁓ ⁓⁓ ⁓ ⁓⁓ ⁓⁓
the masjid, but only of the qua⁓⁓ ⁓ ⁓⁓ ⁓⁓ ⁓⁓ ⁓
situated. A sketch of this ⁓⁓⁓⁓ ⁓ ⁓ ⁓⁓ ⁓⁓⁓
Plate XII, in whose time the ⁓⁓⁓⁓ ⁓⁓ ⁓ ⁓ ⁓⁓ ⁓
was still standing. "From a⁓ ⁓⁓⁓⁓ ⁓ ⁓ ⁓⁓ ⁓⁓⁓⁓
ton gives its date as A.H. 885. Now ⁓⁓⁓ ⁓⁓⁓⁓⁓ ⁓ ⁓ ⁓⁓
true date of the building for ⁓⁓ ⁓⁓⁓⁓ ⁓⁓⁓ ⁓ The
Thántipára Mosque had two ins⁓⁓⁓⁓⁓ ⁓⁓ ⁓⁓ ⁓⁓ outside
measuring 5 feet ⅛ inch by 1 ⁓⁓⁓ ⅛ ⁓⁓⁓⁓ and the other
inside measuring 2 feet 9 inches ⁓⁓ 1 ⁓⁓⁓ ⁓ inches. The
former I take to be the record ⁓⁓⁓⁓ by Creighton, while
the latter must be the small slab w⁓⁓⁓ is now fixed over the
doorway of the court-yard of the Kadam Rasul Mosque, to
which it cannot possibly belong. Now this inscription is also
dated in A.H. 885, and its dimensions agree perfectly with
those of the vacant panel inside the Thántipára Masjid.
The slab measures 2 feet 4 inches by 13 inches, or just 5
inches less than the broken panel both in length and in
breadth. As this would allow a border of one brick thick all
round the slab, which was the usual way of fixing the inscriptions. I think there can be little doubt that it must have belonged to the Thántipára Masjid.

This mosque is an oblong brick building of two aisles,
divided by 4 stone pillars down the middle. It is 78 feet by 31
feet inside, and 91 by 44 feet outside, with an octagonal
tower at each corner. The walls are 6½ feet thick, with five
arched openings in front and two at each end. The outer
faces are ornamented with large panels with projecting flowered borders, each panel being decorated with a pointed arch,
under which is the usual bell-shaped ornament suspended
from a long chain. The towers also are ornamented in the

same style. The battlement in front has the favourite Bengal curve or rise on the centre, above which rise ten hemispherical domes, which are scarcely seen amidst the dense mass of foliage that now covers the roof. To my taste this mosque is the finest of all the buildings now remaining in Gaur. Its ornamentation is rich and effective, and the large decorated panels stand out in high relief against the plain walls. The whole building is of a uniform rich red colour that is much more pleasing to my eye than the gaudy glazed tiles of the Lattan Masjíd.

The Lattan Masjid.

The name of this mosque is universally believed to be derived from *Nattu*, a favourite dancing girl of the king, after whom it was called the *Nattan Masjid*, or, as it is more generally pronounced, the *Lattan Masjid*. Creighton states that it was built in A.H. 880 by Yusuf Sháh, and though he says nothing about any inscription, I feel satisfied that he must have seen one, either attached to the building, or lying somewhere near it, and has forgotten to quote it, as he is always very careful to note his authorities for the dates which he gives. At the time of Francklin's visit the inscription had certainly been removed. The vacant panel in which it was fixed over the middle doorway is 6 feet 6½ inches in length by 1 foot 11¼ inches in height, which I record here in the hope that some day the inscribed slab belonging to the masjid may thereby be identified.

The ground plan of the Lattan Masjid is exactly the same as that of the Chámkatti Mosque. Both are square rooms covered by a single dome, with a verandah or corridor in front. The main room of the Lattan is 34 feet square, and the corridor is 34 feet long by 11 feet wide. The two side walls of the mosque and the front wall of the verandah are each 8½ feet thick, but the front and back walls of the main room are 10 feet 7 inches. The whole building is therefore only 72¼ feet long and 51 feet broad outside. The corridor has three arched openings in front, and one at each end, the middle arch being 6 feet 11 inches span, the side arches 5 feet 5 inches, and the end arches 4 feet 9½ inches. The mosque itself has three openings in the front and sides, of the same dimensions as those of the corridor front. The back wall has 3 niches corresponding to the doors on the other three sides. The square is changed to an octagonal form by arches springing from black stone pillars, 17 inches thick, which seem to be of Hindu workmanship. Above the octagon is a very flat vault, over which rises the hemispherical dome[1]. All the four faces of the outer walls have curved battlements.

The whole surface of the masjid, both inside and outside, was once covered with glazed tiles in various patterns of four colours, green, yellow, blue and white, the pattern being formed of hexagons touching at the angles, with triangular pieces, alternately white and blue in the interstices. Nearly the whole of the outer glazing has fallen off, but the interior glazing is still in fair order, with the exception of the flat dome and floor, both of which have been very much injured by bats, the former by the incrustation of their nests, the latter by their dung. Francklin has given an enthusiastic description of the beauty of this mosque, which he thinks is not surpassed for " elegance of style, lightness of construction, or tasteful decoration, in any part of Upper Hindustân." I freely admit that the general appearance of the building is decidedly pleasing, but I dispute the lightness of construction, and deny altogether the tastefulness of the decoration.

[1] I have been thus particular in stating the measurements of the different parts of this mosque for the purpose of correcting the crowd of errors in Francklin's description which is quoted by Mr. Grote in Ravenshaw's Gaur, p. 32. Thus the verandah, which is 34 feet long by 11 feet broad, is said to be 50 *feet long by 36 feet broad*, while the main room of the mosque is said to be 36 feet square, so that the verandah is larger than the mosque itself. Again, the whole building is said to be 60 feet broad, instead of 51 feet, while the diameter of the dome is also made 60 feet, so that the edge of the dome would have been flush with the outer face of the building, while the dome itself would have been half the difference between 60 and 36 feet, that is, exactly 12 feet in thickness. Further, as he makes the summit of the cupola only 40 feet in height and the semi-diameter 30 feet, the spring of the dome would have been only 10 feet above the ground, while the height of the veranda is said to be 35 feet.

Lightness of construction is just the point in which the Muhammadan architecture of Bengal fails. It is in fact too massive, the thickness of the walls of the domed buildings being generally more than one-fourth of the span of the dome, as in the side walls of the Lattan Masjid itself, while in the front and back walls the proportion is more than three-tenths. It may be granted that the massiveness was a necessity in brick buildings, as I have observed the same proportions in the brick tombs of Badâun. But no attempt has been made to relieve the too massive appearance by recessed mouldings round the doors, which would have given to the great blocks of rectangular piers the appearance of polygonal pillars. On the contrary every doorway is generally a straight passage cut through the wall, like a tunnel driven through a hill.

With regard to the taste shown in the decoration, I will take Francklin's own selection of the *kibla* arch as an example. The arch over the prayer niche is a low, pointed one, with the joints of the white voussoirs marked by thin blue lines. This certainly looks well, but all its good effect is completely spoiled by narrow horizontal lines of different colours in the spandrils, with the same repeated on the wall below the springing of the arch, while the middle of the arch itself is filled with a small chequer pattern in blue and white. The wall below the spring of the arch is divided into three parts perpendicularly, and into a succession of narrow horizontal lines arranged as follows :—

Left.	Middle.	Right.
Green.	Blue.	Green.
Yellow.	White.	Yellow.
Green.	Blue.	Green.
White.	White.	White.
Blue.	Blue.	Blue.
White.	White.	White.
Blue.	Blue.	Blue.
White.	White.	White.
Green.		Green.
Yellow.	[Niche.]	Yellow.
Green.		Green.

Surely this is the very poorest, the most primitive, and the most tasteless style of ornamentation that could be imagined ; nothing but plain horizontal stripes repeated till the eye is fatigued with their niggling monotony. But fortunately all is not like this. The lotus flowers of blue and white in the middle of the spandrils are rich and effective, the cornices are all good, and the battlements round the dome, wherever they have been spared by the weather, show a bold treatment that is wanting in the designs of the interior. The general view of the Lattan Masjid is certainly pleasing ; but for graceful outline, beauty of ornament, and stateliness of appearance, I greatly prefer the Old Minâr, the Thântipâra Mosque, and the Dâkhil Gateway.

The Gunmant Masjid.

This old ruined mosque is not noticed by any of the writers on the antiquities of Gaur, most probably on account of its very ruinous state. It stands near the village of Mahdipur on the bank of the Bhâgirathi or old Ganges, just half a mile to the south of the citadel, and less than half a mile to the west of the Lattan Masjid. It is very briefly noticed by Mr. King as " the Gunnut Mosque, a large stone building without inscription[1] : " Now there is a long inscription of Fateh Shâh, dated in A.H. 889, at present lying in Mahdipur outside a temporary mosque, with a thatched roof, which is said to have been brought from a ruined masjid to the south of the village by a Hindu about 20 years ago. As his son died soon after, the man thought that the stone had brought bad luck, and therefore got rid of it by depositing it at the thatched masjid of his village. It seems probable therefore that this slab may have belonged to the masjid, as it was actually found not far from it.

As the masjid stands on the bank of the river it was easily accessible to pilferers during the rainy season. Nearly one-half of it has accordingly been carried off to Murshidâbâd and other places. All the lower part up to the

---

[1] Proceedings of Bengal Asiatic Society, 1875, p. 94.

springing of the arches was made of stone, rough blocks or boulders inside, with cut facings. The arches and domes were all of brick.

The ground plan of this masjid is similar to that of the great Adina Mosque at Hazrat Pandua, and differs from that of every other mosque in Gaur itself. It consists of a centre room 51 feet long by 16 feet 10 inches broad, extending from the front to the back wall. It is covered by a ribbed vault with gable ends, and has a window high up in the back wall over the prayer niche. On each side there are three aisles with four openings to the front. There are, therefore, twelve squares on each side, which are covered with hemispherical brick domes resting on stone pillars 1 foot 7½ inches square. The four middle piers which support the vaulted roof are octagonal, with bases 4½ feet square, and a pilaster on each face corresponding with the smaller pillars of the aisles.

The whole of the facing of the back wall and only remaining side wall has been stripped off; but as it measures in its present rough state rather more than 7 feet in thickness, it could not have been less than 8 feet originally. The whole building was therefore 140 feet 9 inches in length by 59 feet 4 inches in breadth outside. Apparently the back and side walls, as well as the front wall above the spring of the arches, were all faced with glazed tiles, as I found numerous fragments of different colours lying at the foot of the wall, while several large pieces of battlement in dark blue and white tiles were found in the village of Mahdipur. The mosque also had a corridor along the whole front, as shown by a portion of the vaulted roof which still remains. This would have increased the breadth by about 18 feet, thus bringing it up to 77 feet, which is just the same as that of the Great Golden Mosque.

Barâ Sonâ Masjid.

The *Barâ Sonâ Masjid*, or " Great Golden Mosque," is the largest of all the buildings in Gaur, being 26 feet longer than the Gunmant Mosque. The inscription recording its erection has long been missing; but luckily it was still *in situ* in the time of Creighton and Franklin, who give the date as A.H. 932 in the reign of Nusrat Shâh. The vacant panel over the middle doorway from which the slab has been removed measures 5 feet 2 inches in length by 2 feet 1 inch in height. The following translation is due to Francklin[1] :—

"The Prophet on whom be the blessing of God! has said: He who builds a mosque for God deserves Paradise. This Jâmi mosque was erected by the most illustrious Sultân, Nasir-ud-din-wa-dunyâ Abul-Muzaffar Nusrat Shâh Sultân, son of Husain Shah Sultân, son of Sayyid Asraf the Hussaini,—may God perpetuate his rule :— A.H. 932 (A.D.1526)."

Regarding its popular name of *Bard Sond Masjid*, or the "Great Golden Mosque," Francklin is much puzzled, and has started the strange theory that as it "bears no marks whatever of gold," its name must have "originated in the bulkiness of the materials and the expense of the erection." The natives, however, do not call bulky things golden, but name them after the real or supposed amount of the cost, as in the case of the *Ek-lakhi* mosque at Hazrat Pandua, the *No-lakha* Palace at Lahore, &c. The fact is that the domes were actually gilded, as well as much of the surface ornament. It is true that no gilding is now visible, but the belief is universal amongst the people, and we know that the *Little Golden Masjid* must have received its name for the same reason, as Creighton remarks that the remains of gilding were still visible, and would account for the epithet *Golden* given to both masjids[2]. I have myself also seen the traces of gilding in the Little Golden Masjid.

The common name of the building is *Bâradwâri*, or literally the "twelve doors." But as there are only eleven openings in front, an attempt has been made to explain the name by *Baradwari*, of which no translation is given. Perhaps *Baridwari*, "God's-house," may have been the original form of the name; but its present pronunciation is simply *Bâradwâri*, which is the proper form of the well-known *Bâradari*.

---

[1] See Ravenshaw's Gaur, p. 15, note quoted by Mr. Grote.
[2] Creighton's Ruins of Gaur, Description of, Plate VII.

The masjid is a massive rectangular block of building 168 feet long and 76 feet broad[1], with four small towers at the corners, without any noticeable relief save four insignificant octagonal minârs at the corners, which were crowned with still more insignificant pinnacles. Inside there are three long aisles divided by massive stone pillars, with a corridor running the whole length of the building. In front there are eleven arched openings all of the same size, 5 feet 11 inches, and four openings of 4 feet 10 inches at the south end, with two of the same size at the northern end, and four windows. The walls are of brick faced with stone, both inside and outside, but all the interior arches and domes were of brick only. The walls were 20 feet high, above which the domes rose about 10 feet. The whole building was covered with forty-four small hemispherical domes. Every one of these domes has fallen, and nearly all the stone pillars have disappeared. The bases of many of them are still *in situ*, and the lower parts of three pillars at the northern end still remain. These have perhaps escaped from having been buried in the ruins of an upper room which was screened off for the use of the ladies of the court. The floor of this private apartment, or Takht, was formed of brick vaults, the traces of which are distinctly marked against the end wall of the mosque. The room comprised six bays in the north-western corner, three in the back aisle, and three in the middle aisle. Access to this compartment was obtained through a room on the outside, from which two low doors led into it, there being two similar small doors below leading

---

[1] As the dimensions of this mosque are variously stated by different authors, I will here bring them together for comparison—

Creighton gives the dimensions as 170 × 76 feet.
Franoklin   180
Ravenshaw   .   .   .   .   . 180 × 80
Buchanan   .   .   .   . about 180 × 76
My own measurement of   .   . 168 × 76, which was made in 1871, was verified in 1879. Creighton gives the span of the arches at 6 feet, but I could not find one of this size ; they differed from 5-10¼ to 5-11¼, the mean being 5 feet 11 inches. Similarly I make the walls only 7 feet 11 inches in thickness, while Creighton gives them as 8 feet complete.

into the body of the mosque below the vaulted harem room. The position and size of this apartment will be seen in the accompanying plan. In the back wall there was a prayer niche in each bay between the pilasters, those of the harem apartment much smaller than the others. These niches were originally faced with curved pieces of black basalt, but nearly the whole of the facing has been stripped off.

The mosque stands on the western side of a quadrangle about 200 feet square, with an arched gateway on the north, south, and east sides. Each of these gateways is 38¼ feet by 13½ feet. They were once faced with stone, and ornamented with flowers in glazed tiles of different colours, white, blue, green, yellow, and orange, of which numerous fragments are lying in the ruins at the foot of each gate. One hundred feet to the east of the eastern gate there is a fine tank, 600 feet long by 300 feet broad.

In its present state, surrounded by luxuriant tamarind trees, the Golden Mosque is a very picturesque pile of building when seen from the front, as most of the domes of the corridor still remain intact to break the long horizontal line of battlement. The grand corridor, 150 feet in length, is perhaps the finest part of the anterior, as the dimly-lighted aisles of the mosque must always have been gloomy, more especially in the evening when the sun is in the west. But the sombreness was most probably relieved by a liberal use of gilding, which obtained for this masjid its well-known name of the Great Golden Mosque.

The Kotwáli Gate.

The Kotwáli Gate, or southern entrance of the city, is 1 mile to the south of the Lattan Masjid and 2 miles to the south of the citadel. It is usually called the *Katal Darwáza*, which is perhaps only a corruption of Kotwáli, but which was more probably derived from the execution of criminals at the Kotwáli, or Police station, as *Katal Darwáza* means simply the " Slaughter Gate."

The gateway is a lofty brick arch, 30 feet in height and 16¾ feet span, with a passage of 17 feet 4 inches in length, through the thickness of the wall. On each side of the outer face the wall extends for 21 feet 4 inches to a round bastion, pierced with two rows of loopholes. This gateway appears to me to be of a much earlier style of architecture than that of the citadel gates. On each face, both inside and outside, there are two sloping semicircular towers 6 feet in diameter. On each side of these towers there are deep niches, with pointed arches resting on ornamental pillars. As all these peculiar features, the sloping towers, the deep niches, and the highly decorated pillars, are characteristic of the early Muhammadan architecture of Delhi, it seems to me not improbable that this gateway may belong to the same period, or some time between the conquest of Iltitmish in A. H. 627, and the death of Alá-ud-din Muhammad Khilji, when the influence of Delhi was permanent in Lakhnauti.

19.—THE SUBURBS OF GAUR.

Sadullahpur.

Tomb of Shekh Akhi Sirâj.

The tomb of this very holy saint stands on a high mound near the north-west corner of the Sâgar Dighi tank, in a dense bambu jungle in the suburbs of Sadullahpur to the north of the city. His full name was Shekh Akhi Sirájuddin Usmân. He was a disciple of the famous Nizâmuddin Aulia of Delhi, and having become very learned he was told to go to Bengal, where he died in A.H. 758, or 1357 A.D. The *Haft Iglim* says that Nizâm called him the "Mirror of Hindustan," and that "he only received, when advanced in age, proper instruction from Fakhruddin (Zarrâdi). After Nizam's death he went to Lakhnauti, and all the kings became his pupils."[1]

The date of the tomb is not known, but it is most probably much older than the gateways of the enclosure, which bear two inscriptions of Husen Shah, dated in A.H. 916, or A.D. 1510. The tomb is a square brick building, covered

---

[1] Blochmann, in Bengal Asiatic Society's Journal, Vol. XLII, p. 260.

with stucco, and ornamented with flower patterns in the
panels and borders. As the saint died in A.H. 758, the
tomb may have been erected by Sikandar Shah, a very zealous Muhammadan, who began to reign in the following year,
but who had already been associated with his father Ilias as
early as A.H. 750. If the tombs had been built by Husen
Shah, I think his inscription would have been found in the
long panel over the door. But this has been simply plastered over and is now blank. The three gateways of the enclosure are duly inscribed, one with a sentence of the Koran,
and the others with the record of their erection by Alá-ud-din
Husen. The following are Blochmann's translations made
from my copies of the inscriptions. For " door of the tomb "
I have substituted " gateway," as the records are placed
over the *gateways* of the enclosure, and not over the *doors* of
the tomb itself[1]. The first mentions the name of the saint :—

" The gateway of the tomb of the venerated *Shekh Akhi Sirdj-
uddin* was built by the great and liberal king, *Alaud-dunya-waddin
Abul Musaffar Hussain Shah,* the king, son of Sayyid Asraf-ul-Hus-
saini—May God perpetuate his kingdom and rule! In the year 916
(A.D. 1510)."

The second inscription is, I think, the same as that of
Franklin, which Mr. Grote has quoted[2]. If so, Francklin's
copy was a very imperfect one. My copies of the inscriptions
give the erection of both gateways in the same year A.H.
916, while Franklin's copy assigns one to A.H. 910, which
I cannot believe to be correct.

"The gateway of this tomb was built during the reign of the
exalted and liberal king *Alaud-dunya-waddin Abul Musaffar
Hussain Shah,* son of Sayyid Asraf-ul Hussaini—May God perpetuate
his kingdom and rule, and elevate his condition and dignity, and may
he render his benefits and evidence honorable! In the year 916
(A.D. 1510)."

From these inscriptions over the gateways I infer that
the tomb of Akhi Siraj was already in existence before the
time of Ala-ud-din Husen. In fact the holy man is better

[1] See Ravenshaw's Gaur, p. 8,—note.
[2] Blochmann, in Bengal Asiatic Society's Journal, Vol. XLII, p. 294.

known as *Purâna Pir*, or the "old saint," than by his own name, and if there had been no tomb over him, Husen Shâh would certainly have built one. I do not think that the ornamentation can be of any assistance in determining the date of the tomb, as there is no certainty about its age. It may in fact have been added by Husen himself, as it is most probable that he repaired the tomb at the same time that he added the gateways. Beneath the stucco the walls of the tomb appear to be quite plain, but the long vacant panel above the door looks exactly as if it had been made for an inscription. It measures about 4½ feet by 8 inches. Now there are in the Indian Museum in Calcutta four bricks which were brought from Gaur, each 7 inches in height and 6 inches broad, with beautifully cut Tughra letters, giving the titles of a king, Ghiâsuddunya wa-ud-din, with the date of *Sabamayat*, or 700 of the Hijra. The other parts of the date are lost, but the title of Ghiâs-ud-din is quite sufficient to show that this record must belong to Azam Shâh, the son of Sikandar, who reigned as sole king from A.H. 792 to about 812, and as joint king, either with or against his father, from A.H. 772. Now as these inscribed bricks would exactly fit the vacant panel over the door of Akhi Sirâj's tomb, I think it quite possible that they may once have formed parts of its inscription. The date would agree very well, as Akhi Sirâj died in 758 A.H., and Ghiâs-ud-din was coining money in A.H. 772. Both time and place therefore fit, but as no other evidence is forthcoming, the assignment of the inscription can only be accepted as a probable one.

The letters remaining on the four bricks are as follows :—[1]

1—Brick. ـــ قال النبي صلي االله علينا و صل [م

2—Brick. ـــ عهد غياث الدنيا والدين ابو المظفر

3—Brick.

4—Brick. ـــ شهر محمد اباد * * سعمايه

[1] See Plate XX.

The Jan Janiya Masjid.

This is the latest of all the buildings at Gaur, having been erected only three years before Bengal passed into the hands of the Great Sher Shâh of Delhi. It is an oblong brick building faced with stucço, with three arched openings in front, and octagonal towers at the corners, finished with petty pinnacles above the roof level. The roof consists of three large domes, supported in the inside by stone pillars. Outside, the whole face of the wall is divided by bands of cornice into four parallel rows of uniform panels, placed in regular order one above the other. The cornice bands are all slightly curved in the Bengali fashion. The inscription is on a large slab placed over the middle doorway. From it we learn that the mosque was built by a lady of high position, who conceals her name, but it has been preserved by the people in the familiar appellation of *Janjaniya*, the common form of *Janjan Miyan*, which is applied to the masjid. The building is close to the tomb of Akhi Sirâj, at the north-west corner of the Sâgar Dighi. The following is Blochmann's translation of the inscription[1], from which I infer that the lady must have belonged to the household of the reigning king, Mahmud III.

" The prophet says : ' He who builds a mosque for God will have a house like it built for him by God in Paradise.' This Jami Mosque was built during the reign of the king, the son of a king, *Ghias-ud-dunya wad din Abul Musaffar Mahmud Shah*, the king, son of Husain Shah, the king—May God perpetuate his kingdom and rule ! Its builder is a lady—May she long live, and may God continue her high position !—941 A.H. (A.D. 1534-35.)"

SUBURB OF FIROZPUR.

Chota Sona Masjid.

This building stands at a little more than 1 mile to the south of the Kotwâli Gate of the city, on the side of the high road leading to Kansat on the Ganges, 7 miles distant. It received its present name of the " Little Golden Mosque"

---

[1] Bengal Asiatic Society's Journal, Vol. XLI, p. 339.

from the quantity of gilding employed in its ornamentation, of which some still remains to justify the popular appellation. Creighton first noticed it, and I verified his statement myself by inspecting some remains of gilding found by my servants.

This masjid is another rectangular block of building 82 feet by 52½ feet outside, and about 20 feet high. The interior is 70 feet 4 inches by 40 feet 9 inches, divided into three longitudinal aisles, with five arched doorways in front, the arches being cusped on the outside only. The walls are of brick completely faced with stone outside, but only up to the springing of the arches inside, all the arches and domes being of brick. The three middle bays forming the nave are each roofed with four flat segments of vaulting meeting in the middle ; the six other bays, on each side, being covered with small hemispherical domes. Externally only five domes are visible over the middle aisle ; but they are of different heights, diminishing from the central dome to the end domes. As the bays are of the same size, this exterior lessening of the domes must have been arranged by diminishing their thickness.

The doorways are bordered with broad bands of ornament, but the cutting is shallow, and the carving is not observed till one arrives quite close to the building. Creighton has given sketches of several Hindu figures found on the backs of slabs which formed part of this masjid, which, as he justly remarks, must have "formerly belonged to Hindu temples." The same shallow carvings also occupy niches between the doorways. Many of the designs are pretty, but no amount of prettiness of mere surface ornament can make up for the want of deep and boldly marked mouldings, the absence of which in all the later Muhammadan buildings of Bengal takes away very much from the effect which their massiveness and profusion of ornament would otherwise command.

The whole of the interior of this masjid is covered with carving of the same kind, a specimen of which is given by Creighton in Plate XVI. The ornamental pattern itself is

good, though it lacks both depth and variety. But as we
see it now, it has lost the gilding which once gave effect to
the design. In its original state, therefore, I can easily believe that the interior of the mosque was strikingly rich and
beautiful. In the north-west corner of the masjid a single
bay has been set apart for the use of the ladies. This bay
consists of two storeys, with a small door below and a small
window above. The upper room or takht has been parti-
tioned off by screens of trellis work.

The inscription slab which is placed over the middle doorway has lost both the upper right hand corner and the lower
left hand corner, and with the latter the Hijra date of the
erection of the building; but as the king's name is given, we
know that it was built between the years A.H. 899 and 929,
or A.D. 1494 to 1524. The following translation is due to
Blochmann—

" In the name of God, the element and merciful! God Almighty
says: 'Surely he will build the mosques of God who believes in God
and the last day, and establishes the prayer and offers alms and fears
no one but God. And such, perhaps, belong to those that are guided.'
And the Prophet—May God bless him!—says: 'He who builds a
mosque for God will have a house like it built for him by God in
Paradise.' The erection of this Jámi Masjid took place during the
reign of the King of Kings, the Sayyid of the Sayyids, the fountain of
auspiciousness, who has mercy on Moslem men and women, who exalts
the words of truth and good deeds, who is assisted by the assistance
of the Supreme Judge, who strives on the road of the Almighty, the
viceregent of God with proof and testimony, the keeper of Islam and
the Moslems, *Aláuddunya-wad-din Abul Musaffar Hussain Sháh*, the
King, the descendant of the Prophet—May God perpetuate his kingdom and his rule! This Jámi Mosque was built from pure and sincere
motives and from trust in God, by Wali Muhammad, son of Alí, who
has the title of Majlis-ul Majális Mansur—May God render him
victorious in this world and the next! Its auspicious date is the 14th
day of God's blessed month of Rajab—May its value increase! . . .
(year broken away.)"

In the mid-line of this inscription there are three ornamental circles, each containing a name of God. That in the
middle has *Yá-Allah*, " O God;" that on the right has *Yá*

Háfis, "O Guardian;" and that on the left has *Yá Rahím,*
"O merciful." All these can be seen in Ravenshaw's photograph, plate 22, as well as the loss of the two corners of the
inscription.

At a little distance from the masjid there are two stone
tombs, or sarcophagi, standing on a raised terrace 15 feet
long by 10½ feet broad. Both tombs bear inscriptions at the
head or northern ends; but they contain only extracts from
the Korán. Creighton suggests that the tombs may be those
of "the founder of the mosque and one of his kindred," which
seems very probable on account of their position. The tombs
would therefore belong to Wali Muhammad and his father,
Ali.

Báradwári of Niámat Ullah.

About one quarter of a mile to the north of the little
Golden Mosque is the Báradwárî of Niámat Ullah, a very holy
saint, of whom I could obtain no precise information. His
tomb is a regular Báradwári, or " Twelve Doors," as it is a
square building with three openings on each face. It is 49
feet on each side, with an inner apartment 21½ feet square,
enclosing the actual tomb. Four of the five inscriptions
found here consisted of the usual extracts from the Korán.
The fifth was a loose slab containing a record of Husen Sháh,
dated in A.H. 918, which recorded the building of one of the
fort gateways, and had no connection whatever with the
Saint's Tomb.

Darasbári, or College.

Half a mile to the south-west of the Kotwáli Gate near the
small village of Umarpur, there are some ruins and a very
large inscription 11 feet 3 inches in length by 2 feet 1 inch in
height. The spot is called *Darasbári,* or the " college;" but
the inscription refers to the building of a masjid. It is however
very probable that the masjid may have been attached to the
college, as the stone is much too heavy to have been moved
from its original site. It is a record of the time of Yusuf
Sháh, and is dated in A.H. 884[1].

---

[1] See Plate XXII in which I have been obliged to divide the inscription into
two parts on account of its great length.

20.—MALDAH.

The decayed old town of Máldah is situated on the eastern bank of the Mahánadi River, opposite its junction with the Kalindri River. It is about 3 miles to the north of the citadel of Gaur. The houses are chiefly built of bricks taken from the surrounding ruins, which show the former extent of the old town. As the Kalindri was formerly an important branch of the Ganges, the situation of Máldah was a very happy one, as it had water communication with Devikot on the north by the Purnabhába River, a branch of the Mahánandá, as well as with the Ganges itself, both to the east and the west.

The oldest building now standing is the Jámi Masjid, which was erected in A.H. 1004, during the reign of Akbar as stated in the inscription over the doorway, which reads as follows :—

این قبلة که در عالم معلوم آمد • در هند بنام کعبه موسوم آمد

چون ثانی که به بود تاریخ رغیب • بیت‌الله الحـــرام معصوم آمد

"This place of worship became known in the world, and was called in India by the name of *Kauba*. As it was the second *Kaaba*, the date is disclosed in '*Byt Allah al Harám Masûm*' (=A. H. 1004.)"

This masjid is therefore a comparatively modern building, but it is made of old materials, amongst which I observed many carved stones of Hindu temples, and one stone of some older mosque, with the cusped arched panel containing flowered ornament with the chain and bell, similar to the brick ornament in the panels of the Gaur mosques.

Inland, to the east of the Jámi Masjid, the ground is covered with broken bricks and pottery, and amongst the scattered brick-houses there are several inscriptions belonging to buildings which have long since disappeared.

· The oldest of these inscriptions, which was discovered by Mr. Westmacott, records the building of a mosque by one Hilál in A.H. 859, or A.D. 1455, during the reign of Nasirud-din Mahmud I. It is No. 3 of Ravenshaw's Gaur.

The next oldest inscription was also discovered by Mr. Westmacott at the Sát Mohan or Shák Mohan Masjid. It

records the building of a mosque during the reign of Shamsuddin Yusuf Shâh.   The date is not certain, as many of the
letters are still partly hidden in a mass of indurated filth
which adheres too firmly to the stone to be easily removed.
I think that I can make out *Samân wa Sabaïn wa Samânmayat*,
or 878 A.H., which is just one year earlier than the date
assigned by the histories.   As the imperfect state of this inscription baffled even Blochmann's ingenuity, I may be excused
in not being able to give a perfect text.   But by further cleaning
I have been able to make out several parts that were formerly
obscure.

A third inscription exists in the Huseni Dalân of the katrâ,
where it was found by Mr. Westmacott.   It records the building of a mosque during the reign of Saif-ud-din Firoz Shah,
who reigned from A.H. 896. It is No. 8 of Ravenshaw's Gaur.

A fourth inscription in Chalisapâra records the building
of a mosque in A.H. 899, or A.D. 1494, by Majlis Râhat
during the reign of Alâ-ud-din Husen. It is No. 10 of Ravenshaw's Gaur.

A fifth inscription from the *Fauti* or cemetery masjid
records its erection in A.H. 900, or A.D. 1495, during
the same reign.   It is No. 11 of Ravenshaw's Gaur.   The
masjid is a small one, but is much ornamented with carved
bricks and glazed tiles.

A sixth inscription records the building of a Jâmi mosque
by Alâ-ud-din Husen himself in A.H. 911, A.D. 1505. It is
No. 14 of Ravenshaw's Gaur.

A seventh inscription, which is now at the Dâk Munshi's
house, was found by Mr. Westmacott lying on the grave of a
widow in the *Chalisapâra* division of the town.   It records,
however, the building of a well by a lady named *Bonamalti*
in A.H. 938, or A.D. 1531, during the reign of Nusrat Shâh.
It is No. 24 of Ravenshaw's Gaur.

But the most curious building at Mâlda is the minâr or
tower on the west bank of the Mahânanda River, in the
middle of Nima Sarai, immediately below the junction of the
Kâlindri River.   It is said to have been a look-out tower,
as it commanded a very extensive view up the Kâlindri River,

and both up and down the Mahânanda River. Some people
say that the minâr was a *Chirâgh-dân*, or "Illumination
Tower," and they point to the numerous projecting stones outside in proof of their opinion. But all these projecting
stones are in the shape of elephants' tusks, and their rounded
forms would not lend themselves readily to the support of
little chirâgh lamps; besides, they are about 2¾ feet long. Of
course the chirâghs could be easily set with clay or mud;
but I do not think that the architect would have selected the
rounded form of an elephant's tusk as a support for a lamp;
and I conclude therefore that the minâr was not built as an
illumination tower.

The upper part of the minâr has fallen down long ago;
but the two lower storeys, which still remain standing, are
about 60 feet in height. I was unable to ascertain the exact
height by measurement, as the circular staircase was filled
with wasps' nests. The circumference at the base I found to
be 58 feet 9 inches, which gives a diameter of 18 feet 9 inches·
It is, therefore, almost of the same size as the minâr in Gaur,
which is 19 feet 4 inches in diameter and about 90 feet high.
According to Ravenshaw—

Tradition says that this was an alarm tower on which fires were
lighted in times of danger or invasion, to give timely notice to the
city of Gaur.

This tradition agrees with my own information that it was a
"look-out tower," for which purpose it was well adapted,
both from its position and its height. The elephant-tusk
projections have suggested the possibility that it may have
been a hunting tower, similar to Akbar's Hiran Minâr at
Fatehpur Sikri and Dâra Shikoh's Minâr at Shekohpura, near
Lahore; accordingly, some people call it a Shikâr-gâh. But
whatever its purpose, it forms a very striking and picturesque
object on approaching it, either from the Kalindri River or
from the Mahânanda River.

21.—HAZRAT PANDUA.

Pandua (or *Parua*, as it is generally pronounced) was one
of the old capitals of the Muhammadan rulers of Bengal, on

which account it is called *Hazrat Pandua*, or the " Royal Residence, Pandua," to distinguish it from the other Pandua near Hugli. The original name is said to have been *Panduvyia*, which was gradually shortened to *Panduya*, and eventually to *Pandua*. The Hindus, of course, say that it was so named after the ubiquitous Pândus; but I should think the *Pandubis*, or " water fowl," with which the place abounds, have a much better claim to the honour. *Hanspur* and *Mayurpur*, or " Goose town " and " Peacock town," are well-known names ; and in Buddhist times there were monasteries called after the goose, the pigeon, and the cock's foot. *Pandubiya* would therefore be a most natural appellation for any place in a marshy country.

The earliest mention that I have been able to find of Pandua is during the reign of Alâ-ud-din Ali Shâh, who reigned from A.H. 742 to 746, and who is said to have built the tomb of the famous saint Jalâl-ud-din Tabrezi[1]; but as the saint died just one century earlier, Pandua must have been already a place of note during his life-time, or before A.H. 642. This is proved most incontestibly by the numerous Hindu remains, both of sculpture and architecture, which still exist at Pandua—some lying loose, and others built into the Adina Masjid, the Ek-lakhi Tomb, and the buildings about the shrine of Nur Kutb Alam. Two very fine specimens are given by Ravenshaw in Plate 30.

The next mention of Pandua is during the reign of Iliâs Shâh, who, on the invasion of Firoz Tughlak, is said to have retired from Pandua to Ekdâla. Firoz also marched through Pandua on retiring from the siege of Ekdâla[2]. It would thus appear to have been one of the royal residences as early as the time of Iliâs Shâh, in A.H. 754, or A.D. 1353. But his son Sikandar, who reigned from 759 to 792

---

[1] Blochmann, in Bengal Asiatic Society's Journal, Vol; XLII, p. 253. The coins of this king also give the mint of Firuzabad, which is said to be the name of Pandua ; but if so the name is older than the time of Firoz Tughlak, who is recorded to have given his own name to Pandua.

[2] Tarikh Firoz Shahi, in Elliot's Muhammadan Historians by Dowson, Vol. II, p. 294.

A.H., made it his permanent residence, and here he built the great Adina Masjid, and the tomb in which he was afterwards buried. During the reign of the succeeding dynasty, both Jalâl-ud-din and his son Ahmad would appear to have lived at Pandua, which was the residence of their spiritual adviser, the famous saint Nur Kutb Alam, as well as of his predecessor, Alâ-ul Hak. But soon after the accession of Mahmud I, the court was once more transferred to Gaur, and the city of Pandua began gradually to decay.

It is difficult to ascertain the former extent of Pandua, owing partly to the dense jungle infested by tigers, and partly to the large swamps swarming with mosquitoes, which render any minute examination quite impossible. On the south side, near the tenth milestone from Angrezâbâd, or 7 miles from Mâlda, the fields are seen strewn with bricks, and on each side of the road there is a long line of low mounds,—the ruins of the shops of the old city. The road itself, which is from 11 to 15 feet in width, is paved with brick-on-edge, and runs in a nearly straight line to the north for $4\frac{1}{2}$ miles, to a large embankment which is said to have formed the limit of the town on that side. The breadth of the town no one even professes to know. On the west side of the road it was certainly very confined, as the ground is low and swampy. On the east side, the palace of *Salaisgarh* is just $1\frac{1}{4}$ mile from the Adina Masjid. The northern half, therefore, was certainly $1\frac{1}{4}$ mile broad. In the southern half, Buchanan was informed that remains of buildings could be traced for 2 miles to the east, which would make the breadth of this part not less than $2\frac{1}{2}$ miles[1]. But a very large portion of this great area of $4\frac{1}{2}$ miles in length by 2 miles in mean width must have been covered with tanks and swamps; in fact, the town would appear to have consisted chiefly of one long main street, with many short side streets on both sides. The length, however, as shown by the milestones, is not so much as 5 or 6 miles, as stated by Buchanan, as the remains of brick shops and the paved

[1] Eastern India, Vol. II, p. 648.

road are first observed shortly before reaching the tenth mile-
stone, and the last traces are near the northern embankment, close to the fourteenth milestone. Ravenshaw adopts
Buchanan's estimate of the size of Pandua, which he says—
"must have been about a mile probably in its widest part. Like
Gaur, it is covered with innumerable tanks, some of great age, and
nearly all of them having their greatest length from north to south,
as evidence of their Hindu origin[1]."

Close to this line of paved road stand all the principal
remains of Hazrat Pandua. They consist of four groups,
extending over 1½ mile from the Bardwári at 10½ miles,
to the Adina Masjid at 12 miles from Angrezábad. These
two and the Satáisgarh are on the east side, all the others,
including the Eklakhi and Sona Masjids, and the tombs
of Alául Hak and Núr Kutb Alam, are on the west side.
I will now describe them in the order in which they would be
visited by a traveller coming from Máldah.

Bardwári.

The first building on the right, or east hand, is the
Salámi Darwáza, or "Salutation Gate," leading to the
Bardwári, or shrine of Jalál-ud-din Tabrezi. This gateway
is the western boundary of the land belonging to the shrine,
which is called Báis-hazári, or "twenty-two thousands," from
the number of bighas of land with which it is endowed,
equal to about 7,000 acres. The shrine itself stands 1,200
feet to the east of the gateway. The present building is a
small paltry-looking masjid, plastered and whitewashed, with
a short inscription recording its erection in A.H. 1075.

When Shekh Jalál-ud-din came to Bengal, he began "to
destroy idols—in fact, his vault occupies the site of an idol
temple[1]". He died in A.H. 641, or A.D. 1244. His first
shrine was built by Alá-ud-din Ali, who reigned from A.H. 742
to 746. He is still in great repute, and his shrine is visited
by thousands of pilgrims from all quarters.

[1] Ravenshaw's Gaur, p. 44.
[1] Blochmann in Bengal Asiatic Society's Journal, Vol. XLII, p. 260.

Shrine of Nur Kutb Alam.

The shrine of this saint, being endowed with six thousand *bighas* of land, is generally known by the names of *Chhah Hazári* and *Shash Hazári*, or the " six-thousander." The following is Blochmann's account of this holy saint :—

" He is the son and spiritual successor of Alâul Hak. In order early to practice the virtue of humility, he washed the clothes of beggars and wanderers, and kept the water constantly hot for ceremonial ablutions." He died in A.H. 851, or A.D. 1447.

" The words *shams-ul-hidáyat*, ' lamp of guidance,' are the *tárikh* of his death. He was succeeded by his sons Rufat-ud-din and Shekh Anwar[1]."

The tomb of the saint is a plain sarcophagus with a canopy supported on four red stone pillars, and a fifth pillar at the head with a Persian inscription. To the west of the tomb there is a small building of three doorways with a cook-room attached outside. Here there are four inscriptions, of which three are fixed in the verandah of the mosque and one in the cook-room. The oldest of these is a record of Mahmud I. in the cook-room, of which the following is Blochmann's translation[2] :—

" God Almighty says, ' every creature tasteth ' (Qor., chap. III, verse 182). He also says, ' when their fate comes, they cannot delay it an hour, nor anticipate it' (Qor., chap. X, verse 50). He also says, ' everything on earth fadeth but the face of Thy Lord.'

" Our revered master, the teacher of Imams, the proof of the congregation, the sun of the faith, the testimony of Islam and of the Moslims, who bestowed advantages upon the poor and the indigent, the guide of saints and of such as wish to be guided, passed away from this transient world to the everlasting mansion, on the 28th Zil Hijjah, a Monday, of the year 863, during the reign of the king of kings, the protector of the countries of the Faithful, Nasir-ud-dunya wa-din Abul Muzaffar Mahmud Shah, the king,—May God keep him in safety and security!—This tomb was erected by the great Khan, Latif Khan,—May God protect him against evils and misfortunes !"

[1] Blochmann, in Bengal Asiatic Society's Journal, Vol. XLII, p. 262.

[2] For the texts and translations of this inscription and the two following, see Bengal Asiatic Society's Journal, Vol. XLII, pp. 271, 289, and 291.

The tomb here mentioned I take to be the present tomb of Nur Kutb Alam with the canopy supported on stone pillars. As the saint died in 851 A.H., only 12 years had then elapsed.

The next oldest inscription is one of Mahmud II., which is built into the wall of the masjid over the right-hand door. The following is Blochmann's translation :—

" The Prophet (may God bless him!) says : ' He who builds,' &c., (as before). This mosque was built in the reign of the king of the time (who is endowed) with justice and liberality, the help of Islam and the Moslims, Nasir-ud-dunya wa-din Abul Mujahid Mahmud Shah the king—May God perpetuate his kingdom and rule!—by the great and exalted Khan Ulugh Majlis Khan ...... (illegible.) Dated 23rd Rabi " ......

I read the month as Rabi-ul-awal, and the year as 896 A.H.

The third inscription is of Muzaffar Shâh, dated in A.H. 898, and is inserted over the middle door of the masjid. The following is Blochmann's translation :—

"God Almighty says : ' Verily, the first house that was founded for men is the one in Bakkah (Makkah), blessed, and a guidance to all beings. In it are clear signs: the place of Ibrahîm ; and who entered into it was safe ; and God enjoined men to visit it, if they are able to go there ; but whosoever disbelieves, verily, God is independent of all beings. (Qor., chap. III, verses 90 to 92.)

"In this Sufi building the tomb of the pole (Kutb) of poles was built, who was slain by the love of the All-Giver, the Shekh of Shekhs, Hazrat Nur-ul-Haq Washshara, Sayyid Kutb Alam.—May God sanctify his beloved secret, and may God illuminate his grave! This house was built in the reign of the just, liberal, learned king, the help of Islam and the Moslims, Shams-ud-dunya wa-din Abul Nasar Muzaffar Shah, the king—May God perpetuate his kingdom and rule, and may He elevate his condition and dignity! This house was built during the *khilâfat* of the Shekh-ul-Islam, the Shekh of Shekhs, son of the Shekh of Shekhs, Shekh Muhammad Ghaus—May God Almighty ever protect him !

" Dated 17th Ramzan 898 (2nd July 1493)."

The fourth inscription is a short one of Husen Shâh, dated in A.H. 915. It is fixed over the left hand door of the masjid, and records the building of a mosque.

From the first inscription we learn that the tomb of Nur Kutb Alam was built in A.H. 863 by Latif Khan, one of the nobles of Mahmud Shah I, just 12 years after the death of the saint. The residence, or *chilla*, of the saint's successors was built by Muzaffar Shàh. But there is no trace of either of the masjids mentioned in the other two inscriptions.

On the north side of the chilla there is a small masjid with a long inscription of Yusuf Shàh, dated in A.H. 884, of which the following translation is by Blochmann[1] :—

"The prophet (may God's blessings rest upon him !) says : ' he who builds a mosque for God shall have a castle built for him by God in Paradise.' This mosque was built in the reign of the just and liberal king Shams-ud-dunya wa-din Ab ul Muzaffar Yusuf Shah, the king, son of Barbak Shah, the king, son of Mahmud Shah, the king —May God perpetuate his kingdom and rule !—by the Majlis-ul-Majalis, the exalted Majlis—May God whose dignity is exalted also exalt him in both worlds ! And this took place on Friday, the 20th Rajab— May the dignity of the month increase !—of the year 884, according to the era of the flight of the Prophet, upon whom God's blessings rest !"

The tomb of Nur Kutb Alam and the saint's residence or *chilla* are situated in a square enclosure, which is entered through a doorway called *Behisht Darwàza*, or the " Gate of Paradise." Outside this enclosure, on the east, and between it and the high-road, there is a second smaller enclosure containing the tomb of Alà-ul-Hak, the father of Nur. It is a simple sarcophagus. The following is Blochmann's account of this saint, whose full name was Alà-ud-din Alà-ul-Hak. He was " the son of Shekh Akhi Siràj-ud-din Usmàn (whose shrine is at Sadullapur outside Gaur). According to the *Maarij-ul-Wilayat*, he was a true Quraishi Hàshimi, and traced his descent from Khàlid-bin Walid. He was at first exceedingly proud of his origin, wealth, and knowledge, so much so that Shekh Akhi, complaining, told Nizàm-ud-din Aulià that he was no match for Alà-ul-Haq. But Nizàm told him not to mind it, as Ala would in time become his (Akhis')

---

[1] Bengal Asiatic Society's Journal, Vol. XLII, p. 276.

pupil. It seems that Ala in his pride called himself Ganj-i-Nahat, and when Nizâm heard this he cursed him and said, "May God strike him dumb!" The curse instantly took effect; nor was Ala-ul-Haq's tongue loosed till he became the humble pupil of Shekh Akhi. As Shekh Akhi travelled a great deal on horseback, Ala-ul-Haq accompanied him, walking barefoot, and carrying his master's pots filled with hot food on his head till he became quite bald. Nor did he feel concerned when Shekh Akhi, with a view of humbling him, passed, on his journey, the houses of his brothers who were all Amirs and rich men.

"Alâ-ul-Hak spent large sums in feeding pupils, beggars, and wanderers, but the king of the land got envious, because the public treasury even could not have borne such a heavy expenditure, and he drove the saint to Sunârgâon. He stayed there for two years, and gave his servants orders to spend twice as much as before. And yet he only possessed two gardens, the income from which was eight thousand silver tankas per annum; but as he gave a beggar the land as a present, all money must have been supplied him from the unseen world."

He died on the 1st Rajab A.H. 800, or 20th March 1298. The king who drove him to Sunârgaon was probably Sikandar Shâh, who lived at Pandua, while his son Azam lived at Sunârgaon and ruled the eastern provinces. As Azam was at enmity with his father, the saint when persecuted by Sikandar would naturally have sought refuge with the son, and afterwards in A.H. 792, when Azam succeeded to the throne, Alâ-ul-Hak would of course have returned to Pandua.

Sona Masjid.

The Golden Mosque of Hazrat Pandua stands only a short distance to the north of the Chhah Hazâri Shrine of Nur Kutb Alam. It is surrounded by a dense jungle, and is very much ruined, the whole of the domes having fallen in. The mosque itself is a rectangular block of building 80 feet long by 40 feet broad outside. It is built of roughly-cut stone up to the springing of the arches, above which all is made of brick. It stands on the western side of a court-yard 172 feet long by 127 feet broad, which is surrounded by a brick wall with a stone gateway on the east side.

The front wall of the masjid has the usual Bengali battle-ment with a curved rise in the middle. The walls are 7 feet thick, with five arches in front and two at each end. The interior is divided into two aisles by a row of twelve-sided stone pillars, from which spring the arches to carry the ten domes. The pillars are rough and clumsy; and amongst the brick-work of the arches I observed several fragments with blue glaze upon them, showing that this part of the mosque had been built with old materials taken from other buildings. In the back wall there are five semicircular niches; and to the right of the kiblah niche there is a well-designed pulpit with its canopy in good order. I could not find any traces of the gilding from which the building must have derived its popu-lar appellation of the "Golden Mosque." We know indeed that this was not its proper name, as the builder himself calls it the "Kutb-Shâhi Masjid."

There are three inscriptions belonging to this mosque, all of which are still *in situ*. The oldest, dated in A.H. 990, is over the centre door of the masjid; the next, dated in A.H. 992, is on the pulpit, and the latest, dated in A.H. 993, is over the entrance gateway of the quadrangle. Imperfect copies of the first and last have been given by Ravenshaw, who does not, however, notice the pulpit record. To these Mr. Grote has added the copy of an inscription taken from Major Francklin, who states that it was "on the front of the Golden Mosque at Pandua." But Francklin must have made some mistake in his notes, as not only is there no inscription of Yusuf Shâh on the front of the masjid, but there is no place for it. The text, moreover, as given by Francklin, records nothing whatever, and for this reason I strongly suspect that it is only a portion of an inscription; in fact, either a fragment or an imperfect copy of a longer record.

The mosque was built by Mukhdum Shâh in A.H. 990, or in A.D. 1582, the pulpit was set up in A.H. 992, and the gateway was added in A.H. 993 by the same person. It was

called the *Kutb Shahi Musjid* in honour of Nur Kutb Alam,
who was the ancestor of the builder.

Ek-lakhi Tomb.

The great brick mausoleum, generally known as the Ek·
lakhi Masjid, is a square of nearly 75 feet, with octagonal
towers at the corners. The inside is an octagon of 48½ feet
diameter covered by a single dome. The tomb stands a
short distance to the north of the Sonâ Masjid, and close to
the high road leading northward to Dinajpur. There are
three graves inside, the middle one being almost certainly that
of a female, as it has a plain top, while that on the east side
is larger and is marked as that of a man by the pen-case on
the top. The people differ very much as to the names of the
three persons buried here. Buchanan gives one set of names
and I have received four different series of names. Accord·
ing to Buchanan, they are the tombs of Ghiâs-ud-din, Zein-ul-
Abdin, and Hâj-ud-din[1]. According to my first informant,
the tombs belong to Kans Râja of Sunârgaon, and his two
sons Shams-ud-din and Sirâj-ud-din. Following my second
informant, the names of the two sons of Kans are Ain-ud-din
and Jalâl-ud-din. My third informant called them Kans, and
his son Jalâl-ud-din and his grandson Zein-ul-Abidin. My
latest informant assigned them to Jalâl-ud-din and his son
and daughter. The author of the Riyâz-us-Salatin gives the
tombs to Jalâl-ud-din and his wife and sons, while Ravenshaw
assigns them to Ghiâs-ud-din, his wife and his daughter-in-law.
After comparison of these names I think there can be no doubt
that the great Ek-lakhi Tomb was built by Jalâl-ud-din, the son
of Raja Kâns, who reigned from 816 to 831 A.H. The middle
tomb I take to be that of the king's wife, and the western
tomb may be that of Jalâl-ud-din's son Ahmad, who bore the
title of Shams-ud-din. We know that Jalal-ud-din lived at
Pandûa, and as he was a jealous Musalman, it is very pro-

[1] Eastern India, Vol. II, p. 649. Buchanan gives the last name as Wahuz-ud-
din ; but at the bottom of his plate of the tomb the name is written Wa Haj-ud-
din, that is simply " and Haj-ud-din. " There is a fatal objection to the assignment
of the tomb to Ghias-ud-din, that he has a very handsome tomb at Sunârgaon.

bable that he would have selected a burial place near the
tomb of the famous saint Alá-ul-Hak, who died in A.H. 800,
and close to the dwelling-place of his spiritual guide, the
equally famous Nur Kutb Alum. There is no inscription of
any kind on the building.

The inside of the tomb has once been decorated with
flowers and other ornaments painted on the plaster. But no
amount of surface painting can make up for the want of
mouldings and panels. In this respect the interior is a complete contrast to the exterior, which is very highly ornamented
with fine mouldings, and an infinite variety of flowered designs
in carved brick, or terra-cotta. The walls are 13 feet thick,
with an arched doorway of 7 feet 1 inch span on each of the
four sides. The arch is 14 feet in height; but under it there
is a regular Hindu doorway, with a horizontal lintel, both lintel
and jambs having Hindu figures carved upon them. All the
walls have curved battlements of the Bengal fashion, the rise
in the middle being about 3 feet as nearly as I could measure
it, and the total height of the wall 27 feet. There are two
broad bands of ornament below the cornice, following the
curve of the battlement. The cornice itself is very rich, and
at the same time very bold for a brick building, as it stands
out well from the wall supported on small balusters, which
have once been coated with glazed tiles, but very few portions
now retain their colour. On each side of the doorway there
are three projecting faces of 7 feet 2 inches, and two recessed
faces of 2 feet 8 inches. The recessed portions are ornamented with continuous bands right up to the cornice; but
the projecting faces have only two large panels, with cusped
arches in the niches, surrounded by highly decorated borders,
and crowned by ornamented battlements. Two specimens of
the niche decorations are given in the accompanying Plate [1].
The ornamentation is very rich and very varied, the same
pattern being rarely repeated, except in some of the borders.
Whether the whole of the terra-cotta ornament was originally
glazed I could not ascertain; but from the small number of

[1] See Plate XXVI.

pieces of glazed tile that I was able to pick up at the foot of
the walls, I do not think that the whole could have been
glazed. The cornices certainly were so, and perhaps the
niches also.

The great dome, as well as the flat roofs of the corners,
is entirely covered with trees, which will no doubt eventually
destroy the building; but at present the interlaced roots of
the pipal trees seem to hold the walls together. The dome
itself is scarcely visible amongst the dense foliage. The
drawing given by Buchanan is very inaccurate, as the dome
is made too high and very much too narrow. Its span is 48
feet, or very nearly two-thirds of 75 feet, the outside square of
the building. If we allow a thickness of 5 feet, the outside
diameter of the dome will be nearly four-fifths of the outside
square, whereas Buchanan's drawing makes it only three-
fifths. The pointed appearance of the summit of the dome,
as shown by Buchanan, I take to be only the ruins of the old
pinnacle.

The Adina Masjid.

The Great Adina Mosque of Hazrat Pandūa is looked
upon by the Bengalis as one of the wonders of the world.
But bigness is not grandeur, and the Adina Masjid is little
better than a gigantic barn. Outside it is an oblong quadrangle, 507½ feet in length by 285½ feet in breadth. Inside it
consists of four great cloisters surrounding a court 497 feet in
length by 159 feet in breadth. On the west side the cloisters
are five aisles in depth, forming the masjid ; on the other
sides they are only three aisles in depth. In the middle of
the west side the cloisters are divided into two wings by a
large room which forms the nave of the mosque. This room
is 64 feet 4 inches in length and 33 feet 8½ inches in width.
On each side it has five archways opening into the five aisles
of the cloisters. The roof was a long vault, a simple con-
tinuation of the front arch which spanned the whole breadth
of the room. Both arch and vault have now fallen down, but
the outline of the vaulted roof is distinctly marked against
the top of the back wall. The cloisters on all four sides were

roofed with a succession of small domes, amounting to 378.
Not many of these are now standing, except over the two-
storeyed portion of the mosque set apart for the king and his
family[1].

The exterior of the masjid is very plain, the slight mouldings and weakly marked niches being lost sight of in the
great length of the wall. The front wall of the masjid also
is plain, all the architect's strength having been reserved for
the inner side of the back wall, which is highly decorated.
The patterns, however, are much too small and too shallow for
the great extent of wall over which they are spread. But all
this lavish ornamentation is expended in vain, as it is only
dimly visible even at a short distance. In the forenoon, when
the sun shines slantingly upon this wall, the ornamentation
looks well, as all the petty details are sharply defined by the
light and shade. But this effect is not due to the architect
but to the falling in of the roof, which has brought into broad
daylight what the architect himself had hidden in the gloomy
obscurity of a five-aisled arcade 62 feet in depth.

The most remarkable feature about this great masjid is
the total absence of any entrance gateway. There are two
small doors in the back wall, but these are mere posterns or
private entrances for the convenience of the king and the
mullahs. There is also a small arched opening in the middle
of the east side, which was no doubt intended for public use ;
but this is only a simple doorway or passage through the walls,
unmarked by any projecting wings or rising battlements.
The real public entrance I believe to have been at the south-
east corner of the cloisters, where the three archways at the
eastern end of the south cloister are left open, so that the
people could enter at once into the south and east cloister from
the outside. As this arrangement utterly spoils the sym-
metry of the building, it was most probably an afterthought,
when the single small door in the middle of the east side was
found utterly insufficient.

---

[1] See Plate XXV. The private room for the use of the haram lies to the east
of the tomb, which could only be approached from this side.

Viewed from the outside the back of the masjid, with its feebly marked niches placed high up, recals the appearance of a great ship with its portholes closed, while the strongly marked line between the lower 12 feet of stone wall and the upper 20 feet of brick wall might be taken for the water line. But the front view of the masjid from the eastern cloisters must have been a complete contrast to the back. It is true that nearly the whole front has fallen down, but many of the pillars still remain, as well as the two piers that supported the great central arch. This arch was 33 feet in span and upwards of 60 feet in height; and on each side it was flanked by a line of 15 arches of 8 feet span, making a grand front of nearly 400 feet in length. I presume that the bare outside view of the vault was screened by a lofty battlemented propy-lon, which would have given dignity to the whole building.

The back wall of the central vault has the usual *kibla*, or prayer-niche, in the middle, with a pulpit on the north side. The whole of the back wall is very richly decorated, but the carving is shallow, and affords a strange contrast to the deep cutting of some Hindu door-jambs, which are placed hori-zontally in a single line touching end to end, just below the two lines of Arabic writing, containing sentences from the Korân in ornamental Kufic and Tughra characters. The steps leading up to the pulpit have fallen down, and, on turn-ing over one of the steps I found a line of Hindu sculpture of very fine and bold execution. This stone is 4 feet in length, and apparently formed part of a frieze. The main ornament is a line of circular panels $7\frac{1}{4}$ inches in diameter, formed by continuous intersecting lotus stalks. There are five complete panels, and two half-panels which have been cut through. These two contain portions of an elephant and a rhinoceros. In the complete panels there are (1) a cow and calf; (2) human figures broken; (3) a goose; (4) a man and woman, and a crocodile; (5) two elephants. The carving is deep, and the whole has been polished. In the niche itself, the two side pillars which support the cusped arch are also pickings from Hindu temples.

This great mosque was erected by Sikandar, the son of Iliás Sháh, in A.H. 770, or A.D. 1369. The inscription recording its erection is placed on the outside of the back wall, facing towards the high road. The inscription, forming a single line of beautifully executed Tughra characters, is thus translated by Blochmann :—

This * * * * mosque was ordered to be built in the reign of the great king, the wisest, the justest, the most liberal of the kings of Arabia and Persia, who trusts in the assistance of the Merciful, Abul Mujáhid Sikandar Sháh, the king.—May his reign be perpetuated till the day of promise! He wrote it on the 6th Rajab of the year 770 [14th February 1369.]

In the northern half of the masjid, but close to the pulpit, is the Bádsháhi Takht, or royal seat, for the king and his family. It occupies six bays in the three back aisles, or altogether eighteen bays. To form this apartment, the round stone pillars of 18 inches were exchanged for massive stone octagonal piers, 3½ feet in diameter, to carry the heavy stone floor of an upper storey. In the royal apartment itself, the pillars become circular with twelve convex flutes. The niches also are ornamented with sentences from the Korán. This is the only part of the masjid, with the few adjacent bays on the south and east, that still retains its roof. The domes most probably owe their safety to the massive pillars of the lower storey, which gave extra stability to the arches above them, while at the same time they offered no temptation to the spoiler to carry them off. The tall shafts of 10 feet in the cloisters of the masjid were not difficult to remove, and, in consequence, several scores of them have disappeared.

Tomb of Sikandar Sháh.

Attached to the northern half of the back wall of the masjid stands the roofless tomb of Sikandar Sháh, the founder of the mosque. The building is a square of 41 feet 9 inches inside, with walls 6 feet 8 inches thick. There are three openings on the north and south sides; but these must have been trellised windows, as the floor of the tomb is on the same level as the floor of the Bádsháhi Takht in the

mosque. Between them there are three openings through
the back wall of the masjid, which apparently formed the
only access to the tomb. The sarcophagus is in ruins, and
the inside of the vault, in which the body was deposited, is
now exposed.*

Satáis-ghar.

One mile to the east of the Adina Masjid are the ruins of
a building called *Satáis-ghar*, which the people say was the
palace of Sikandar Sháh. Buchanan calls it *Satas-ghar*, or
the " sixty towers ;" but the name given to me was certainly
Satáis-ghar, or the "twenty-seven rooms." The ruin now
standing seems to have formed the humáms or baths of the
palace : There is an octagonal room, 24 feet in diameter,
with a small room on each of the eight sides. From one of
these I traced a passage into a large oblong room, 25 feet by
7 feet; and beside it, on the north-west, a separate room 11
feet square. On the east side there are numerous remains of
walls, which are much too broken to afford any satisfactory
plan. Altogether, there is nothing now remaining to repay the
trouble of a visit.

22.—DEVTHALA.

Devthala, or *Devasthala*, the " Deva's abode," is an old
Hindu place on the high road to Dinájpur, 15 miles to the
north of Pandua. There is one very fine large tank and several
small ones, and here, as in every other old Hindu place
throughout Bengal, there stands a Muhammadan shrine on
the very site of a temple, and built with the stones of the
ruined temple. At Devthala this shrine is the Takiya, or
" resting-place, " of Jalál-Sháh. Beside the Takiya there is
a small white-washed masjid, with a court-yard containing
several small tombs. Over the entrance gateway of the
enclosure there is a neatly-cut inscription on a black basalt
slab, recording the erection of a Jámi Masjid in the year
A.H. 868, during the reign of Bárbak Sháh. There are
several Hindu pillars lying about the enclosure, and I was

fortunate enough to get a fine standing figure of Vishnu with four arms, which is represented in the accompanying plate[1].

The inscription is a very fine specimen of the curious style of writing which prevailed at this period, in which all the perpendicular strokes of the letters are prolonged upwards and arranged at equal distances so as to look like a railing[2].

23.—DEVIKOT.

The old fort of Devikot is situated on the left or eastern bank of the Purnabhâba River, 33 miles to the northeast of Pandua, 18 miles to the south-south-west of Dinâjpur, and 70 miles to the north-north-east of the citadel of Gaur. According to the belief of the people, Devikot was the citadel of the ancient city of Bân-nagar, which stretched along the left bank of the Purnabhâba for a length of 2 miles. It was still a place of consequence when the Muhammadans first entered Bengal, as Ghiâs-ud-din Iwaz, who ruled the country from A.H. 608 to 624, made an embanked road the whole way from Lakhnauti (or Gaur) to Deokot, as the Muhammadan writers always call it.

The fortified portion of the old city consisted of three distinct parts separated by broad ditches, and surrounded by massive earthen ramparts. The citadel, which the people call Devikot, is about 2,000 feet square, and is so filled with dense jungle that it is quite impossible to penetrate any distance inside except in the very hottest weather, when the grass and underwood have been burnt, and the tigers and leopards have sought shelter elsewhere. In the south-east corner of the citadel stands the Muhammadan shrine of Sultân Shâh, with the two Hindu wells named *Jiva* and *Amrita*, or " Life" and " Immortality."

To the north of Devikot is a walled enclosure about 1,000 feet square, and to the north of this there is a second fortified enclosure of about the same size. Both of these are surrounded by massive earthen ramparts and broad ditches. At the north-western corner of the northern enclosure are the ruins of the shrine of Shâh Bokhâri, standing on the top

---

[1] See Plate XXVII.   [2] See Plate XXIII, No. 2 inscription.

of a lofty mound, which was certainly the site of a great
Hindu temple[1]. Here I found brick walls and many fragments of moulded bricks, together with six stone pillars of
Hindu workmanship. On the opposite bank of the Purnabhâba River there is a high mound, and at a short distance
further up is the shrine of Pir Bahâ-ud-din. There are no
inscriptions at any of these places.

The whole length of the fortified city is nearly 1 mile,
extending from the 16th mile-stone to within a short distance
of the 17th mile from Dinâjpur. To the south lies the
Muhammadan quarter of Damdamma, or the cantonment,
extending in a straggling way down to the 18th mile. From
this point there is an embanked road leading to the east
past the two great lakes called Dahal Dighi and Kâla Dighi.
The former is supposed to be of Muhammadan construction,
as its length lies from east to west, while the former is
claimed by the Hindus, because its length lies from north
to south. The Kâla Dighi is about 4,000 feet long by 800
feet broad, and is said to have been named after Kâla Râni,
the wife of Bân-Asur. The Dahal Dighi is about the same
length, but rather broader, but no derivation is given for its
name. I suspect, however, that it may be only a corruption
of *Dhola* or the "white" water, in contradistinction to the
Kâla Dighi, or "black water." Both lakes are about 1 mile
distant from the citadel of Devikot, the former lying to the
south and the latter to the south-east.

On the north bank of the Dahal Dighi there is a Muhammadan shrine of a very holy saint, Mulla Atâ Shâh, or
Maulâna Atâ. His exact date is not known, but he must
have lived before the time of Sikandar Shâh, who ruled
Bengal from A.H. 759 to 792, as he is mentioned in Sikandar's
inscription, dated in A.H. 765, as the founder of the building
(*gumbas*) which was completed by Sikandar himself. This
gumbas was no doubt the tomb of the saint, which, as seems
to have been the custom in Bengal, was soon converted
into a mosque. There is even now a grave in the eastern

[1] Buchanan, Eastern India, Vol. II, calls this saint, Pir Hava Khari, which is
probably only a misprint.

half of the building, while the western wall has the usual
kiblâh, or prayer niche of a masjid.   The building itself is a
square of 26 feet 10 inches inside, with walls 5 feet 9 inches
thick.   The lower part of the walls, for three courses in height,
is of coarse grey stone; all above is of brick.   The dome
has disappeared long ago.   The western niche is very highly
ornamented with carved bricks.   Numerous remains of rough
terra-cotta horses and elephants are scattered about inside.
These are the usual offerings at the shrine, and betray a
lingering remnant of Hinduism amongst the people, the
greater number of whom are no doubt the descendants of for-
cibly converted Hindus.   In front of the tomb to the south,
towards the lake, there is an open court-yard, with a room at
each end.   That to the west appears to have been the *chilla,*
or resting-place of the saint, while the eastern room was
most probably his kitchen.

There are four inscriptions fixed in the walls of the tomb
and court, and there is an empty panel, which must have
contained the fifth inscription seen and described by Buchanan.[1]   This missing record was of Fateh Shâh, the son of
Mahmud I. ; but the date of A.H. 845, given by Buchanan,
is certainly wrong, as Fateh Shah did not succeed to the
throne until A.H. 885 or 886, and died in 892.   The remaining inscriptions I will now describe, premising that the tomb
of Atâ, and consequently all the inscriptions, are at Devikot
or Damdamma and not at Gangârâmpur, as Blochmann was
led to believe.   Gangârâmpur is 3 miles distant to the south,
and was formerly the police station of the district, by which
the civil officers are in the inconvenient habit of describing
all places no matter how far distant.

No. 1 is a well-preserved record of the reign of Kai Kâüs,
dated in A.H. 697.   It describes the building of a mosque
by a noble named Zafar Khân Bahrâm Aitigín ; but there is
no trace of such a building now remaining.   The following
translation is by Blochmann[2] :—

"This mosque was built during the reign of the king of kings

---

[1] Buchanan's Eastern India, Vol. II, p. 661.
[2] Bengal Asiatic Society's Journal, Vol. XLI, p. 103.

Rukn-ud-dunyâ wa-din, the shadow of God on earth, Kai Kâûs Shâh, son of Mahmud, son of the Sultân, the right hand of the Khalifah of God, the helper of the Commander of the Faithful—May God perpetuate his rule and kingdom !—at the order of the Lord of the age, by Shihâb-ul-haqq wa-din, a second Alexander, the Ulugh-i-A'zam Humâyûn, Zafar Khân Bahrâm Aitigîn—May God perpetuate his rule and king-dom, and may God prolong his life !—under the supervision (batauliyat) of Salâh Jîwand of Multan.   On the 1st Muharram 697 A.H. (19th October 1297)."

The second inscription is a very fine specimen of Tughra writing of the time of Sikandar, A.H. 765. The following is Blochmann's translation of this record, which refers to the tomb (*gumbas*), as having been begun by Maulâna Atâ him-self, and completed by Sikandar :—

" [Verse]—In this dome, which was founded by Ata—May the building be a house for both worlds ! angels sing an account of its erection till the day of judgment, ' Banaina fauqakum Saban Shidada.'

"[Prose)—Through the grace of the maker of the wonderful seven places, ' who has created the seven heavens one above the other' His name be praised ! the building of this lofty dome was completed. It is a copy of the dais of the vault of glory.   And we have adorned the heaven of the world with lights in the blessed shrine of the pole of saints, the unequalled among enquirers, the lamp of truth, and law and faith, Moulana Ata—May God Almighty bestow His grace upon him in both worlds ! (The building was completed) by order of the Lord of the age and the period, the causer of justice and liberality, the guardian of countries, the pastor of the people, the just, wise, the great king, the shadow of God on earth, distinguished by the grace of the merciful, Abul Mujahid Sikandar Shah, son of Ilyas Shah, the king. May God perpetuate his kingdom !

" (Verse)—The king of the world, Sikandar Shah, for whom people string pearls in prayer, and chant, May God illuminate his worth, and say, ' May God perpetuate his kingdom.'

'¹ Dated A. H. 765 (A.D. 1363) done by the slave of the throne, Ghias, the golden handed."

The third inscription is one of Shamsuddin Mozaffar. Blochmann was unable to decipher the date, but he guessed it correctly as A.H. 896. The letters of the inscription are a good deal broken, and the word Samânmayat or 800 is carved in small letters on the border between the two lines of the inscription. The king's *Kunyah* title of *Abul Nasr* has been misread as Abu'l *Muin*, but my copies of the inscription are no doubt much better than that which Blochmann had before him. The same *Kunyah* title of Abu'l Nasr occurs in my Hazrat Pandua inscription of this king, as read by Blochmann himself[1]. The following is his translation of this Devikot inscription[2] :—

" This mosque was built in the time (fi'ahd) of the renowned saint Maulâna Ata ! May God give him affluence and may He make paradise his dwelling-place ! During the reign (fi'ahd) of Shamsuddunya waddin Abul Nasr. Muzaffar Shah, the king, May God perpetuate his rule and kingdom ! In the year 896.''

The first *fi'ahd*, "in the time of" puzzled Blochmann, but it appears to me to be a repetition of the statement made by Sikandar that the building was actually begun by the saint himself. What Muzaffar did is however not stated, but he most probably repaired the tomb. Some word appears to have been lost in the beginning, between *haza* and *alimârat*, as there is a vacant space with a broken surface. The inscription is coarsely cut, and the letters are rudely formed.

The fourth inscription, which is placed immediately over the entrance door of the tomb, records the building of a mosque and a minâr in A.H. 918, during the reign of Alâud-din Husen. From the position of this inscription, it would appear that the present "tomb-mosque" must have been built at that time, and that the two other inscriptions must refer to some previous building which had become ruinous. Of the minâr here mentioned no trace now remains, and the people know nothing about it. The inscription is thus translated by Blochmann[3]—

" The mosque and minaret were built by the Khân-i-Azim Rukn Khan (son of) Ala-ud-din of Sarhat, cup-bearer out of the palace.

[1] Bengal Asiatic Society's Journal, Vol. XLII, p. 291, where Blochmann says that the date is "not legible.''

[2] Bengal Asiatic Society's Journal, Vol. XLI, p. 107.

[3] Bengal Asiatic Society's Journal, Vol. XLI, p. 106.

Vazir of the town known as Zafarabad, Commander-in-chief, High Kotwal of the town known as Firuzabad, Munsif of the Diwan of books in the town mentioned, during the reign of Ala-ud-dunya waddin Abul Muzaffar Husen Shah, the king, a descendant of the prophet, in front of the door of the Shekh of Shekhs, Shekh Ata. He who keeps up and renews this pious grant will be renewed by God, and will find favour with the Shekh.   A.H. 918 (A.D. 1512)."

The old name of the district in which Devikot is situated was *Devikot Sahashir*.   Now *Sahasra viryya*, or " one thousand strong," is a title of the Asur Bâna, who had one thousand arms; and this name, applied to the whole district, shows that the traditions about the city of Bân-nagar must be of ancient date.   In the Haimakosa and also in the Trikanda Sesha, *Devikot* is said to be one of the synonyms of *Sonita-pura*, or the " Red City," which is also called *Bânapura*, *Kotivarsha*, and *Ushavana*, or *Umavana*[1].   Now the name of *Sonitapura*, or the " Red City," is specially applicable to Devikot, as the ramparts are made of red earth.   I believe therefore that this Devikot or *Bânanagara* is the city of *Sonitapura* referred to in the Vishnu Purana.   Of its antiquity there can be no doubt, as it possesses numerous Hindu remains in the shape of stone pillars and sculptures and large mounds of brick ruins, besides the great fortress of Devikot nearly half a mile square.   The story of Bâna Asura and his daughter Usha will be found in the Vishnu Purâna.

24.—KHETLÂL.

Khetlâl, or Khyetlal, according to Buchanan, is a large village and police station, situated on the high road leading from Dinâjpur to Bagraha (Bogra).   It is 59 miles to the south-east of the former place, and 24 miles to the north-west of the latter.   Its name, however, is not to be found in the maps, as it is included in the cluster of villages called Kasbâh Kismat.   The site is certainly an old one, as there are several mounds of brick ruin and a great number of fine tanks, besides numerous pieces of sculpture.   Sometimes the name is written

[1] Wilson's Vishnu Purana by Hall, Vol. V, p. 112.

Kshetra-nála, as well as *Kshetra-ídla*, but I could learn nothing as to its origin.

There are only two places that possess remains of any interest, one at half a mile to the south of the thanna, the other at three quarters of a mile to the west of it.   At the first place there is a small mound 3 feet high, with the remains of a brick temple 11½ feet by 9 feet.   Here are three pieces of sculpture, 1st, a standing male figure now firmly imbedded in the folds of a pipal tree; 2nd, a standing figure of Vishnu with four arms, 1 foot 10 inches high by 11 inches broad; 3rd, a sculpture, 1 foot 10 inches long, bearing a female figure lying on her left side on a bed, with her head resting on her left hand and both knees bent.   On the bed in front of her is a small child.   At the head of the bed there is a female attendant with a *chauri*, or fly-whisk, and at the foot of the bed a second female attendant is shampooing the lady's feet.   In her right hand she holds a flower, and overhead there is a small lingam, and small figure of Ganesa seated, and a second small figure not identified.   Beneath the bed there is a basket of flowers, and a bowl full of fruits.   Over her feet there is a short inscription in mediæval Nâgari, reading : " *Vansonigralatima*," the meaning of which I have not yet been able to discover.   Close by there is a broken octagonal pillar 10 inches in diameter.

At the other site, near the Pushkarini Tank, there is a ruined lingam temple, and traces of other ruins.   Here there are four principal figures, all of which have been described by Mr. Westmacott; 1st, a female figure lying on a bed with a child beside her, and two female attendants, one at the head of the bed and the other at the foot, as in the sculpture at the first site.   Above there is the lingam and the figures of the nine planets, or *navagraha*.   This sculpture is 2 feet 6 inches in length and 1 foot in height; 2nd, a group of *Hara-Gauri*. Hari with four arms chucking Gauri under the chin; 3rd, a four-armed figure of Vishnu, standing 3 feet 3 inches in height, with two female attendants carrying a *Vina* or " Lute," and a *chauri*, or " fly-whisk ; " 4th, a small sitting figure, which Mr. Westmacott thought was a Buddha.   There is happily no doubt on the subject, as the broken pedestal bears a part of the Buddhist creed in mediæval Nágari letters :

"*Ye dharmma hetu prabhavá hetu teshán.*"   The rest is lost.

The figures at these two sites show that the prevailing worship was that of Vishnu and Siva, and chiefly, I think, that of the former, as the two principal sculptures of the female and child seem to be intended for Devaki and the infant Krishna.   But the single figure of Buddha shows that the Buddhist religion existed at the same time.   This we know from other sources, as the Pâla Râjas in their inscriptions declare themselves to be Buddhists.

25.—BHASU-BIHÂR.

Thirteen miles to the east-south-east of Khetlâl, and on the east bank of the Nagor River, there is an old village named Bihâr, which possesses a very large mound of brick ruins, 700 feet in length by 600 feet in breadth, with a large tank tó the north surrounded by high embankments.   To the west of the tank is the *Bári*, or residence of the *Chaudrân*, the widow of the former zemindâr, who owns all the lands of Bihâr and Mahâsthân.   About three quarters of a mile a little to the east-of-north is the village of *Bihâr*, and at a short distance further north is the village of *Bhâsu Bihâr*. Opposite this village, on the west, there is a great mound 30 feet high, covered with very thick jungle. With the guidance of the villagers I made my way over this mound, and discovered that it was a large brick stûpa. Beyond this, to the north, there is a second mound with the ruins of a temple in carved brick. Still further to the north there is a very fine sheet of water called *Sosong Dighi*, or " Rajah Sasângka's tank."

One of my objects in visiting this part of the country was to search for the ancient capital which Hwen Thsang calls *Paundra Vardhana.*   I had already decided that Mahâsthân must be the place, partly on account of its name, which means simply " the capital," and partly because Hwen Thsang describes a monastery named *Po-shi-po,* as situated at 4 miles to the west of the city, which is exactly the position of Bihâr with respect to Mahâsthân. But I did not hear of *Bhâsu Bihâr* until my arrival at Bihâr itself, when the name at once struck me as being the very one intended by the pilgrim's *Po-shi-po*. Julien renders the Chinese syllables by *Vashpa,* which means "vapour," and also "iron;" but I think that the name must be connected with *Bhâsu,* "the sun," and mean the "splendid or resplendent" monastery. It may be a contraction of *Bhaswat,* "splendid, shining." The name of the village is not entered in the atlas sheet, No. 119, but it will be found in the Revenue Survey map of the Bagraha (Bograh) district, on the scale of 1 mile to 1 inch, of which a copy is given in Plate XXIX.

Here the pilgrim found a grand monastery, remarkable for the size and height of its towers and pavilion[1]. It was occupied by no less than seven hundred monks, who studied the Mahâyâna; and men famous for their learning flocked here from the eastern districts.

At a short distance from the monastery there was a stûpa built by Asoka, on the site where Buddha had explained his law to the Devas. Near this was a spot where the last four Buddhas had taken exercise and rested, and the traces of their foot-marks were still to be seen.

Not far from the last place there was a temple containing a statue of Avalokiteswara, which manifested its divine powers by prodigies.

Now each of these buildings has its representative in the still existing remains at Bihâr.

The great monastery I would identify with the mound of Bihâr itself, which is 700 feet by 600 feet broad. The southern half is higher than the northern portion, and there I would place the monastery. The brick walls have been dug out to furnish materials for the *bâri,* or residence of the zamindâr; but many trenches still remain open to show the position of the walls. An old *bâri* and two masjids are also said to have been built with those bricks, which are of large size, 11 by 6

---

[1] Julien's Hwen Thsang, Vol. I., p, 180; and Vol. III., p. 75.

by 3 inches. At the south-west corner of the mound there is an off-set of about 200 feet, but it is not so high as the main mound. I am inclined to identify this mound with the fort of *Basankot*, which was founded by Ghiasud-din Iwaz.

The stûpa is well represented by the solid brick mound of Bhâsu Bihâr, which is still 30 feet in height. It is covered with very thick tree-jungle, and would consequently be exceed-ingly difficult to excavate, even if the owner of the land would permit it, which is generally very doubtful in Bengal. To the east of the mound there is a large tank.

The vihâra containing a statue of Avalokiteswara is well represented by the ruined temple to the north of the stûpa. It is a small building only 13 feet by 11 feet inside; but the walls are 4 feet thick, and it is surrounded by a wall forming an enclosure 104 feet long from north to south by 64 feet broad. The entrance is on the south side towards the stûpa. No remains of sculpture could be found; but there were plenty of carved bricks, both *in situ* in the walls, and scattered about the ground. Some of the courses were formed by bricks on edge, presenting their broad carved faces as panels of orna-ment and separated by others presenting their ends.

The people know nothing about these ruins, and have not even a tradition regarding them.

26.—MAHÂSTHAN.

The old fortified city of Mahâsthân stands on the right or western bank of the Kâratoya River, 7 miles to the north of Bagraha (Bogra). In the maps its name is written *Mustan-garh,* which is only a corruption of *Mahâsthân-garh*, which means simply the "chief city" or "capital." Most of the names in Bengal are corrupted, as for instance the *Kâratoya* River, which is here called *Kartiya.* Mahâsthân is only the title of the city as the metropolis of this part of the country, but the people know no other name.

The ruins of the old city of Mahâsthân, or "capital," consist of an oblong mound of about 15 feet general elevation above the country, with ramparts rising to 35 feet at the corner

bastions. It is 4,500 feet in length from north to south by
3,000 feet in breadth. The ramparts generally are covered
with rather thick jungle, and so also are most of the brick
mounds, but all the rest of the place has been cleared and
divided into fields.

It was originally surrounded by a broad ditch on the north,
south, and west sides, and was no doubt protected by the
Káratoya River on the east, as the low lands come right up
to the foot of the rampart.

The people speak of four gates, one on each of the four
sides ; but according to my observation there must have been
six gates, each of the longer sides having two. The people
call the gates as follows :—

> To *East.* —Dáráb Sháh.
> ,, *South.*—Buri ka Darwáza.
> ,, *West.* —Támbá, or Támrá Darwáza.
> ,, *North.*—Sanátan Sáheb ka gali, near a saint's tomb.

Now, the Dáráb Sháhi Gate is near the south-east corner
of the enclosure, and I conclude that there must have been
another gate in the east side, near the north-east corner, which
would lead direct to the Silá Devi Ghát, on the Káratoya River
—in fact I found a similar opening, by which I descended to the
road outside, although the path was nearly hidden by jungul.

The south-east gate now leads, by a curved road 10 feet
wide, paved with brick, to the shrine of Sháh Sultán, but immediately opposite the opening is the great mound on which
lies the massive door-sill of a Hindu temple, which is now
worshipped under the name of *Khuda-ka-pathar,* or "God's
stone." The stone most probably owes its sanctity to its great
weight, which effectually prevented its removal by the Muhammadan conquerors, and there it now lies in its original position
facing the east, and there it will most likely remain, as it is
11 feet long, 2 feet 9 inches broad, and upwards of 1 foot in
thickness. It therefore contains rather more than 30 cubic
feet, and must weigh nearly three tons and a half. Both
Hindus and Muhammadans take off their shoes before they
approach it. A few other massive pieces of granite are lying

about the mound, but, from the great quantity of bricks, I infer that the mass of the temple must have been of brick.

About 600 feet to the north there is another large mound, known as *Mân-kali-ka-kundi*. The kund refers to a deep tank lying at its foot, and the builder of the temple is said to have been Raja Mân Singh, who, with his brother Tân Singh, preceded Raja Parasurâma. No stones were noticed on this mound, which forms an oblong brick ruin lying from east to west, and is no doubt the remains of a temple which faced the east. Many carved bricks were obtained here, and several *terra-cotta* figures in *alto relievo*, which once decorated the walls.

Twelve hundred feet still further to the north is another brick mound known as *Parasurâmka Bâri*, or " Raja Parasurâma's Palace." It is similar in appearance to the Mân-kali mound, but it contains several stones and possesses a famous well called *jivat-kund*, or the " water of life," with which the Raja resuscitated his soldiers as fast as they were killed by the Muhammadan invaders.

In the south-east corner of the fort stands the Muhammadan shrine of Pir Sultân Mûhi-sawâr, or Sultân Shâh-mâhi-sawûr, " the Fish-rider." The origin of this strange title is quite unknown. He is said to have come from Balkh, and several different versions are current regarding his settlement at Mahâsthân; but they all agree in the two main points as to the name of the Raja, Parasurâma, and his overthrow by the Muhammadan Saint. The story told to Mr. O'Donnell was as follows[2] :—

" A humble *fakir*, or religious mendicant, appeared before Parasurâma, and begged for as much ground as he might cover with his *chamra*, or skin, kneeling on which he might say his prayers. The Hindu prince granted his request, and the *fakir*, turning towards the west, began to pray. Scarcely had he done so when the skin began to expand,–and before he had done it covered nearly the whole principality. Parasurâma called his troops together and attacked the *fakir*, but to no purpose, as he and they perished in the battle. Parasurâma

[1] See Beveridge, in Journal Asiatic Society, Bengal, 1878, p. 94.
[2] Bengal Asiatic Society's Journal, Vol. LIX, p. 185.

had one daughter, the beautiful Silâ Devi, whom the conqueror, who bore the title of Shâh Sultân Hazrat Auliya, now claimed as his prize. The Hindu princess, pretending to accept her fate, found an opportunity of stabbing him, and then threw herself into the Kâratoya. A steep part of the bank, where there is now a flight of stairs, still bears the name of Silâ Devi's Ghât, and in Hindu hymns the favourite name of Mahâsthân is ' *Silá Dwipa*,' or the " Island of Sila."

The story which I heard differs in several of the details, but the result is the same : " On coming to Mahâsthân, Mâhi-sawâr sat down to rest at *Mâni-de-Chauk*, where he spread out a leather hide on the ground and began to pray. As he prayed the hide became larger and larger until it reached the palace of the Raja. Then Parâsurâma came out to kill the Pîr, but his followers were struck down by the holy man. The Raja, however, revived them by giving them water from the *Jivat-kund*, or " Well of Life." The secret of their revival was betrayed·to the saint by the Raja's sweeper, named Harpâl, and the Pîr then sent a *Bhavan-Chila*, or kite, to drop a piece of *Gaomâns,* that is, cow's flesh, or beef, into the well. The water then lost its power, and the Raja and all his followers were killed. The Raja's daughter, *Silâ Devi*, begged for her life, and was allowed to go to the Kâratoya River to bathe; but she jumped into the deep water and was drowned, and has ever since been worshipped as a goddess. An annual *méla* is held at Silâ-Ghât on the Kâratoya, on the new moon of Chaitra, when people from all parts assemble to bathe. At the ghât there is a " stone wall " from 25 to 30 feet in length, with one large carved stone inserted, which no doubt once formed part of a Hindu temple. The name of Silâ Devi is most probably connected with the name of the district *Silbâris*, in which Mâhasthân is situated.

Mâhi-sawar's tomb, or *asthân* as it is generally called, is a common whitewashed square building covered by a low dome. The entrance door is very small, but each of the jambs has a short inscription in mediæval Nâgari letters, reading *Sri Nara sinha dâsasya*, " of Sri Narasinha's slave." The two records are the same, both unworn and quite distinct,

but on rough chisel-marked stones. The letters were partially filled with several coats of whitewash, which no doubt
prevented Mr. O'Donnell from reading the inscription. In
the court-yard there is a battered Jain statue without feet.
I recognized it by the position of the arms hanging down close
to the sides, and reaching below the knees. As the figure is
naked, there can be no doubt whatever as to its being one
of the twenty-four Jain pontiffs. It has been deliberately
chiselled all over by the Muhammadans. Close by there is
the pedestal of a large figure of the Varâha Avatâra, of which
only the feet remain, trampling on a Nâga, or a Nâgni. It is
this human-bodied Nâga ending with a serpent's coils which
Mr. O'Donnell describes as a figure of a girl, with a long
fish's tail, half reclining on " her left side." The left foot of
the god rests on the head and upraised right hand of the
Nâga, while the right foot is treading on the serpent's coils.
The pedestal is 2 feet 1 inch across the front, with a tenon
below, 13 inches in depth and 11 inches in height, for fixing
it in position. Judging from the length of the foot, the
figure must have been of life size.

There are also two *arghas* of lingams with the usual
spouts, one circular, of 4 feet 5 inches diameter; the other
oblong, 3 feet 9 inches by 2 feet 4 inches. The lingam of the
former was 11 inches in diameter. Its base is surrounded by
eight small holes, and there are nine similar holes inside the
rim of the argha. They look as if they were intended for the
insertion of metal work.

Here also I found half a man's head in blue stone of life
size, but there was nothing to show the nature of the statue
to which it belonged.

From the *Mân-kali-ka-kundi* I obtained a considerable
number of carved bricks, such as are always found in the
ruins of temples, and which still exist *in situ* in the fine brick
temple of Bhitargaon. There were mouldings of cornices of
many varieties, portions of undulated eaves, and of *amalaka*
fruits of the pinnacles of a temple. I got also twelve square
terra-cotta alto-relievos, and one small pilaster or baluster,
which formed the upright of two of these panels of a long frieze.

Three of the large-size terra-cottas are shown in the accompanying plate, along with one of the smaller ones and its accompanying baluster'. They are all of coarse workmanship and of soft red brick. There is, however, much variety in the designs, as will be seen in the following list :—

> Nos. 1, 2, 3.—Men in various positions.
>   ,,   4.—A wheel, or the sun.—See Plate.
>   ,,   5, 6, 7.—A ram, a bull, and a tiger.
>   ,,   8.—A caparisoned horse.
>   ,,   9, 10.—A parrot, and an unknown bird.
>   ,,   11.—Lion sitting to front.—See Plate.
>   ,,   12.—A circular lotus flower.

Along with these I obtained two old bronze figures of Ganesa and Garuda, and a fragment of blue stone pedestal with the end of an inscription in mediæval Nâgari characters reading *nâgrahâra*, which would seem to show that the great mound of Mânkali-ka-Kundi was part of an ancient *agrahâra*, or " endowment of land " belonging to Brahmans. The name of Mânkali is referred to Raja Mân Singh, one of the predecessors of Parasurâma.

The palace of the last Raja, called Parasurâm ka bâri, is another high mound covered with brick ruins, with a fine well 14½ feet in diameter, which is the famous *Jivat-Kund*, or " Well of Life." It is now filled with bees' nests, and I was unable to obtain its depth, as my measuring of the width had already disturbed the bees. The descent to the water was made by isolated stones projecting from the wall like steps.

It will be seen from this account that not a single fragment of anything Buddhist has been found in Mahâsthân itself. Mr. Beveridge also could find nothing Buddhist at Mahâsthân². But the place is so extensive, and is in many parts (especially amongst the brick ruins), so thickly covered with jangal, that it is quite impossible to make any satisfactory exploration, save at a great waste of both time and money.

---

¹ See Plate XXXI.
² Bengal Asiatic Society's Journal, Vol. XLVII, p. 94.

*

In my account of Bhâsu Bihâr, 4 miles to the west of Mahâsthân, I mentioned that the Buddhist remains at that place corresponded both in description and position with those noted by Hwen Thsang at the *Po-shi-po* monastery, which was situated just 4 miles to the west of the capital city of Paundra Varddhana. This city the pilgrim places at 600 *li*, or 100 miles, to the east of the Ganges, near Râjmahal. Now this description corresponds exactly with the relative positions of Râjmahal and Mahâsthân, the latter being just 100 miles to the east of the former. The natives of the country are unanimous in their opinion that Mahâsthân was the ancient capital of Barendra, or Eastern Gauda. According to Hwen Thsang the city was about 30 *li*, or 5 miles, in circuit. This is very considerably in excess of the size of the fortified city, which, according to my survey, is only 4,500 feet long by 3,000 feet broad, or 15,000 feet in circuit. But there are extensive remains on the north, south, and west sides, showing the limits of the old suburbs of the city. Including these outlying portions, the city would have been about 7,000 feet in length from north to south by about 4,500 feet in breadth, or rather less than 4½ miles in circuit.

Mahâsthân possesses one characteristic feature in the great number of its pân gardens, which, according to my observation, are the never-failing accompaniments of an old Hindu city. But here they are in greater numbers than in any other places that I have seen. To the westward, for upwards of 2 miles to the bank of the Nagor River, the country is covered with several hundred Pân gardens which extend down to Chand Miyan on the south-west.

Mr. Westmacott has proposed Bardhan Kuti, 12 miles to the north of Mahâsthân, as the probable representative of Paundra Varddhana ; but, according to Mr. Beveridge, " Bardhan Kuti is a comparatively recent place," and is never mentioned by the people as a large city, while Mahâsthân is the recognised traditional capital, which is known to everybody far and near. In fact the very name of *Kuti* shows that it must have been a small place, as every large fort is invariably called *Kot*, and not *Kuti*. Now we know that in the time of

Bakhtiyar Khalji *Bardhan Kot* was the name of a " city," to
which Ali-mech conducted the Muhammadan invader[1]. But
according to the universal belief of the people, Mahâsthân
was the capital of Barendra or Eastern Gauda at the time
of the Muhammadan occupation. Accepting the tradition
as correct—and it is amply supported by the size of the ruined fortress—the Bardhan Kot of the Muhammadan historian
must be the same place, as Mahâsthân. The name of Bardhan Kuti, which is applied to the Râjbâri, or King's palace,
12 miles to the north of Mahâsthân, may have been given tò
it to distinguish it from other Râjbâris, just as we have a
Kashmiri Shâlimâr, a Lahori Shâlimâr, and a Delhi Shâlimâr.

The earliest mention that I have found of the city of
Paundra-Varddhana refers to the end of the eighth century
A.D., when Jayapida Raja of Kashmir (A.D. 779 to 813)
visited Gauda. At that time the king of Paundra-Varddhana was named Jayanta, but there were no less than five
other " Kings of Gauda" whom Jayapida is said to have
conquered. Now this is exactly the state of the country
which is described by Târanâth immediately preceding the
establishment of the Pâla dynasty[2].

" A Odivicha (Orissa) du Bengale et dans les cinq autres provinces
de l'Orient, chaque Kshatriya, Brahman et Marchande(Vaisya) se fais-
ait roi de ses aleutours, mais il n'y pas de roi gouvernant le pays.
L'auteur raconte comment la femme de l'un des defuncts rois, assas-
sinait, la nuit, chacun de ceux qui avaient été choisis pour être rois,
mais eusuite apres un certain nombres d'années, *Gopala*, qui avait
été élu pour un temps, sedelivra d'elle, et fut fait roi pour toujours.
Il commença par reguer au Bengale, et ensuite il reduisuit aussi
Magadha sous son pouvair."

The author goes on to relate how *Varendra*, and afterwards Orissa, were conquered by Deva Pâla, the son of Gopâla.
From these two accounts it would appear that the province
of Barendra was divided amongst several petty chiefs shortly
before the establishment of the Pâla dynasty in the beginning

---

[1] Raverty's translation of Tabakât-i-Nâsiri, p. 561.
[2] Vassilief's Taranath, translated by La Comme, p. 54—note.

of the ninth century. Tradition gives us the name of Parasurâma Raja of *Mahâsthân*, and at a later date of Kansa Raja
of *Bhaturia* (the father of Jalal-ud-din Muhammad). The
remaining four chiefships were probably Gauda, Santosh,
Devikot, and Rangpur.

Hwen Thsang's account of Paundra Verddhana is very
meagre[1]. He simply notes that there were about twenty
Buddhist monasteries containing some 3,000 monks, who
studied the Hinayana, or the lesser means of advancement,
and about one hundred Brahmanical temples ; but the greater
numbers of the heretics were *Nirgranthas* who went about
naked. In my description of the ruins I have already noticed
the traces of the Brahmanical worship of Vishnu and Siva,
and to these I may add a temple of Kârtikeya, which Jayapida is said to have visited on his arrival at Paundra Varddhana. The pilgrim mentions no king, and his silence on
this point may be taken as evidence that Barendra was in his
time one of the dependent provinces of the vast dominions
of Harsha Varddhana of Kanauj. The king of the neighbouring country of Kâmrup, or Assam, named Bhâskara
Varmma, is duly noticed, but as he was certainly tributary to
Harsha Varddhana, I conclude that the intervening province
of Barendra had been annexed to the kingdom of Kanauj.

Hwen Thsang notices that the country was low and moist,
and this leads me to suggest that the name of the district of
Silbaras, in which Mahasthan is situated, must be *Silavar-
sha*, or the "wet or moist district." Following the same descriptive explanation, I think that the name of Kotivarsha
applied to Devikot must mean simply the "fort district."

The name of the whole country was *Pundra*, or *Paundra-
desa*, or the "land of the red sugar-cane." Now another
name for this same red cane is *Kântâra ;* and amongst the
countries mentioned as being tributary to Samudra Gupta, I
find the name of *Mahâ Kântâra* under its king, *Vyâghra*.
This country I would identify with *Paundra-desa*, partly because the two names are perfectly synonymous, and partly

---

[1] Julien's Hwen Thsang, Vol. III, p. 74.

because the country to the west of the Káratoya River is still called *Kayár*, which I think may be possibly a contraction of Kántár.   This identification first suggested itself to me on finding that several other names connected with the province of Barendra bore the same direct reference to a sugar-cane country.   Thus *Gauda* must have derived its name from *gur*, "raw sugar," so also the name of the parganah of *Audumbara* in which Tanda was situated must have been derived from the *Audumbara*, or red-coloured (literally copper-hued) sugar-cane, and not from the *Udumbara* tree, which is very rarely found there.   This suggests the probable derivation of the name of the *Tameræ*, a people placed by Ptolemy to the east of the head of the Gangetic delta, from *Tamra*, "copper."   The *Tameræ* would therefore be the people who occupied the country of the "red or copper-hued sugar-cane," as *tamraka* is a synonym of *Audumbara*.

But it is not only the sugar-cane that is red, for the soil on which it grows is even redder than the cane.   As Mr. Beveridge justly remarks, the Káratoya River forms the boundary between two distinct kinds of soil.   "On the west, Bagura (Bogra) is a veritible land of Edom, the soil being almost as red as blood.   It is at the same time so hard and tenaceous that ditches cut in it retain their sharpness of outline for years, and that the walls of the peasants' huts are almost invariably made of earth.   The ant-hills, so common on the edges of the fields, testify to the peculiarity of the soil, for they stand up in sharp and many-pointed pinnacles and are like Adens in miniature.   On the east of the Karatoya, however, all is sand and alluvium, and the ryots have to construct the walls of their houses with reeds or mats.   This difference of soil is said to affect the crime of the district, for burglaries are reported to be rare in the western thanás, as it is no easy matter for thieves to break through and steal when the walls of the houses are so thick and hard as they are in the '*khiar*' land."   Closely connected with this redness of the soil is the fact that the western gate of the fort of Mahásthán is still known as the *Támra Darwáza*, which, as I believe, simply refers to the "red land" on the west to which the gate leads in contradistinction to the light, sandy soil on the eastern side of the fort. But if this suggested identification of Ptolemy's *Tameræ* with the people of the "red land" or red sugar-cane land be correct, it follows that their capital named *Tagma metropolis* must be looked for in Eastern Barendra away from the Ganges. As it is seated on the western bank of a large river, I think it may be Mahâsthân. It is true that the Kâratoya River is now a comparatively small stream, but, as Mr. Beveridge has justly remarked, "in old times it was a great river and formed the boundary between Bengal and Kâmrup[1]." In fact the Kâratoya was one of the ancient beds of the Tista River, which has changed its course several times since it received its Sanskrit name of *Trisrota*, or the "three channels." The three old channels, according to my observation of the river system of Barendra, must have been the Purnabhâba, the Atreyi, and the Kâratoya. The first name, as I believe, actually means the "old channel," as Purna is only a contraction of Purâna. The Atreyi is still a fine large stream, from 250 to 300 feet broad and 3 feet deep in the cold season. But its bed is that of a much larger river, and I have no doubt that the people are quite correct in their belief that it was once the main channel of the Tista. The Kâratoya has a much smaller stream than the Atreyi, but its bed appeared to me to be larger. And here also the people have a tradition that this was on an old channel of the Tista, and Mr. Beveridge has quoted the tradition of Sherpur Bagurâ having been called *Das Kâhania*, because the river was so broad that the ferry toll for a single passenger was *ten Kâhans*, which, at the present day, would be equal to 12,800 kauris, or one rupee. But the usual valuation of the kâhan is 16 panas or "handfuls" of kauris, or 16+80—1,280 kauris, and in Calcutta the four-anna piece or quarter rupee is still called kâhan. But the common *Kâhan* is the copper *Kâhapana*, which, in ancient times, was equal in value to only 80 *kauris*, so that 10 *kâhans* would have been only 800 *kauris*, or just two annas and a half of the

---

[1] Bengal Asiatic Society's Journal, Vol. XLVII, p. 89.

present day. The ferry toll over the Ganges at Rajmahal is only two annas even now, so that the *Das Kâhania* seems a fair toll for a large river.

As for the name of Barendra, the people have no derivation of any kind. Varendra in Sanskrit is a title of Indra, but there is no legend to connect the god with the name of the province, such for instance as we have about Banâsur with his thousand arms, and the names of Bânnagar and Sahasbir. The old name of the district was certainly Paundra-desa, as the Paundras are mentioned by Manu and also in the Mahâbhârata¹. I have a suspicion that the name of Barendra may be connected with the establishment of the twelve chiefships of the " Bârah Bhuihârs." Wilford calls them the twelve Bhumiyas, Bhattis, or principalities, but the common tradition of the country, as related by Buchanan, and repeated by O'Donnell, and heard by myself on the spot, is that twelve " persons of very high distinction, and mostly named *Pál*, came from the west and settled " at Mahâsthân.² Buchanan says that they were of the *Bhungiya* tribe, to which the Rajas of Benares and Bettiah belong. The name Bhuihâr is said to have been shortened from *Bhumihâra*, a title given to certain Brahmans who became degraded as " tillers of land." They are perhaps more generally known as Bâbhans, which is a very strong testimony in favour of their Brahmanical origin, as Bâbhan is a common pronunciation of Bâhman or Brâhman. This is their own statement of their claims, but their enemies say that they are the descendants of men of low caste whom Jarasandha raised to the priesthood. According to Wilford it was Ripunjaya who drove away the real Brahmans, and installed men of the lowest tribes, such as *Kaivartas*, *Pulindas*, and *Madrakas*, as priests. These *Bhuihars* must not be confounded with the *Bhuiyas*, who are aborigines.

The Bâbhans form a very large part of the population of Magadha, the chief representative of the clan being the Raja

---

¹ In Manu's code, Chap X, Vol, the Paundras are called Mlechbas.
² Buchanan's Eastern India, Vol, II, pp. 118, 119—O'Donnell in Journal of Bengal Asiatic Society, Vol. XLIV, p. 184.

of Tikári.   On this account I am led to suspect that the
Pála Rajas, who ruled for so long a time over Bengal,
Barendra and Magadha, must have been of this caste, as
they would appear to have been descendants of some of the
Bára Bhuihár Páls, while in their inscriptions they are silent
as to their ancestry.   According to Buchanan there are ten
thousand families (or about fifty thousand persons) of these
Bábhans or zamindar Brahmans in the Bhágalpur district
alone, and he thinks that they may be the Brachmani of
Pliny.   They are famed for their contentious and brawling
dispositions; and their quarrelsomeness has passed into a
proverb—

> *Bábhan, kuta, háthi,*
> *Tinon ját ka ghátí.*
> " Bábhans, Dogs, and Elephants
> Are all three ready combatants."

The first notice of Varendra that I have been able to find
is in Táranath's account of the Pála kings.   To Gopála, the
first king, he assigns the conquest of Bengal and Magadha,
and to his son Deva Pála the subjugation of Varendra and
Orissa. This was about the middle of the ninth century. The
name is never mentioned in any of the inscriptions, the kings
being called only lords of Gauda and Paundra-desa.   This
omission is, I think, rather favourable to my suggestion of its
being a popular name derived from the *Bára Bhuihar* chiefs,
rather than a pure Sanskrit name imposed by the Brahmans.

Ancient coins are occasionally found in Mahásthán and
its suburbs.   About 1862 a number of gold coins were found
at Báhmanpára, out of which Mr. Beveridge obtained two,
which he forwarded to the Asiatic Society in Calcutta
for identification.   They were both Gupta coins, one of
Chandra Gupta II, and the other of Kumára Gupta.   The
latter coin was wrongly attributed by Babu Rajendra Mitra
to a fabulous Mahendra Gupta.   But Mahendra was the title
of Kumára Gupta; and as the Babu quotes a part of the
legend on the obverse of the coin as *Sri Mahendra Sinha*, I

am able to give a more complete reading of the legends on
both sides from a coin in my own collection—

Obv.—Sri Mahendra Sinha Parâkrama.

Rev.—Kumara Gupta ⁎   ⁎—

"In 1874 a pot of old rupees was found in Mahâsthân
itself by a labourer, who was digging a ditch in a *pân*
garden." One of these coins belonged to Ilias Shâh, and
the others to Mahmud I. I also obtained three of these
rupees found in Mahâsthân. One of them belonged to Jalâl-
uddin Muhammad, and the other two to Mahmud I. One of
them is dated in A.H. 846, and the other in A.H. 848. The
first coin is in very fine order.

27.—PAHARPUR.

A brief notice of the great mound of Pahârpur has been
given by Buchanan, and his opinion that it was a Buddhist
stûpa has been adopted by Mr. Westmacott[1]. The mound
had also been described to me by some of the railway officers
as being a solid mass of bricks, and they had no doubt
inspected it carefully with an eye to railway ballast, as it is
only 4 miles to the west of the Darjîling Railway, opposite
Jamâlganj. It stands 29 miles to the west of Mahâsthân, and
20 miles to the east of Patnitolah on the Atreyi River. Buchanan estimates the height of the mound rather vaguely at
"from 100 to 150 feet;" but according to my measurement
it is not more than 80 feet above the country, and only 70
feet above the level of its own court-yard. On the south is
the good-sized village of Pahârpur, or "Hill-town," which
derives its name from the mound. To the north-west is the
small village of *Gwâl Bhita*, which is erroneously printed in
Buchanan's account as *Gopal Chitar Pahar. Gwâl Bhita*
means simply the cow-herd's mound, *Gwâla* being the contraction of *go-wâla*, or "cow-keeper." Buchanan always spells
this word as *goyâl*, but the common pronunciation is better
represented in the name of *Goâlpâra* in Assam.

[1] Buchanan, Eastern India, Vol. II., p. 669, and Westmacott, in Bengal
Asiatic Society's Journal, Vol. XLIII, p. 189.

The great mound stands in the middle of a large enclosure, about 1,500 feet square outside, formed by a massive earthen embankment, about 150 feet broad on the east side, and not more than 100 feet on the other three sides. I forced my way on to the top of the southern embankment on an elephant; and in the same way I was able to examine several parts of the broad eastern embankment, which is everywhere covered with bricks, and the remains of walls. On the low ground inside the enclosure the jungle was so high and so dense that it was quite impenetrable to a man. I forced my way through on an elephant to the foot of the mound, and ascending a short distance on the south-east side to a small clear spot, I was able to examine the site at leisure. With the exception of a few tanks, there was nothing to be seen but thick jungle. On the slope we found several broken terracotta alto-relievos and pieces of carved brick. A party of coolies was then set to work to clear the jungle on all the slopes of the mound, and to make a rough path up to the top. In cutting the jungle two leopards were disturbed, but they slunk away to the opposite side, where they were seen again on the following day. ·

I had intended making some extensive excavations in the mound, and I had brought some skilled labourers with me for this very purpose, but on my return to my tent I found an agent from the zamindar owner of the land, Raja Kishen Chandar Rai, of Bolihâr, 9 miles to the south, who prohibited all excavations. I then set all the men to work to clear the jungle, and by the evening I got a pretty fair view of the mass of the mound, and was also able to climb to the top of it. Here I made a few superficial excavations, which showed that the upper part of the building was a square tower of 22 feet side, with a projection in the middle of each face. A few feet lower down the side was 28 feet, below which the wall could not be traced, as the slope was too steep for the workmen to find a footing. The slope of this upper part was 3 inches in ten courses of bricks, equal to 30 inches in height, or just 1 in 10. On the east side, however, from about half down the slope is long and gentle. I conclude therefore that the mound is the ruin of a large Brahmanical temple, with its entrance to the east, and its highest point, the spire covering the sanctum, on the west. The whole length of the ruin from west to east is about 200 feet, the highest point being 50 feet from the western base and 150 feet from the eastern base. There was ample room therefore for the usual *Mahá-mandapa*, or assembly hall, between the sanctum and the entrance.

I have ventured to call the temple a Brahmanical one, because one of the terra-cotta sculptures represented the skeleton goddess Kâli. The other terra-cotta figures give no indication of the nature of the building. They are all 14 inches in height by 10 in breadth. The best preserved specimen is shown in the accompanying plate[1]. It is apparently only a fancy figure representing a man sitting in an uneasy-looking position, with both arms raised. A third figure has the right hand raised and the left hand resting on the hip. A fourth figure is accompanied by a monkey. A fifth terra-cotta panel of smaller size, 10 inches by 8, was filled with an ornamental circle, while a sixth of still smaller size, or 6 inches by 6, was decorated with some neatly designed foliage. All of these must have belonged to the long lines of friezes with which all the finer Hindu temples are decorated. There were also numerous pieces of moulded and carved bricks, which formed the cornices and smaller bands of ornament.

On the very top of the mound a considerable number of wedge-shaped bricks were found, the smaller ones being ornamented at the broad or outer end. The largest of these bricks was 15½ inches in length by 10⅞ inches at the broad end, and 8⅜ inches at the narrow end. Others were only 11⅜ inches in length by 9 inches at the broad end, and 8 at the narrow end. From the position in which these wedge bricks were found, it is clear that they must have belonged to the *Kalas*, or pinnacle of the temple, which is always of a circular shape. I made out from an examination of the different sized pieces that the neck of the *Kalas* must have been about 9 feet in diameter, gradually swelling to about 12 feet by successive projections of the upper courses. As the top of the

[1] See Plate XXXII

square mass of the spire could not have been less than 12 feet, or the diameter of the *Kalas*, while the slope was 1 in 10, the height of the square portion may have been about 5 feet above the point where I was able to measure it as having a side of 22 feet. This would make the total height of the square body of the spire just 85 feet, and if we allow 15 feet for the pinnacle, the whole height of the building would have been just 100 feet. The temple was therefore an exceptionally large one, and, to judge from the quantity of carved and ornamented bricks, must have been a very fine one. I was therefore much disappointed in being prohibited from exploring the mound. But almost everywhere in Bengal I have found the same "dog-in-the manger" conduct on the part of the zamindars. In the present instance the Raja's agent repeated what I had previously heard from the people of the surrounding villages, that a great treasure was buried in the mound. This is the general belief all over the country, but it is in Bengal alone that the owner of the land will neither dig up the treasure himself nor allow anybody else to make any excavations. In 1876 an excavation was actually begun on the north side by a man named Ghansyâm, which was promptly stopped by the zamindar Raja. I examined the spot, but I saw no trace of any chamber, such as the people had mentioned to me. There was a large clear space covered with broken bricks, amongst which there was one large dark-grey stone. Apparently this is the spot noted by Buchanan where he saw three stones. At the back of the cutting the wall was quite broken by the roots of trees. According to the people, three separate doorways of black stone were uncovered, leading into different rooms. But I could not find any traces of these doorways, and I am inclined to think that they must have been only niches. The stones were of course removed by the zamindar.

28.—JOGI-GUPHA.

On the bank of the Jabuna River, 8 miles to the west-north-west of Pahârpur, and the same distance to the south-west of Mangalbâri, the true site of what is erroneously called the Budal pillar, there is a curious half-sunken lingam temple called *Jogi-gupha*, or the "Jogi's cave." It is said to be connected with a similar temple, 9 miles to the south-west of Mahásthán, by a subterranean passage. This temple is usually called *Jogi-Bhawan*, but in the large map of the Revenue Survey I see that it is also called *Jogi-gupha*. The Jabuna temple stands on a large low mound of brick ruins, which is said to have been "the house" of Raja Deva Pála, according to Buchanan. But the name given to it by the people is *Raja Deva Pála ka Chhatri*, which is the usual term for a mausoleum built over the ashes of a person of consequence. I think, therefore, that this must be the place where Raja Deva Pála died, and where his body was burned.

The Gupha is a small oblong room, only 6 feet wide, containing a Siva lingam. To the right and left of the entrance there are two small platforms, one bearing the holy tulsi, or basil, and the other the trident of Siva. In front is the Jogi's residence, and to the right there are two small shrines, one with a common plain lingam, the other with a four-faced lingam, called "Brahmá lingam." But there should be a fifth face on the top to represent Siva. Outside the Gupha temple there is a four-armed figure of Vishnu, 3 feet 7 inches in height, and a broken figure of a female lying on a bed with a child by her side. Mr. Westmacott thinks that the "stone carvings are of undoubted Buddhist origin;" but the recumbent female cannot be, as he supposes, Máyá Devi, as he admits that the sculpture is similar to one which he saw at Khetlál. Now the Khetlál recumbent female figures, as I have already pointed out, are certainly Brahmanical, as they are accompanied by lingams; and I believe that they represent Devaki with the infant Krishna by her side.

29.—AMARI, OR AMAI.

About 3 miles to the south-west of Jogi-gupha there is a large scattered village called Amári or Amai, which possesses several sculptures and fragments of sculpture, and has evidently been a place of some consequence in former days. The village extends for upwards of a mile in length from east

to west in small collections of houses, with numerous old
tanks between them. At Brindûban, 1¼ mile to the north-west
of Amâri, there are several sculptures collected under a pipal
tree, of which the best is a slab containing the figures of the
Ashta-sakti, or "eight female energies" of the gods. At
Siv-Tala, near Kâdipur, there is a fine figure of Vishnu, 3 feet
3½ inches in height, besides several fragments of sculpture
enclosed in the roots of a pipal tree. A mêla, or fair, is held
there in the month of Chaitra.

30.—GHATNAGAR.

Ghâtnagar is another large scattered village, 12 miles to
the west-south-west of Patni Tola on the Atreyi River. It
is an old site, as evidenced by the numerous sculptures and
quantities of old bricks to be seen in all directions. At half
a mile to the south there is a Muhammadan tomb without
roof, but with an ornamented doorway of carved bricks containing parrots and flowers. The designs, however, are only
slight alterations of one pattern, and all are of low relief and
of poor execution. Close by there is one large tank and
several small ones.

To the south-west, at about 1¼ mile, is the zamindar's
kacheri, in the wall of which is fixed a sculptured slab containing standing figures of Brahma, Vishnu, and Siva, with
two small figures between. The kacheri itself stands on a
rising ground, and is built of old bricks. A single stone pillar,
square below and octagonal above, was found here. Nothing
whatever is known about the history of the place, every
Bengali, as usual, professing entire ignorance. I tried to
ascertain why the place was called *Ghâtnagar*, but without
success.

31.—DEBAR DIGHI.

Nine miles nearly due north from Ghâtnagor there is a
fine large sheet of water called *Debar Dighi*. It is noticed
by Buchanan, who ascribes it to one "*Dhivor Raja*, who lived
about one thousand years ago." In the Atlas map, sheet
No. 119, the village is called *Deebur*, but the name given to

me was *Debar*, which I take to be a corruption of *Dev Pal,* the third Prince of the Pâla dynasty, who must have reigned just about one thousand years ago, in the latter half of the ninth century. According to Târanâth, he was the conqueror of Varendra.

The lake is a fine sheet of water, upwards of 1,200 feet square, or nearly one quarter of a mile, and 12 feet deep. In the middle there is a stone pillar standing 10 feet out of the water, and as the water is 12 feet deep the height of the shaft above the bottom is 22 feet, while its full length cannot be much short of 30 feet. Buchanan, indeed, says that it is 22½ cubits, or 33¾ feet, in length, and 6¼ cubits, or 9 feet 9 inches, in *diameter*. The last is no doubt a mistake for circumference, which would reduce the diameter to 3 feet 1¼ inches. My servant, who measured the pillar, made a similar mistake about the diameter, which he recorded as 9 feet. But on examining his other measurements I found that the pillar had *nine* sides of 12 inches each, which would give a diameter of 29 inches. Buchanan calls the pillar *octagonal*, and as he speaks of cubits instead of feet, I infer that his Pandit's measurements were made with the small arm of the Bengali himself, of about 17 inches. This would make his circumference just 110½ inches, or 8 feet 10 inches, or within an inch and a half of my servant's measurement in English feet. Similarly, his 22½ cubits of length would be reduced to 31 feet 10½ inches. I regret that I did not visit the place myself, as no single shaft of such large size as 30 feet in length and 2½ feet in diameter has yet been found of later date than the time of Asoka; and it seems to me quite possible that this may be one of Asoka's monoliths. There is, however, no inscription on the upper 10 feet above the water level; but as the inscriptions of the Asoka pillars are always in the middle of the shaft, any record on this column would be below the water level.

32.—PANDUA.

Pandua is an old town in Western Bengal, situated about half-way between Bardwân and Calcutta. It possesses a

very curious old tower, about 125 feet in height, a large long
masjid, and also a square masjid, near the famous tomb of
Shâh Safi-ud-din. The town is sometimes called Chhota
Pandua, or " Little Pandua," to distinguish it from the more
famous Hazrat Pandua near Mâldah.

The square masjid was built in the year 882 of the Hijra,
during the reign of Yusuf Shâh of Bengal. The occupant
of the tomb is named Hazrat Shâh Safi-ud-din, and is said to
have been a nephew of Firoz Shâh of Delhi. This, however,
is quite impossible, as Firoz died in A.H. 791, or just 91
years before the date of the inscription on the tomb. But
it is not improbable that the masjid and minâr may have
been built by a nephew of Firoz, as the style of the long
masjid is very like that of other mosques built during his
reign. I may instance the old masjid in the fort of Jaunpur,
which was built in A.H. 778, during the reign of Firoz. This
is 130 feet long by 23 feet broad, the aisles being supported
on Hindu stone pillars. The Pandua masjid is much larger,
being 231 feet long by 42 feet broad; but the proportions are
almost exactly the same, and the aisles are supported in
the same way on Hindu pillars. The great tower I take to
be the *Mâsina*, or Muazzin's Minâr, for calling the faithful to
prayer, as its entrance is on the west *towards the masjid*. I
think, therefore, that the square masjid and tower may belong
to the first half of the ninth century of the Hijra, and that
the tomb may belong to the son of the square mosque builder, who may have been a nephew of Firoz. But whether it
be so or not, I believe that the founders of these three
Muhammadan buildings were closely connected, and that the
mosques and the tower all belong to the same century of
the Hijra.

The great masjid is a long low building of three aisles,
with 21 openings in front, and a roof of 63 small domes
resting on brick arches, which spring from single Hindu pillars
of many different kinds. Most of the pillars are out of the
perpendicular; but they are kept in position by the great
weight above them, and will remain so until one of the walls
gives way, or until some of the arches are destroyed by the

roots of trees. The curious appearance of the massive brick arches, resting on single slender shafts of basalt, is well shown in the drawing given by Blochmann in his account of Pandua. The arches spring at once from the walls without any pilasters or even imposts. The outer face of the front wall is profusely ornamented with small patterns in carved brick. These are pretty enough in design, but they are all small, and are quite lost sight of on a long wall of 230 feet. The back and end walls are perfectly plain. The mosque stands on a mound once the site of a Hindu temple, the pillars of which now support this mean-looking barn-like masjid. There is no inscription of any kind attached to it.

The second mosque is a square of 25½ feet inside with walls 6 feet 10¼ inches in thickness. It has three arched openings in front, and one on each side, with three prayer niches in the back wall. At each of the four corners there is a square minár of 4½ feet side, projecting 3⅛ feet from the building. It is covered by a single dome, which is completely overgrown, and the branches of the tree hang down in front, partly concealing the inscription. The tops of the four towers have been nearly destroyed by the trees. In the interior the square is made into an octagon by cutting off the corners with pointed arches springing from octagonal pilasters. The angles of the octagon are filled up by overlapping pendentives, to form a circle for the spring of the dome.

Outside, the walls are decorated with panels of carved bricks, but much of the carving has been obliterated by repeated coats of whitewash. The mosque, however, must have been white outside from the beginning, as it is still called the *Kauriya Masjid*, a name which I believe to have been derived from the fine white plaster made from cowrie shells.

High up over the central arch of the Tomb there is an inscription dated in A.H. 882 during the reign of Yusuf Sháh. The following translation of this record is by Blochmann[1]:—

" God Almighty says :—' Surely the mosque belongs to God. Do not call on any one besides Allah.' And he upon whom God's bless-

[1] Bengal Asiatic Society's Journal, 1873, p. 276.

ing rests, says, ' He who builds a mosque in the world will have seventy castles built for him by God in the next world.' This mosque was built during the reign of the king of the age, who is assisted by the assistance of a Supreme Judge, the viceregent of God by proof and evidence, the king, the son of a king, who was the son of a king, Shamso-dunyâ-waddin Abul Muzaffar Yusuf Shâh, the king, son of Bârbak Shâh, the king, son of Mahmud Shâh, the king—may God perpetuate his kingdom and rule ! The mosque was built by the Majlis-ul-Majâlis, the great and liberal Majlis, the lord of the sword and pen, the hero of the age and the period, Ulugh Majlis-i-Azam May God Almighty protect him in both worlds !

"Dated Wednesday, 1st Muharram, 882. Let it end well ! "

The minâr of Pandua is a very curious structure, quite different from all others that I have seen. It is a round tower of five stages or storeys, each lessening in diameter from 60 feet at the base to 15 feet at the top. The dimensions of the several stages will be best understood by being placed in a tabular form—

	Diameter. feet.			Height. feet.
Upper Storey	12 0	above		18
	15 0	below		
4th Storey	23 10	above		18
	26 0	below		
3rd „	34 8	above		30
	37 5	below		
2nd „	47 6	above		25
	48 1	below		
Basement	58 2	above		25
	60 0	below		
				116
	Pinnacle .	.	.	9
				125

The outer face of each storey is ornamented with very flat convex flutes. In the centre of the building there is a circular staircase leading to the top. At the base of each

---

[1] According to my own Tables as well as those of Jervis and James Prinsep the 1st day of Muharram in A.H. 882 was *Tuesday*, the 15th of April.

successive storey there is a doorway leading out to a narrow
terrace on the outside which runs all round. The entrance
door of the basement storey is on the west side towards the
masjid, which is 175 feet distant. On this account I believe
it to have been the mázináh, or Muazzin's tower, from the
top of which the faithful were called to prayers. There is no
inscription on the building, and the people of course refer its
erection to the holy saint Safi-ud-din, whose tomb is close by.

33.—DHAKKA.

The city of Dhakka has been supposed by some writers
to be comparatively modern, but its happy position on the
bank of the Buri Ganga, or old Ganges, shows that it must
have been established long before the river changed its
course.   Indeed I think it not impossible that Dhakka
may be the *Tugma metropolis* of Ptolemy, as it is close to
the point of junction of the old Ganges with the Lakhia River,
· an old bed of the Brahmaputra.

The city is said to have derived its name from a temple of
the goddess Durgâ, under the title of *Dhakka Seri*, which is
also the name of one of the western quarters. The whole
length of the river-front is about 4 miles; but its breadth
only extends to 1 mile in a few places. It is said to have possessed 52 bazars and 53 streets (*Báwano Basar aur Tipano
gali*). Dr. Taylor notes that one of these bazars, called the
Bangla Bazar, still exists, and is known throughout the country as one of the most ancient places of trade in Bengal.
He thinks, apparently with good reason, that it may be the city
of Bangâla, mentioned by European travellers of the sixteenth
and seventeenth centuries[1]. What tends to confirm this
opinion of the identity of Dhakka and Bangâla is, he says,
the circumstance that—

" only one of them is ever mentioned by the same traveller. Methold,
in enumerating the principal cities of Bengal for instance, mentions
Rajmahal and Bengalla, which he designates ' faire cities,' while
Herbert and Mandelso, who travelled about the same period, specify
Dhakka and Rajmahal, but make no mention of Bengalla. It may fur-

[1] Topography and Statistics of Dacca, by Dr. James Taylor, p. 92.

ther be remarked that the opinion of this city having been carried
away by the river is not supported by any tradition in this part of the
country. The natives, who are well acquainted with the sites of the
ancient places of note in the district, and of the changes occasioned
by the inroads of the rivers, mention two cities, called Serripore
(Sripur) and Kotesar, as having been thus destroyed, but of the existence of Bengalla they have never heard a circumstance that tends to
support the opinion that the name was originally used by foreign
traders instead of ' Bawan Bazar and Tipan Galee' or of Dhakka,
which latter appellation appears to have been exclusively applied to
the western quarter of the town in the vicinity of ' Dhakka Seri.'
Bengalla is described by Vertomannus in the year 1503 as a place
' that in fruitfulness and plentifulness of all kinds may in manner
contend with any city in the world. '   The region, he further says,
is so plentiful in all things, that there lacketh nothing that may serve
to the necessary uses or pleasures of men, for there are, in manner,
all sorts of beasts, and wholesome fruits, and plenty of corn, spices
also in all sorts. Likewise of bombasin and silks so exceeding great
abundance, that in all these things I think there is none other region
comparable to this."

The only building of any consequence now existing at
Dhakka is the tomb of Bibi Peri, the daughter of Shaistah
Khan, and the grand-daughter of Asaf Khan, the brother
of Nûr Jahân. According to Taylor, she was married to
Sultân Muhammad Azim, the third son of Aurangzeb; but,
according to my information, she was not married. She died
in A.H. 1095, or A.D. 1684, while her father was governor
of Bengal. The tomb stands in a large enclosure called the
Lâl Bâgh, which is 2,000 feet long by 800 feet broad. In
the middle there is a fine tank 235 feet square, and to the
west of it, distant 130 feet, there is a small dwelling-house
70 feet broad. Still farther to the west, at a distance of
275 feet, stands Bibi Peri's tomb; and beyond that, at 170
feet still farther to the west, there is a small three-domed
mosque 65 feet long by 32½ feet broad. The south face of
the enclosure was formerly washed by the river; but the
stream has now receded some distance, leaving a long low
piece of meadow land which is partially occupied by huts.
On the north face of the enclosure, opposite the tomb, there
is a gateway leading into the town.

According to Dr. Taylor, "the palace of the Lál Bágh was commenced in 1678 by Sultán Muhammad Azim, the third son of the Emperor Aurangzeb, and was left by him in an unfinished state to Amir-ul-Umra Shaistah Khan, his successor in the government[1]." It was apparently never finished; and Taylor notes that when Tavernier visited Dhakka, Shaistah Khan was residing in a temporary wooden building in its court. But as the English translation of his travels was printed in London in 1678, Tavernier must have visited Dhakka some years before.

"The governor's palace," he says, "is a place enclosed with high walls, in the midst whereof is a pitiful house, built only of wood. He generally lodges in tents, which he causes to be set up in a great court of that enclosure[2]."

Apparently his first visit took place in A.D. 1666, as he was at the junction of the Gandak and Ganges on the 1st January of that year. But he so mixes up the dates of his different visits that it is difficult to disentangle them. Thus he "parted from Patna in a boat for Dhakka the *nine and twentieth* of January," and arrived at Dhakka on the *thirteenth* of the same month. He distinctly mentions two visits, for he says—"When I travelled last to Dhakka, the Nabab Chalest Khan (Shaistah Khan), who was then governor of Bengala," from which it seems probable that Shaistah Khan was not the governor at the time of his first visit. Shaistah Khan succeeded to the Governorship of Bengal some time after the death of Mir Jumla in March 1663. I conclude, therefore, that Tavernier must have paid his first visit to Dhakka some time before 1663, and that his second visit took place in January 1666, shortly after Shaistah Khan had arrived from the Dakhin to take charge of his new government. This would account for his living in tents, as he had not been there long enough to build himself a house. I have no doubt, however, that he did build a palace within the great quadrangle, as there are numerous traces of buildings that have

[1] Taylor's Topography of Dhakka, p. 95.
[2] Tavernier's Voyages, Part II, Book 1, p. 55.

been removed, besides several ranges of houses that must have been occupied by his followers.

The tomb of his daughter is built entirely of stone, of black basalt from Gaya, grey sandstone from Chunar, and white marble from Jaypur. It consists of nine rooms, namely, a central room 19 feet 3 inches square, four central side rooms 24 feet 8½ inches long by 10 feet 8½ inches broad, and four corner rooms 10 feet 8¼ inches square[1]. The walls of the central room are of white marble, panelled with black lines, and the floor is laid out in a small pattern of the same material. The walls of the four central side-rooms are also of white marble, but the walls of the corner rooms are decorated with glazed tiles. The colours of the panels are dark-blue, orange, green, and purple on a yellow ground, with borders of orange and lilac flowers on a green ground. But the most curious part of this tomb is its roof, which is built throughout in the old Hindu fashion of overlapping layers. I am inclined to attribute the adoption of this primitive style of dome to the ignorance and utter want of experience of the Bengal masons, who did not know how to cut the voussoirs of a dome. To the same cause I attribute the unsightly mixture of brick domes and arches resting on stone walls, which are found in the mosques and tombs throughout Bengal, at Pandua, Gaur, Malda, and Hazrat Pandua. But in all the old Hindu examples, as well as in those of the early Muhammadans, these overlapping domes are either hemispherical or paraboloidal in shape, whereas this Dhakka example is a simple straight-lined octagonal pyramid. The walls supporting the roof are 5 feet 8½ inches thick, and 14 feet 4 inches high, and the roof rises by thirteen overlaps to 19 feet 11 inches in height. Outside, on the top of the pyramid, there is a small octagonal dome or lantern about 10 feet in diameter, covered with copper plates, which have once been gilt.

All the side-rooms are roofed after the same fashion by seven overlaps, rising from 7 feet 8 inches to 13 feet 6 inches, with a flat terrace above.

[1] See Plate XXXIV for a Plan and Section of the Tomb.

The sarcophagus in the centre room is of white marble, 7 feet 3½ inches long by 5 feet 4 inches broad. It is formed in three steps, each of 9½ inches in height, the upper part being 3 feet 6½ by 1 foot 7 inches. The faces of the steps are ornamented with flowered work, but the cutting is shallow.

The sandal-wood doors of the tomb are also of Hindu design, as the panels form regular *swastikas,* or mystic crosses.

Outside there are the following inscriptions on the eastern and western faces :—

Middle of west face.

الله محمد عمر علي عثمان
از سنه ١٠٩٥

محمدي عربي كابوى مر دوحراست
كسي كه خاك درش نيست خاك برمر او

غزاء واز و عبدالكبير

بر زمين كه نشان كف پاي تو بود
ساها سجده صاحب نظران خواهد بود

34.—BIKRAMPUR.

The rich district of Bikrampur is bounded by the little river Isâmati on the west, the Dhalaseri river on the north, the Megna river on the east, and the Ganges on the south. The whole district is now to the north of the Ganges; but at some former period, when the main stream flowed down the Dhalaseri Channel, Bikrampur was to the south of the river, which is here more commonly known as the Padda or Kirti-nâsa. As the latter name means the "fame destroyer," I

think that it may possibly have reference to some destruction
caused by the change in the course of the Ganges. The
names of the *Karmandsa*, or "works destroyer," and the
Varnandsa (Bands), or "caste destroyer," seem to point to
some special signification having once been attached to the
Kirtindsa. Before the change in the course of the Ganges,
Bikrampur formed part of the extensive district of *Bagdi* or
Samatata, but afterwards it was included in *Banga* along
with *Dhakka* and Sunârgaon.

Bikrampur was the residence of the early Sena Râjas
before the aggrandisement of the family by the conquest of
Barendra and Rârh. The site of the old capital is still pointed
out near the great lake of Râmpâl Dighi, to the north of
which is the Ballâl-bâri, or Palace of Ballâl Sen. To this
place the Hindu Râja retired on the invasion of the Muhammadans and the consequent capture of his chief cities of
Gaur and Nadiya. The people of the country know only
the one name of Ballâl Sen, who they say was the opponent
of the Musalmân invaders. According to Târanâth this
king was named *Lava Sena*, while the Muhammadan historians call him *Lakhmâniya*. But his true name was most probably the same as that of his grand-father, *Lakshmana Sena;*
and as this is frequently pronounced Lakhan Sen, I believe
that it is really the same name as the Lava Sena of Târanâth.
Ballâl Sen was the great aggrandiser of the family, to whom
several places are attributed, as well as the foundation of the
famous city of Gaur. The palace of Ballâl-bâri at Bikrampur was quite sufficient to preserve the name of Ballâl, while
the name of Lakshmana, having been forgotten, all the events
of consequence in the history of the Senas would naturally
be referred to the founder of the family.

The only remains of this old Sena capital are the Ballâl-
bâri, with its Agnikund, and the great lake called Râmpâl
Dighi, and at a short distance to the north, the masjid and
tomb of Bâba Adam, one of the first Muhammadan invaders
of the district.

The ruins of Ballâl-bâri consist of a large earthen fort
about 750 feet square, with a broad ditch of about 200 feet

all round. The entrance is on the east side by a causeway leading through an oblong outwork 300 feet in breadth, which was most probably the site of the servant's houses. The whole circuit of the enclosure, with its ditches and outwork, is just 1 mile. No bricks are now to be seen; but Dr. Taylor states that there are "mounds of bricks and the foundations of walls" both in the vicinity and in the country around, to the distance of many miles.

Half a mile to the west of Ballâl-bâri there is a small square tank called *Pushkarini* and Agnikund. Close by there is a small masjid with a stone figure of Bhairava lying in front of the entrance for the faithful to tread upon. The figure is much mutilated. The Agnikund is held in much veneration by the Hindus as the scene of the voluntary cremation of the last Râja and his family. There are several versions of the story, differing only in some of the details. According to Dr. Taylor—

"Tradition states, that the Râja, when he went out to meet the invaders of his territory, carried with him a messenger pigeon, whose return to the palace was to be regarded by his family as an intimation of his defeat, and a signal, therefore, to put themselves to death. He gained the victory, it appears, but unfortunately, while he was stooping to drink from the river after the fatigues of the day, the bird escaped from the part of his dress in which it was concealed, and flew to its destination. The Râja hurried home; but arriving too late to avert the consequences of this unhappy accident, he cast himself upon the funeral pile smoking with the ashes of his family, and thus closed the reign of the last dynasty of Hindu princes in this part of India[1]."

Inside Ballâl-bâri there is a small tank called *Mitha-pokhar*, or the "sweet-water tank," but which is never used by the people, as it is believed that the ashes of the last Râja and his family were thrown into it.

Half a mile to the south of Ballâl-bâri there is one of the largest and finest sheets of water that I have seen. It is called *Râmpâl Dighi*, and is about 1,800 feet in length from north to south by 800 feet in breadth. The water is deep

[1] Taylor's Topography and Statistics, p. 102.

and clear and the banks are covered with large old trees. The royal elephants are said to have been kept at the northern end. The land at the south end is still held by descendants of the old Rájas.

About half a mile to the north of Ballál-bári stands the much venerated tomb of Bába Adam, or Adam Shahíd, or the " Martyr," as he is generally called. The story of Bába Adam is thus related by Dr. Wise' :—

" Bába Adam was a very powerful Darwesh, who came to this part of the country with an army during the reign of Ballál Sen. Having encamped his army near Abdullapur, a village about 3 miles to the north-east, he caused pieces of cows' flesh to be thrown within the walls of the Hindu prince's fortress. Ballál Sen was very irate and sent messengers throughout the country to find out by whom the cow had been slaughtered. One of the messengers shortly returned and informed him that a foreign army was at hand, and that the leader was then praying within a few miles of the palace. Ballál Sen at once galloped to the spot, found Bába Adam still praying, and at one blow cut off his head."

The holy man is commonly called *Bábardam*, and the story of his death is told with many slight variations. Some say Bába Adam came alone ; others say that he was accompanied by an army. According to one version, *"muni,* or holy man, came to warn the Rája of the approach of the Muhammadans, but the Rája was asleep and could not be disturbed. The *muni* came a second time, and a third time, but each time with the same result. He then picked up a dry stick and stuck it in the ground, and saying 'it is the fate,' went away, and was no more seen. In the morning the dry stick had become a flourishing green tree. Then came Bába Adam and knelt down in prayer before the Raja's palace, and retired to the spot where the masjid and tomb now stand. When the Raja was informed about the *muni* and his words, and about the Bába and his prayers, he became angry and sent men to kill the Muhammadan saint. He was found engaged in prayer, and his head was at once struck off on the very spot where the tomb now stands just outside the masjid.

' Bengal Asiatic Society's Journal, Vol. XLII, p. 285.

Then came the Muhammadan army and put an end to the rule of the Hindus.

The masjid of Bâba Adam is a highly ornamented brick building covered by six domes. It is small, being only 43 feet long by 36 feet broad outside. The walls are 6 feet 6¾ inches thick, with a Bengal curved battlement both in front and behind. There are three arched doorways in front, opening into a double aisle supported on octagonal stone pillars, 1 foot 8 inches in diameter, with corresponding pilasters on all four sides. In the back wall there are three richly decorated semicircular niches, and in each of the side walls two rectangular niches.

On the outside I noticed that one of the ornamented bricks is placed upside down. This may possibly have been accidental ; but from the place which the brick occupies I inferred that some old materials may have been used. This is the more probable as the masjid does not belong to the period of the first Muhammadan invasion, but was erected in the reign of Jalâl-ud-din Fateh Shâh, as recorded in an inscription placed over the middle doorway. The following is Blochmann's translation[1] :—

"God Almighty says : ' The mosque belongs to God.' ' Do not associate any one with God.' The Prophet, may God bless him! says : ' He who builds a mosque will have a castle built for him by God in paradise.'

"This Jami Masjid was built by the great Malik, Malik Kafur, in the time of the king, the son of the king Jalâl-ud-dunya wa-ud-din Fateh Shah, the king, son of Mahmud Shah, the king, in the middle of the month of Rajab 888 A.H. (August 1483, A.D)."

The actual tomb of Bâba Adam is a common plastered brick sarcophagus, standing on a platform 25 feet square.

35.—SUNARGAON, OR SUVARNA-GRAMA.

Sunârgaon, the capital of Eastern Bengal under the Muhammadans, is traditionally said to have been the residence of one of the twelve Bhûmihâr chiefs. Its name of

---

[1] Bengal Asiatic Society's Journal, Vol. XLII, p. 284.

Suvarna-grâma, or "Gold Town," proves that it must have been a Hindu city, although there are only a few fragments of Hindu work now left to attest the fact. The earliest notice of the place that I have been able to find is during the reign of the Emperor Balban, when the rebel Governor of Bengal, Mughis-ud-din Tughral, retreated beyond Sunârgaon, near which he was overtaken and killed. The district was then ruled by a Hindu Chief named Dânuj Rai, with whom the Emperor made an arrangement to prevent the escape of Tughral by water. This Dânuj Rai is said to have been one of the Bhûmihâr chiefs. After the death of Balban, Sunârgaon formed part of the kingdom of Bengal, which then became an independent State under Bughra Khân and his descendants. Bâhâdur Shâh, the last of these princes, was defeated and put to death by Tughlak Shâh in A.H. 722, or A.D. 1322, and Bengal was again attached to the empire of Delhi. In A.H. 737—A.D. 1336-7, on the death of Bahrâm Khân, the imperial Governor of Sunârgaon under Muhammad bin Tughlak, his silahdar or armour-bearer, Fakhr-ud-din Mubârak, seized the government and declared himself independent. "He was in the first instance defeated by the troops sent against him from Lakhnauti, but finally succeeded in maintaining his authority, and, as the coins prove, in retaining his hold on Sunârgaon and its dependencies throughout the nine years from 741 to 750 A.H., comparatively undisturbed. The history of the period is confused, and the dates given by the native authors prove of little value ; but the coins establish the fact that in 751 another ruler, designated Ikhtiâr-ud-din Ghâzi Shâh, presided over the mints of Eastern Bengal[1]."

Much light has been thrown on this dark period of Bengal history by Mr. Thomas in his very valuable chronicles of the Pathan kings. From him we learn that much about the same time Ala-ud-din Ali Shâh made himself independent in Lakhnauti, on the death of the Imperial Governor, Kadr Khan. Ali Shâh was assassinated by his foster-brother Haji Ilias,

---

[1] Thomas's Chronicles of Pathan Kings, p. 263.

who took the title of Shams-ud-din. Mubárak was succeeded by his son Ikhtiár-ud-din Ghází, who in A.H. 753 or A.D.
1352, was overcome by Ilias Sháh, of whom we have coins
minted at Sunárgaon in the same year. From this time
Sunárgaon formed part of the independent kingdom of Bengal,
and was generally ruled by one of the sons or brothers of the
reigning king. Sometimes these Governors openly rebelled,
and made themselves virtually independent, as in the case of
Azam Sháh the son of Sikandar. Again, in the reign of
Akbar, it was the chief city of Isa Khan, who maintained his
independence for several years. He was still in power when
Ralph Fitch visited the city in A.D. 1586. After Isa Khan's
death it became a part of the great Mughal empire.

The old town of Sunárgaon is situated 2 miles to the
north of an old branch of the Megna River, and 3 miles to
the west of the present course of the stream. When the site
was first selected, the Brahmaputra flowed 3 miles to the
westward, between the Lakhia River and the present course
of the Megna. It was therefore situated in the fork of these
two great rivers, in a most favourable position for monopolis-
ing the commerce of all the rich country to the north. By
the present road it is about 15 miles to the east of Dhakka.

The modern town has been described at some length by
Dr. Taylor, whose account I will now quote[1] :—

" Painám is the ancient city of Sunárgaon, the Haveli Sunárgaon
of the Muhammadan rulers of this part of the country. It is situated
about 2 miles inland from the Brahmaputra creek, in a grove of areca,
tamarind, mango, and various other trees, interspread with dense
thickets of bamboos, which completely conceal the village from view
until within a few yards of it. This sequestered spot is approached in
the dry season by narrow winding foot-paths; but during the rains
it is partially inundated, and is almost inaccessible except by small
boats, or to a person on an elephant or horse. Painám at this latter
season is surrounded by numerous stagnant creeks and ponds, and by
a vegetation rank and luxuriant in the extreme. From the thick
foliage of the trees which exclude the sun's rays, the village at this
time presents a most gloomy aspect, and in the sickly emaciated
appearance of its inhabitants it certainly realises the character so

[1] Taylor's Dacca, p. 106.

that *Firozah Minár* means si
the turquoise-coloured glaze
style of architecture is similar
Dákhil Gate, which I have
divided in the same five storey
of the door); it has the same
the same proportion to its dia
Dákhil Gateway. I think, th
as old as the time of Mahmud

Franklin found a broken in
Factory, which, on the streng
thought might have belonged
of the tower. That this brol
minár is, I think, highly proba
Franklin that the letters are
vacant panel from which the ins
3 feet 11 inches in length b
would exactly suit an inscripti
inches in height. Unfortunatel
with the title of the King Saif-u
in doubt whether it should be
zah, who reigned from A.H. 6
Froz, who reigned from 893 t
Firozah Minár, if derived from
in favour of the later prince Sai
style of the building is against
view of its early date is suppor
Mr. Fergusson, I think it more
belongs to the earlier prince S
of this view also I can point t
coins of the two Princes on w
Abul Mujáhid, as in the broken
the title of Abul Muzaffar.

The minár stands on the
350 feet long from north to

[1] Franklin notices this "blue and
note by Mr Grose.
[2] See History of Indian Architecture

ere is a fine tank, which was no doubt made for the ... of obtaining earth for filling ... the ... ... building which once stood on the mound. ... been cleared away, but I picked ... ...ed bricks and many fragments of ... ... of the ... on the south-west ... are ... ... the middle of the mound, ...tral doorway of a temple. ... explain ... ... one of ... ... I ... ...

on
own
the
illars,
of a
th-east
stening
sacred
mmadan

is a fine
ascribe to

generally ascribed to it of its being one of the most unhealthy places in the district. It consists of two narrow streets of straw huts, and good brick-built houses of two and three storeys in height. Surrounding it there is a deep muddy and stagnant canal, which appears to have originally been a moat for its protection. Upon an old bridge across this ditch (the only avenue leading to the village), are the remains of a gateway, which in former times, when there was more wealth in the place than at present, was shut every night, and no person was allowed to enter or leave the town until the following morning. In the immediate vicinity of Painâm there are several mosques and buildings in ruins, which, in all probability, constituted the place of residence of the early Muhammadan Governors, though not more than a mile distant from Painâm. This spot is almost inaccessible from being buried in the midst of dense jungle infested with tigers and leopards, which renders it unsafe for a person to approach the place, except he is mounted on an elephant."

The difficulty of the approach to Painâm has not been exaggerated by Dr. Taylor, in fact he has omitted to mention the most formidable of all the obstacles, namely, the gigantic tough canes which cross the narrow paths in all directions, and with their long, sharp, flat, thorns, just like lancets both in size and shape, most effectually bar the passage of the stoutest elephants. At all these places our elephants had to quit the raised pathway, and take to the ditch, where they stirred up the fœtid mud of ages, and filled the air with a most horrible stench. In the dense jungle there were numerous patches of wild plantain trees, on which the elephants feasted with evident pleasure.

About a mile to the south of Painâm, and close to the village of Khâsnagar, there is a very fine tank, about 1,200 feet long from north to south, by 600 feet in breadth. Dr. Wise says that it is now gradually silting up, and that in the month of April it is only 6 feet deep. Its age is unknown, but from its longer sides, lying north and south, it must belong to the Hindu period.

Sunârgaon was formerly noted for its fine muslins, but with the falling-off in the demand the art of making them gradually decayed, and is now lost. Only common *malmal*, or coarse muslin, is now woven, and even that is made with

English thread. In the time of Ralph Fitch, A.D. 1586, Sunárgaon and Sripur produced "the best and finest cloth, made of cotton that is in all India." These were the famous Dhakka muslins, for the purchase of which the East India Company established a factory at Painám. This building is still standing, but in a very ruinous condition. But there are other signs of an old city in the great numbers of mango trees, and the numerous *pán* and betel gardens. The mangos are still famous, the best kinds being known as *Sháh-pasand*, or "the king's favourite," "*Shiya-pasand*," or the "Shiya's favourite," and *Senduria*, or the "red" mango. The best kind of betel is called *Kafuria pán*, from its faint scent of camphor. It is said to be in great demand at Lucknow. The *dahi*, or curd, of Sunárgaon is also in great repute all over North-eastern Bengal.

The few remains of any antiquity at Sunárgaon have already been described by Dr. Wise, under whose kind guidance I was able to visit them all[1]. A few notes will be sufficient for each, which I will now describe in the order adopted by Dr. Wise.

1.—*Panj-pir Dargáh.*

These are five small brick tombs arranged in one line on a platform about 4 feet high. Nothing whatever is known about the holy men who are entombed in them. Along the edges of the platform there are some unfinished brick pillars, which look as if they had been intended for the support of a roof, or perhaps only a trellised railing. To the south-east there is a small neglected brick mosque, now fast hastening to ruin. Dr. Wise notes that this dargáh is held " so sacred that even Hindus saláam as they pass, and Muhammadan pilgrims resort to it from great distances."

2.—*Tomb of Azam Shah.*

About 1,000 feet to the east of Panj-pir there is a fine massive stone sarcophagus, which the people ascribe to

[1] Notes on Sunárgaon by Dr. Wise,—Bengal Asiatic Society's Journal, Vol. XLIII, p. 82.

Ghias-ud-din Azam Shâh, the rebellious son of Sikandar Shâh of Bengal. It has once been surrounded by a pillared enclosure, of which many portions are still lying on the ground close by[1]. The sarcophagus itself is richly carved, but the design has the same fault that is common to all Bengali ornament in a monotonous repetition of the same petty forms. Dr. Wise urges the propriety of repairing this tomb. He says :—

"There is no old building in Eastern Bengal which gives a better idea of Muhammadan taste than this ruined sepulchre, and there is none, when properly repaired, which would so long defy the ravages of time. The Muhammadans of Sunârgaon are too poor to reconstruct it themselves. They take great pride in showing it, although they know nothing about it but the name of the Sultân who is buried there, and they take every care that none of the stones are carried off. Unless Government undertakes the re-erection of this handsome tomb, it is not likely that anything will ever be done."

I most heartily endorse this opinion, and I would suggest that the work should be put in hand at once. The sarcophagus is a single block of hard, black basalt, and will last for ages.

3.—*Tomb of Manna Shâh Darwesh.*

The tomb of Pir Manna Shâh Darwesh stands in the midst of the village of Magrâpâra, on the bank of the creek between the old Brahmâputra and Megna rivers. This is said to have been the actual site of the ancient city of Sunâr-gaon. Here there is a large and lofty mound now known as *Damdama*, or the "Bastion," which I think must have been a look-out tower. "Every orthodox Muhammadan," says Dr. Wise, "as he passes the tomb stops and mutters a prayer." A lamp is lighted every night at his tomb, but no one knows anything about him. Close by, on the east and west, there are several other smaller mounds, but they are apparently the remains of separate buildings, and not of a continuous line

---

[1] A very good view of this tomb, taken from a photograph by Mr. Brennand, is given with Dr. Wise's account of Sunârgaon,—Bengal Asiatic Society's Journal, Vol. XLIII, Plate VIII, and p. 85.

of ramparts. At a short distance, on the north, are the remains of the *Khamkah* of Sheikh Muhammad Yusuf and
the tombs of Yusuf himself and his son, Sheikh Mahmud.
Here also is a square brick masjid, said to have been built by
Sheikh Mahmud; but the inscription over the entrance,
which is dated in A.H. 1112, shows that the building is a
modern one. There is however a second inscription let into
the wall of the enclosure, which most probably belonged to
the original mosque attached to these tombs. This inscription was thickly coated with numerous layers of whitewash,
to a depth of nearly 2 inches, which were laid on the stone
under the following singular belief. Whenever a theft occur-
red, the person who had been robbed applied a coat of whitewash to the holy stone, when not only was the thief discovered, but the stolen property was got back again. The
following is Blochmann's translation of this inscription[1] :—

" God Almighty says, ' Surely, the mosques belong to God. Do not
call on any one besides Allah,' and the prophet says ; ' He who builds
a mosque in the world will have seventy castles built for him by God
in the next world.'—This mosque was built during the reign of the
great and exalted king, Jalâl-ud-dunyâ waddin Abul Muzaffar Fateh
Shâh, the king, son of Mahmud Shâh, the king—May God perpetuate
his kingdom and rule ! The builder of the mosque is Mugarah ud-dau-
lah, Malikmud-din, the Royal Keeper of the Wardrobe outside the palace, the Commander and Wazir of the territory of Mazummâbâd, also
known as Mahmudâbâd and Commander of Thanah Lâwâd. This
took place during Muharram 889 (A.D. 1484)."

At a short distance from these tombs there is a loose slab
bearing a record of the time of Alâ-ud-din Husen, dated in
A.H. 919. This probably belonged to a large masjid which
formerly stood just outside Magrâpâra. The foundations of
the walls were 8 feet thick, and one of the *Mihrabs*, or arched
niches, of the back wall, which is still standing, was richly
ornamented with carved bricks.

In Magrâpâra also there is a ruined gateway which is said
to have been the *Nauhat Khana* of the Muhammadan governors.

[1] Bengal Asiatic Society's Journal, Vol. XLII, p. 286.

4.—*Tomb of Ponkai Diwánah.*

To the north of Magrâpâra, near the village of Gohatta, there are three earthen tombs of Shah Abdul Ala and his wife and son. He got the nickname of *Ponkai Diwánah,* or the "white-ant madman," because he sat for twelve years in the forest so absorbed in his devotions that he was unconscious of the lapse of time. When found, he had to be dug out of the mound the white-ants (*Panka*) had raised around him, and which reached to his neck. The same story is told of Válmiki, the sage and others. This Pir must have died near the end of the last century, as his son Shah Imâm Bakhsh, *alias* Chulu Miyan, came, within the recollection of many living, from Sylhet to die at Sunârgaon. Father and son lie buried close together. At the head of the former is placed the lattice stone on which he spent his memorable twelve years. The tombs are otherwise of no interest. They are merely mud heaps kept carefully clean and covered over with grass thatch[1]." He is said to have died about sixty years ago.

5.—*Tomb of Pagla Sahib.*

Near the village of Habibpur, to the east of Magrâpâra, stands the tomb of an unknown saint, called *Pagla Sahib,* or "the crazy." "Various stories," says Dr. Wise, "are told of the reason why this Pir received such a singular name. One is that he became '*must,*' or light-headed, from the intensity of his devotions. Another, that he was a great thief-catcher; that he nailed every thief he caught to a wall, and then beheaded him. Having strung several heads together he threw. them into an adjoining '*khal,*' which has ever since been known as the *Munda Mala,* i.e., necklace of heads. This tomb is so venerated that parents, Hindu and Muhammadan, dedicate at the tomb the '*choti,*' or queue, of their child when dangerously ill[2]."

[1] Notes on Sunârgaon, Eastern Bengal, Bengal Asiatic Society's Journal, Vol. XLIII, p. 90.

[2] Notes on Sunârgaon—Bengal Asiatic Society's Journal, Vol. XLIII, p. 91.

6.—Mosque of Bari Mukhlis.

This is a modern masjid with an inscription dated A.H. 1182, or A.D. 1768.

7.—Painâm Bridge.

Over the ditch, surrounding the square enclosure of Painâm, there is an old brick bridge, called the *Dalâlpur Pul*, or "Brokers' Bridge," which leads directly into the main street of the town. Inside there are two gate pillars of brick, with a single black stone carved with flowers as a step.

8.—Gwâl-dih Mosque.

In the dense jungle, three quarters of a mile to the west of Painam, and 1½ mile to the north of Magrâpâra, there is a small village named *Gwâl-dih*, which possesses two brick mosques, one built in A.H. 995, during the reign of Husen Shah, and the other as late as A.H. 1116, or A.D. 1704.

The older mosque is a small brick building 16½ feet square inside and 26 feet 2 inches square outside. It is, however, very richly ornamented with carved bricks, both inside and out, in the style of the buildings at Gaur and Hazrat Pandua. In the back wall there are three semi-octagonal niches, and in each of the side walls there is a door with two rectangular side niches. The stone pilasters of the prayer niches support richly carved pointed arches ornamented with deep cusps. But they betray their descent from Hindu pillars in having four bracket capitals, of which the front brackets have nothing to support. The whole building, however, is a very fine specimen of the ornamental brickwork which prevailed in Bengal for several centuries of Muhammadan rule. The inscription slab, which was once fixed over the entrance door, has fallen from its place, but is now carefully preserved inside. The following is Blochmann's translation of this record[1] :—

"God Almighty says, 'surely the mosques, &c. (as in last),' and the Prophet says (as in last). This mosque was built in the reign of the

---

[1] Bengal Asiatic Society's Journal, Vol. XLII, p. 293.

king of kings, Sultan Husen Shâh, son of Saiyid Ashraf-ul-Husaini.—
May God perpetuate his kingdom and rule! This mosque was built
by Mulla Hizabr Akbar Khân, on the 15th Shaban, 925 (12th August
1519)."

9.—Sâdipur mound.

Lying on a low mound near the village of Sâdipur, to the
north of Magrâpâra, there is a loose slab bearing an inscription of Nusrat Shâh, the son of the Husen Shâh. The following is Blochmann's translation of this record[1] :—

"God Almighty says, 'Surely the mosques belong to God; worship
no one else besides God.' The Prophet says, 'He who builds a
mosque for God, seeking thereby the reward of God, will have one
like it built for him by God in Paradise.'

"This mosque was built in the reign of the great, the liberal king,
the son of a king, Nâsir-ud-dunyâ waddin Abul Muzaffar Nusrat Shâh,
the king, son of Husen Shâh the king, the descendant of Husain [Ali
Husani].—May God continue his kingdom and rule! It was erected
in order to obtain the reward of God, together with the well, by
the Malik-ul-Umara wal-Wuzara, the chief of the lawyers and teacher
of the Hadîs, Faqi-ud-din, son of Ain-ud-din, known as Bâr Malik-ul-
Majlis, son of Mukh-târ-ul-Majlis, son of Sarwar.—May God preserve
him in both worlds! In the year 929 A.H. [A.D. 1523]."

The only other buildings of any note are two very small
masjids near Bed Bazar, where the old creek joins the Megna
River, beyond the 17th mile-stone on the road from Dhakka.
The larger is 12 feet square outside, but the smaller one,
which is said to have been built by a nautch girl, is only 6 feet
square outside. Both have been deserted by the Muhammadans, and are now used by the Hindus. The smaller one
will probably last for a long time, as it is completely laced
over by the roots of the pipal tree.

On the bank of the old Brahmâputra River, 2 miles to the
west of Painâm, there are two bathing ghâts held in great
reverence by the Hindus on account of their supposed connection with the history of the Pandus. *Nângalband,* or
"plough-stopped," is the place where Balarâma checked his
plough, when he ploughed the bed of the Brahmâputra from

---

[1] Bengal Asiatic Society's Journal, Vol. XLI, p. 337.

its source.   Close by is *Panchami Ghât*, where the Panch Pandava, or five Pandu brothers, used to bathe during their twelve years' wanderings.   As Dr. Wise notes, "these ancient legends appear to point to a period when the cultivated land terminated at Nangalband.   The red laterite soil, which extends from the Garo Hills through the Bhowal jungles, crops up here and there in the northern parganahs.   In Sunârgaon, however, no traces of it are visible.   That the alluvium washed down from the hills should first of all be deposited at the termination of this hard formation is most probable, and it was perhaps on this account, as well as on the inaccessibility of the place itself, that the Hindu princes expelled from Central Bengal were induced to found a city here[1]."

The annual fair is held on the 8th of Chaitra, Sudi.

36.—NOTES ON THE HISTORY OF BENGAL.

A few centuries after the Christian era the fertile province of Bengal, or the country occupied by people speaking the Bengâli language, was divided into the four separate districts of *Barendra* and *Banga* to the north of the Ganges, and *Rârh* and *Bâgdi* to the south of the river.   The first two were separated by the Brahmâputra, and the other two by the Jalinghi branch of the Ganges:—

1. *Barendra* was bounded by the Mahânanda River on the west, the Brahmâputra on the east, and the Ganges on the south, and by Kuch-Bihâr, the most westerly province of Kâmrup, on the north.   Its chief cities were Lakhnauti, or Gaur, on the Ganges, Devikot on the Purnabhâbha River, and Mahâsthân on the Kâratoya, or old channel of the Tista River.

2. *Banga* was bounded by the Brahmâputra on the west, the Ganges on the south, the Megna on the east, and the Khasia hills on the north.   It contained the old cities of Dhakka and Sunârgaon.

[1] Notes on Sunârgaon ; Bengal Asiatic Society's Journal, Vol. XLIII, p. 93.

3. *Rárh* or *Rádha* was bounded by the Rájmahal Hills on the west, by the Ganges on the north, and by the Jalingh branch of the Delta on the east. Its southern boundary is unknown, but it probably extended to the banks of the Bará-kar and Damuda Rivers. Its chief towns were Agmahal (now Rájmahal), Kánkjol, and Nadiya. The great city of Murshidabad is now included within its boundaries.

4. *Bágdi* comprised the delta of the Ganges and Brahmáputra, lying between the rivers Jalinghi and Megna, with the sea on the south. It corresponds with the district called *Samatata* by Hwen Thsang, and by Samudra Gupta in his Allahábad pillar inscription. In the Akbar-náma it is called *Bháti*, and is said to be called by the Hindi name because it lies "lower than Bengal." *Bhathi* literally means "lower down the river," and under this name was included the whole of the country around Jessore, extending "nearly 400 *kos* from east to west" "and nearly 300 from north to south." As the Akbari *kos* was as nearly as possible 1 mile and 3 furlongs, the dimensions here given would be equal to 550 miles by 312 miles, which is considerably more than double the size of the province.

The chief town in this division was Bikrampur. This place is now to the north of the Ganges; but in former days, when the river flowed down the Dhalaseri channel, Bikrampur was on the southern bank. Krishnanagar and Murali (or Jessore) were also large towns of this district, which now includes the great city of Calcutta.

Nothing whatever is known of the early history of the country, the people being content with the puerile tales of the ubiquitous Pandus, who are said to have visited numerous places in Barendra and Banga during their twelve years' exile. The name of Bikrampur has of course suggested a connection with the famous king of Ujain. All the rivers also have legends connected either with their names, or with the changes that have taken place in their course. Thus the *Káratoya* River is said to derive its name from *Kar*, the hand, and *toya* water, because the water which was poured into Siva's hand at his marriage with Párvati, when thrown upon the ground, became the source of this stream. So also the great Brahmâputra River, when wooed by the two maiden streams, Lakhia and Jabuna, is said to have joined the former and slighted the latter. Now this story must have been invented several centuries ago when the main stream of the Brahmâputra flowed down the channel of the Lakhia. But at the present day the great Brahmâputra has deserted the Lakhia, and joined the Jabuna. There must also be some story attached to the *Kirtinâsa* River, or "Fame-destroyer," but I failed to learn anything about it. It is said, however, that the two cities of Sripur and Kotesar were destroyed by the Kirtinâsa River, and if the name is not an old one it may refer to this event. It is the local name of the lower course of the Ganges, just above the junction of the Megna.

Real tradition begins with the Bhûmihârs, or Bâra Bhûmihâr, who are said to have come from the west to attend a great religious festival on the Kâratoya River, but as the time had gone by before they arrived, they remained in the country for the return of the next period, and eventually settled themselves permanently. These twelve chiefs, who were mostly named Pâl, are said to have been Brâhmans, who, when they became agriculturists, received the name of *Bhûmi-hâras,* or "land-tillers," now shortened into *Bhuihâr.* But they still retain their old name of Brâhman or Bâhman under the slightly altered form of *Bâbhan.* To this caste belong the Brahman Rajas of Benares and Bettiah, and of Tikâri in Magadha near Gaya. Dr. Taylor says that they were the ancestors of the Pâla dynasty of kings of Bengal. I had already formed this opinion myself, but at present I am not aware of any direct proof of it. In their inscriptions the Pâla Rajas make no mention of their caste. Three of the twelve emigrants are said to have settled in Rangpur, Dinâjpur, and Bhaturia (near Nator). My impression is that Barendra derived its name from the "twelve chiefs" who then settled in the country lying to the north of the Ganges and to the west of the Brahmâputra. Their descendants afterwards spread over the neighbouring districts, and occupied both Banga and Bâgdi.

We get a glimpse of the state of things which prevailed during this period in the brief statement of Târanâth. Immediately preceding the establishment of the Pâla dynasty under the first king, Gopâla, he says that " in Orissa, Bengal, and five other provinces of the east, every Kshatriya, Brahman, and merchant (Vaisya) made himself the chief of the surrounding districts ; but there was no king ruling the whole country." This account is confirmed not only by Hwen Thsang's silence as to any ruler of the country about a century and a half earlier, but also by a statement of the Raja Tarangini immediately before the establishment of the Pâla Rajas. In this Kashmir History it is said that during Jayapida's visit to Paundra-desa, he conquered " five kings of Gauda," and made them tributary to his father-in-law, the chief of Paundra-Varddhana. From this statement we learn that in the time of Jayapida (A.D. 779 to 813), there were no less than six petty princes in the province of Gauda or Barendra.

Târanâth then goes on to describe the extinction of these petty chiefs and the rise of the Pâla dynasty of Bengal as follows :—

"The widow of one of these departed chiefs used to kill every night the person who had been chosen as king, until after several years Gopâla, who had been elected king, managed to free himself and obtained the kingdom. He began to reign in Bengal and afterwards conquered Magadha. He built the temple of Nalandara near Otantapura, and reigned 45 years."

According to Târanâth the establishment of Gopâla's power took place when Sri Harsha Deva was king of Kashmir. But as there is no Harsha in the list of Kashmirian Rajas before A.D. 1100, we must look for some other synonymous name. This I think may be found in Lalitapida, as Lalita and Harsha have much the same meaning. Now Lalitapida reigned from A.D. 813 to 825, and I would therefore fix the date of Gopâla's rise to power about A.D. 815, which is the very year that I had previously adopted by calculating backwards from Mahipâla, whose date is known.

The Pâla dynasty, the descendants of Gopâla, lasted for about four hundred years. For upwards of two centuries

and a half they held undisputed sway over Bengal and
Bihâr with occasional supremacy over Kâmrup and Orissa.
In the beginning of the eleventh century under Mahipâl their
dominion was extended to Benares, and included all the
provinces to the north and south of the Ganges from the
junction of the Jumna to the Indian Ocean.   But towards
the end of the century, Barendra or Gauda was wrested from
them by the Sena Rajas Ballâla and his son Lakshmana.   As
the date of Lakshmana's death forms the initial point of an
era, which is reckoned from A.D. 1107, the two reigns of the
father and son most probably covered the whole of the latter
half of the tenth century.   But some members of the Pâla
family still continued to reign in Magadha or Bihâr until the
end of the twelfth century, as I have found inscriptions of
Govinda Pâla Deva dated in S.1232 and S.1235, or A.D.
1175 and 1178, the former date being the fifteenth year of his
reign.

The genealogy of the earlier Pâla kings, as given in their
inscriptions, is as follows—

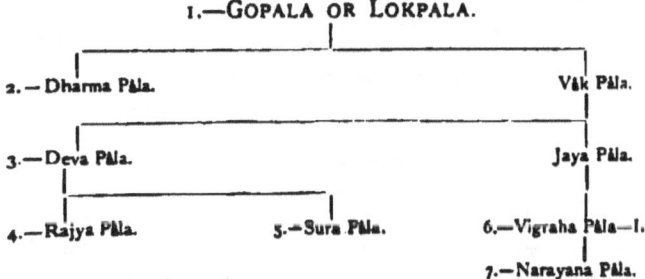

1.—GOPALA OR LOKPALA.

2.—Dharma Pâla.   Vâk Pâla.

3.—Deva Pâla.   Jaya Pâla.

4.—Rajya Pâla.   5.—Sura Pâla.   6.—Vigraha Pâla—I.

7.—Narayana Pâla.

From Narayana we have only the succession of kings given
in the Amgâchi copper-plate.   These are as follows :—

8.—Raja Pâla [or Râjya Pâla].
9.— *'# Pâla Devâ.
10.— Vigraha Pâla, II.
11.—Mahi Pâla.
12.—Naya Pâla.
13.—Vigraha Pâla, III

After this last Prince we have only a few isolated names
obtained from some of the shorter inscriptions.   These are—

14.—Mahendra Pâla Deva.
15.—Râma Pâla Deva.
16.—Madana Pâla Deva.
17.—Govinda Pâla Deva.

Of the first king *Gopâla* we have only one short inscription,
dated in the seventh year of his reign[1]. This record is chiefly
valuable for its place of discovery Nâlanda, which proves
that Gopâla, even at this early period, had already conquered
Magadha. Târanâth says that he began to reign in Bengal
and " afterwards subjected Magadha," and this short record
shows that his statement is correct. According to Târanâth,
Gopâla reigned 45 years, while Ferishta gives 55 years to
Bhupâla, the founder of the dynasty. I would reduce these
long periods to the more reasonable length of a single reign
of eighteen years, and place him between A.D. 813 and 831.

Gopâla was succeeded by his son Dharma Pâla, of whom
we have only one short inscription, which I obtained at Maha
Bodhi (or Bodh Gaya) in November 1879. A translation of
this record has already been published, but the learned trans-
lator, Babu Rajendra Lal, to whom I made it over, has failed
to notice the valuable aid which the mention of the week
day affords for fixing the date of Dharma Pâla's reign[2]. As
I have already given the translation, I need now only quote
the date, which is " the 26th year of the great king Dharma
Pâla, on Saturday, the 5th of *Bhadra-bahula*," or the waning
moon of Bhadrapada. Now the accession of Dharma Pâla
having been fixed approximately in the year 831 A.D., his 26th
year will fall in A.D. 856, in which year the 5th of Bhadra
badi was a Saturday as stated in the inscription. The only
other years near this period, in which this was the case, were
A.D. 836, 853, 863, 870, and 880. The first date is much

[1] This inscription was not discovered by Mr. Broadley as Babu Rajendra Lal
seems to think. It was seen by Buchanan seventy years ago, and was *copied by*
myself ten years before Mr. Broadley saw it. I may mention here what Mr.
Broadley has omitted to state, that all the copies of his inscriptions forwarded to the
Asiatic Society were made for him by my servants under my superintendence.

[2] Bengal Asiatic Society's Journal, Vol. XLVII, p. 407.

too early, as it would place Dharma Pâla's accession in A.D.
811. The next two periods, 853 and 856, also seem to be
the most probable, as they would place Dharma Pâla's accession either in 828 or 831. I prefer the latter, which gives a
full reign of 18 years to Gopâla. The adoption of any of the
later periods of 863, 870, and 880 would, I think, curtail the
interval between Dharma Pâla and Mahi Pâla too much, and so
shorten the reigns of the intermediate kings. I am inclined
therefore to take A.D. 856 as the 26th year of Dharma Pâla's
reign in preference to any of the others, and if we allow him
two years more, or 28 years altogether, his death would have
taken place in A.D. 858. Târanâth has transposed the
names of Dharma Pâla and his son Deva Pâla, making the
latter the predecessor of the former. To the successor of
Gopâla he ascribes the subjugation of the kingdoms of
Varendra and Orissa. In the Bhâgalpur plate record Dharma
Pâla is said to have conquered Indra Raja, and as Varendra
is only another name for Indra, I take this statement as a
confirmation of the conquest of Barendra. Dharma Pâla
married Ranna Devi, daughter of Parabala, " Raja of many
countries."

His son and successor was *Deva Pâla Deva*, of whom we
possess a long record known as the Mongir copper-plate
inscription, which was translated by Wilkins[1]. As this is dated
in the 33rd year of the king's reign, we may safely give him
a period of 35 years from A.D. 858 to 893. To him the
inscriptions assign the conquest of Kâmrup and Orissa, and
other countries from the source of the Ganges to the Ocean.
To the conqueror of Kâmrup Târanâth assigns the subjugation of Gauda and Tirabhukti, and of the whole of North
India between the Himâlaya and Vindhya mountains from
Jâlandhara to the Ocean. His contemporary in the west was
Chakrayodhya. All the warlike expeditions of Deva Pâla are
said, in one inscription, to have been conducted by his brother,
Jaya Pâla, whose descendants eventually succeeded to the
throne; but in a second inscription his Braman miniesth

---

[1] Asiatic Researches 8vo edition, Vol. I. p. 123.

takes the credit of having rendered them tributary by his policy[1].

The immediate successor of Deva Pâla would appear to have been his son *Râjya Pâla*, who, in the Mongir inscriptions, is said to have been appointed "to the dignity of Yuva Raja." No records of him have yet been found, and it is possible that he may have died before his father. But as the inscription is dated in the 33rd year of Deva Pâla, which was most probably near the end of his reign, I am inclined to identify Râjya Pâla with Taranath's Rasa Pâla, whom he calls the son of Deva Pâla. He could, however, have reigned only for a short time, say from A.D. 893 to 895.

His successor would appear to have been *Sura Pâla*, another son of Deva Pâla, of whom we possess two short records, of which one is dated in the 13th year of his reign. We may therefore safely assign him a reign of fifteen years, or from A.D. 895 to 910.

To him succeeded his cousin, Vigraha Pâla I., the son of Jaya Pâla. A long inscription of this king will be noticed presently. Only one short record of him has yet been found, dated in the twelfth year of his reign. But from the Bhâgalpur copper-plate inscription of his son, we learn that he married the Haihaya Princess Lajja. As the Haihayas were Rajputs, I accept this fact as a testimony that the Pâla Rajas must have asserted their Brahmanical descent. Another Haihaya Princess, Mahâdevi, the daughter of Kokalla I., of Chedi, married Krishna Raja, Râshtrakuta, much about the same time, or between 900 and 925 A.D. As Vigraha Pâla had been preceded by his two cousins, it is most probable that his reign was not a long one. I would, therefore, limit him to fifteen years, and fix his reign between A.D. 910 and 925. In fact he must have abdicated, as he is said to have addressed his son with the words "Let penance be mine, and the kingdom thine," which were in ancient times addressed by Sagara to Bhagiratha. There is a long inscription of this king, 27 inches long by 21 inches high, now lying near the Akshay-bat

---

[1] See the Bhâgalpur Plate for the first statement, and the Mungalbâri (or Buddal) Pillar for the second.

Temple at Gaya. Unfortunately the lower right corner is broken off, leaving the unfinished word *samvatsa* to show that it once had a date. It is generally in very bad condition, and I doubt if it can be deciphered satisfactorily.

After Vigraha came his son Nârâyana Pâla Deva, of whom we have a long record in the Bhâgalpur copper-plate, dated in the seventeenth year of his reign. His minister was the Brahman, Gurava Misra, who set up the Mangalbâri Pillar near Buddal. As Nârâyana would seem to have had a long reign, I would assign him the full period of a single generation of twenty-five years, from 925 to 950 A.D.

Up to this time five generations have passed away in 950—813—137 years, giving an average of 27·4 years. During the same period there were seven reigns, giving an average of upwards of 19½ years each. After this we have only the bare succession of reigns as deciphered on the Amgâchi copper-plate, the relationship not having been made out. Between Narayana Pâla's death and Mahipâl's probable accession there are three names to cover the space of 60 years, between 950 and 1010 A.D., which allows 20 years to each prince. These three kings are Raja Râjya Pâla II., [?] Pâla, and Vigraha Pâla II. Of the last we have a short record, dated in the twelfth year of his reign.

Of Mahi Pâla we have several records, of which the most important is the short inscription from Sârnâth, near Benares, which is dated in the Samvat year 1083, or A.D. 1026. In another record we find mention of the tenth and eleventh years of his reign. According to Târanâth, Mahi Pâla reigned fifty-two years. This is most probably correct, as there is an inscription on a brass image, dated in the 48th year of his reign. He may therefore have reigned from A.D. 1008 to 1060. Veracharya, Raja of Orissa, is said to have been tributary to him ; but there is no such name in the list of kings given by Dr. Hunter, which are—

A.D. 999.—Nritya Kesari.
   1013.—Narsinh Kesari.
   1024.—Kurma Kesari.
   1034.—Matsya Kesari.
   1050.—Varâha Kesari.

Amongst these the only name at all like Veracharya is that of Varâha Kesari; but as his reign did not begin until A.D 1050, the identification would show that the reign of Mohipâl must have extended to A.D.1055 or 1060.

The successors of Mahi Pâla, named in the Amgâchi copper-plate are Naya Pâla and his heir apparent, Vigraha Pâla III. Of the former there exists a single long inscription fixed on the gate pillar of Krishnadwârika Temple in Gaya. If we allow thirty years for the reigns of these two princes, their sway will cover the period between A.D. 1060 and 1090.

It was some time during this period, or about the middle of the eleventh century, that the Sena Rajas of Bengal rose to power and wrested the eastern provinces from the Pâla kings leaving them only Magadha and a portion of Rârh or Râdha. Their chronology will be discussed presently; and I will now note all that is known of the few remaining Pâla kings whose names are known only from a few inscriptions. The order of succession of the first three is not known, but they must certainly have preceded Govinda Pâla, whose reign began in A.D. 1161. As the interval between A.D. 1080 and 1161 is greater than would be covered by the average reigns of three kings, it is probable that two or three names still remain to be discovered.

Of *Mahendra Pâla Deva* we possess two inscriptions, one discovered by Kittoe at Gunariya, dated in the ninth year of his reign (not nineteenth as read by him), and a second found by myself at Ram Gaya, dated in his eighth year.

Of *Râma Pâla Deva* also we possess two inscriptions. one discovered by Broadley at Bihar, dated in the second year of his reign, and the other found by myself at Chandi-mau. dated in his twelfth year.

Of *Madana Pâla Deva* there are two inscriptions, one found by Broadley at Bihar, dated in the 3rd year of his reign, and the other found by myself at Jaynagar, near Lakhi Serai, dated in his 19th year. There was a Rathor king of the same name reigning about the same time at Kanauj, of whom there are inscriptions, dated in S. 1158 and 1166, or A. D. 1101 and 1109. I believe, however, that the Kanauj dominion was not extended as far as the Son River until near the end of his son's reign, about half a century later. I therefore accept the two records noted above as belonging to one of the Pâla dynasty of Magadha.

Of *Govinda Pâla Deva* there are also two inscriptions, both dated in the Samvat era of Vikramâditya. The earlier one is attached to the temple of Gadâdhar at Gaya, and consists of fourteen horizontal lines and one perpendicular line. "It begins with the invocation *Swasti namo Bhagavatî Vasudevaya*." Buchanan gives the following account of this record, which is particularly valuable for the minute precision of its date :—"The inscription is dated Samvat 1232 (A. D. 1175), in the 14th year of Sri Govinda Pâla Deva. It would appear from this inscription that Vidyadhara, the grandson of Ullan came to Gaya, gave daily sixteen *kahans* of cowries to the *dwijas* (brâhmans), took to witness fifty worshippers of Vishnu, especially Nrisinha, Sridhara, and Devadhara," &c. In this brief account Buchanan has omitted to notice the peculiarity of recording the year of the Vrihaspati cycle of sixty years, which gives such precision to the date. In the original the date is thus given :—*Samvat 1232, Vikâri Samvatsare, Sri Govinda Pâla Deva gata râjye chaturddasa samvatsare Gâyayam.*

"In the Samvat year 1232, the year Vikâri, 14 years of the reign of the fortunate Govinda Pâla Deva having elapsed in Gaya." The year 1232 of Vikramâditya Samvat is equivalent to A. D. 1175, which corresponds with Vikâri, the 33rd year of the Vrihaspati cycle in northern India. As 14 years of the reign of Govinda had then elapsed (*gata*), his accession must have taken place in A.D. 1161'." The second inscription is only 3 years later, S. 1235, A. D. 1178. Now, the two protests of Pratâpa Dhavala cut on the rock at Sahsarâm, show that the Rathor kings of Kanauj had already occupied Kârushadesa, or Shâhâbâd, in Samvat 1225, or A.D. 1168, just ten years before the date of Govinda Pâla's latest inscription. It seems probable therefore that the old Pâla

---

[1] Archæological Survey of India, Vol. III, p. 125.

58

that *Firosah Mi...*
the turquoise-col...
style of architect...
Dákhil Gate, wh...
divided in the sa...
of the door); it...
the same proport...
Dákhil Gateway,...
as old as the tim...

Franklin foun...
Factory, which, ...
thought might h...
of the tower. ...
minár is, I think...
Franklin that th...
vacant panel fro...
3 feet 11 inche...
would exactly su...
inches in height...
with the title of ...
in doubt whethe...
zah, who reigne...
Firoz, who reig...
Firozah Minár, ...
in favour of the ...
style of the bui...
view of its early ...
Mr. Fergusson, I...
belongs to the e...
of this view also ...
coins of the two ...
Abul Mujáhid; as...
the title of Abu...

The minár sta...
350 feet long fro...

¹ Francklin notices ...
note by Mr. Grote.
² See History of I...

River until near the end ...
ury later. I therefore ...
belonging to one of the ...

ere are also two inscriptions.
of Vikramáditya. The ...
of Gadádhar at Gaya, and on
and one perpendicular ne. ...
... the
llowing account of his reign.
... the
... Ram Deva. I would ...
... the grandson of ...
... ... of ... being
... ... worshippers of V...
... Devadhara," &c. In the
... to notice the peculiari...
... Vrihaspati cycle of sixty year
... the date. In the ... the
... 1232, *Vikrá ...
rájye chatur... ...

1232, the ...
Govinda ...
of Vikra ...
h corre...
cle in ...
had ...
lace.
rs le...
apr
...
...

dynasty of Magadha may have come to a sudden end shortly
after the date of the last inscription in A.D. 1178. In fact the
only inscription of a later date prior to the Muhammadan
invasion seems to belong to another family, as the descendants of Hulkâra *Bhupâla*, named Krishna and Garuda
Nârâyana, are spoken of as the "inveterate antagonists" of
the king of kings, Asoka Chandra Deva. This Bhupâla is
almost certainly the founder of the Pâla dynasty, who is
called Bhupâla by Abul Fazl, a name absolutely synonymous
with the Gopâla of the inscriptions. The title of *Hulkâra*
may, I think, be a misreading of *Bhumihâla*, the *Bhumihâra*,
the caste name of the Pâla family. The date of this inscription as I read it is equivalent to A.D. 1180, the second year
immediately following the latest inscription of Govinda Pâla
Deva.

The Sena Rajas of Bengal.

The power of the Pâla Raja was at its zenith during the
reign of Mahipâla Deva, who was certainly reigning in A.D.
1026, and whose reign may be fixed between the years 1010
and 1060 A.D. As his grandson Vigraha Pâla still called
himself king of Pundra Varddhana or Barendra, the decay of
the Pâla power, and the final loss of the great province of
Gauda cannot be placed earlier than A.D. 1050. According
to the chronology of the Sena Rajas, which will be examined
presently, this event must have taken place during the reign
of Vijaya Sena, who, in the inscriptions, has the titles of king
of Gauda, and conqueror of Kâmrup and Kalinga.

Only three records have yet been found of the Sena dynasty, which are known from their places of discovery as the
Deopâra, the Tarpan-dighi, and the Bâkarganj inscriptions.

The Deopara inscription gives the descent of the Sena
dynasty from one *Vira sena*. "In that same family," says this
record, "was born Samanta Sena, whose son was Hemanta
Sena, whose son was Vijaya Sena." It is nowhere said that
Samanta Sena was the son of Vira Sena, and the expression
"born in his family" simply means that Samanta was one of

the descendants of Vira Sena. The name of Varendra is distinctly mentioned in the last verse of the record.[1]

The Tarpan-dighi plate gives the genealogy of the Senas from Hemanta Sena through Vijaya Sena and Ballâla Sena to Lakshmana Sena, in whose 7th year the record was engraved'.

The Bâkarganj copper-plate gives the genealogy from Vijaya Sena, who is styled Sankara Gaudeswara down to his great-grandson Kesava Sena. It is dated in the year 3, to be counted from the death of his father Lakshmana Sena, which had become the initial point of a new era styled the Lakshmana Sena era[3].

There is also a fourth inscription, which certainly belongs to the period of the Sena rule, but which cannot, I think, be assigned to any member of the family. This is a record of king Asoka Chandra Deva, and is dated in the year 74 of the Lakshmana Sena Samvat. It is true that Bâbu Râjendra Lâl has identified this Prince with Lakshmaniya, the last independent Sena King of Gauda; but this has been effected chiefly by the bold manœuvre of changing the king's name to Asoka *Sena*. Prinsep read Chandra, but it seems to me to be *Balla Deva*.

Having stated all our existing authorities for the genealogy of the Sena family, I will now examine the chronology to which Bâbu Râjendra Lâl has already devoted several pages of his essay on " the Pâla and Sena Rajas of Bengal." In this paper the learned Bâbu points out that the credit of first discovering the era of Lakshmana Sena is due to Colebrooke, to which he afterwards adds that had the date of Lakshmana Sena been "calculated by the datum given by Colebrooke," it would have been settled at once. " But this was not done," says the Bâbu, and he then proceeds to assign " the credit of utilising the date and bringing it to bear on the history of Bengal," to Bâbu Raja Krishna Mukerji, who had " announced that the era of Lakshmana Sena was still current

[1] Bengal Asiatic Society's Journal, Vol. XXXIV, p. 128.
[2] Bengal Asiatic Society's Journal, Vol. XLIV, p. 1.
[3] Journal of Bengal Asiatic Society, Vol. VIII, p. 40.

in Tirhut, and its date in 1874 was 767." This date he is said to have made use of in an elementary History of Bengal, published in 1795.

At a meeting of the Asiatic Society held in April 1878, Mr. Blochmann read the following extract from a letter from Dr. Mitra announcing the discovery of a new era :—

" I have made a great discovery, nothing less than a new era, that of Lakshmana Sena. It is still current among the pundits of Tirhut. It will settle the age of the Senas beyond all cavil, upsetting at the same time Cunningham's date of the Pâla kings of Bengal."

I will now examine this " grand discovery " of the era of Lakshmana Sena, which has " settled the age of the Senas beyond all cavil " at the same time that it has upset my date of the Pâla kings of Bengal—

1.—Colebrooke's notice is as follows :—

" Halayudha the spiritual adviser of Lakshmana Sena (a renowned monarch who gave his name to an era, of which six hundred and ninety-two years are expired) is the author of Nyaya Survaswa[1]."

Now Colebrooke's Digest of Hindu Law, from which this extract is taken, is dated 17th December 1796, from which year, deducting the 699 years stated by him to be " expired," we get A.D. 1104—0, and A.D. 1195—1, or the first year of the Lakshmana era.

2.—On turning to Dr. Buchanan's account of the Puraniya District, I find it stated that the year A.D. 1810 was the year 706 of .the Lakshmana era " *according to the almanacs of Mithila*[2] "—Now 1810—706 gives A.D. 1104—0, exactly as stated by Colebrooke.

In another place, however, he gives a slightly different statement as follows :—

" In Mithila the year is lunar (*i.e.*, luni-solar), and commences on the first day after the full moon of Ashâdha. Here they say that Saka was the same as Sâlivâhan, and this year, 1810, is reckoned the 1732nd year of his era. It is also the 1866th year of Samvat, who, according to them, is the same with Vikrama. In these two points they agree with the Brahmans of the south, and differ totally from those of Ben-

---

[1] Colebrooke's Essays.
Buchanan's Eastern India, Vol. III, p. 41.

gal. They have still another era called after Lahshmana King of Gour, and of which this is the 795th year."

As Bâbu Rajendra admits, that if "the date of Lakshmana Sena given by Colebrooke had been consulted, it would have been settled at once," I can only suppose that as he has adopted a later date, he must have taken Colebrooke's statement without any examination as to whether it agreed with his own newly found date or not.

I will now examine the Bâbu's own date of the Lakshmana Sena era as recorded in different places of the Journal of the Bengal Asiatic Society, Volume XLVII, which I will distinguish by the letters A. B. C. D. E.

A—On page 398, he states that "the era must have commenced in January 1106 A.D."

B—Lower down on the same page he says, "*Beginning* with 1106, Lakshmana had a very prosperous reign."

C—But on page 397 he adopts Bâbu Râja Krishna's statement that in 1874 the date of the Lakshmana era was 767, which places the first year of the era in 1874—766=108 A.D.

D—Again, on page 398, I find him stating that the era is "still current," and in the present year reckons 771. As his paper was written in 1878, the first year of the era must have fallen in 1878-770-1108 A.D.

E—Lastly, on page 201 of his work on Buddha Gaya, I find the following statement regarding the Lakshmana Samvat—"In the present year it numbers 770. Its initial date must therefore correspond with A.D. 1108."

Here then we have three different dates for the beginning of the Lakshmana Sena era, namely A.D. 1104 (of Colebrooke, A.D. 1106 (A. and B.) and A. D. 1108 (C. D. and E.) of which the last two disagree altogether with Colebrooke's statement (A.D. 1104) "which, had it been consulted, would have settled the date at once."

I will now turn to a much more curious account of this era which the Bâbu has inadvertently given in the same paper, namely, that the epoch was both the *beginning* and the *end* of Lakshmana's reign.

The first statement which I have already quoted says "*Beginning* with 1106, Lakshmana had a very prosperous reign of many years."

But in his translation of the inscription of Asoka Chandra Deva, he gives the date as follows:—

"On Thursday, the 12th of the wane, in the month of Vaisákha, Sam, or year 74th, *after the expiration of the reign* of the auspicious Lakshmana Sena Deva."

I would now ask the learned Bábu which of these two periods is it, the *end* or the *beginning* of the reign, that "settles the date of Lakshmana Sena on *infinitely more reliable data* than what we have for any other Hindu Sovereign of the pre-muhammadan era." I would also ask whether it is the *end* or the *beginning* of Lakshmana Sena's reign that has "upset" my date of the Pála Kings. I certainly do not admit the upset, and I now proceed to show that the first year of the Lakshmana Sena era was A.D. 1107.

A copper-plate inscription of Siva Singha Deva, Raja of Tirhut, gives the following dates, *Lakshmana Samvat 293, Srâvana Sudi 7 Gurau,* coupled with *Saka 1321* and *Samvat 1455.* The Saka date is equivalent to A.D. 1399, but the Vikrama date of 1455 gives A.D. 1398. The difference between the two dates is only 134 years instead of 135. This difference was also noticed by Buchanan, who states that Kamala Kânta, the most learned Brahman in the Rangpur district, made the Samvat era begin 134 years before that of Saka[1]. In the Mithila district he found the same, as he notes (see No. 2) that the year 1810 A.D. was reckoned as Saka 1732 and Samvat 1866, with only 134 years' difference. As the Saka date is the correct one, I have adopted it in preference to the Samvat date, which is but little used in Bengal. But the best proof of its accuracy is the fact that it agrees with the *week-day* mentioned in the copper-plate. I have calculated the date, which comes out Thursday, 10th July A.D. 1399, Old style.

[1] Eastern India, Vol. III, p. 506

I will now cite Bâbu Rajendra himself to show that in other places he has admitted the accuracy of my date of Mahipâla, as well as the general correctness of my description of the extent of his dominions.

PALA DYNASTY.

Cunningham.	*Bábu Rajendra.*
A. D. 915—Nârâyana Pâla.	A. D. 935—Nârâyana Pâla.
„ 940—Râja Pâla.	„ 955—Râja Pâla.
„ 965— Pâla.	„ 975— Pâla.
„ 990—Vigraha Pâla.	„ 995—Vigraha Pâla.
„ 1015—Mâhi Pâla.	„ 1015—Mâhi Pâla.
to	to
„ 1040———	„ 1040———

But long before the publication of Bâbu Rajendra's essay, I had already drawn up an amended chronology of these Pâla Rajas, which has been printed in my Report of a tour in the Gangetic Provinces, forming Vol. XI of the Archæological Survey of India.   This amended list is as follows compared with Bâbu Rajendra's list :—

Pâla Dynasty.

		Cunningham.				*Bâbu Rajendra.*	
1.	A.D.	815	Gopala.		A.D.	855	Gopâla.
2.	„	830	Dharma Pâla.		„	875	Dharma Pâla.
3.	„	850	Deva Pâla.		„	895	Deva Pâla.
4.	„	885	Râjya Pâla.	omitted.			
5.	„	887	Sura Pâla.				
6.	„	900	Vigraha Pâla 1.		„	915	Vigraha Pâla.
7.	„	915	Nârâyana Pâla.		„	935	Nârâyana Pâla.
8.	„	940	Raja Pâla.		„	955	Raja Pâla.
9.	„	965			„	975	Raja Pâla.
10.	„	990	Vigraha Pâla.		„	995	Vigraha Pâla.
11.	„	1015	Mahi Pâla.		„	1015	Mahi Pâla.
		1040				1040	

As the Bâbu has omitted the reigns of the two brothers Râjya Pâla and Sura Pâla, of whom the latter certainly reigned 13 years, according to an inscription which I have already published, the discrepancy between my date of Gopâla, A.D. 815, and that of my critic, A.D. 855, will be considerably lessened.   But as in my account I have shown good reason for placing Gopála as early as A.D. 813, I adhere to my own chronology.

With regard to the country over which Mahi Pála ruled, I stated in my Report of 1871-72[1] that "according to Táranáth, the Raja of Orissa was tributary to Mahi Pála, and as he certainly held Benares, his dominions were very extensive. But the Pála dynasty did not retain their power beyond the end of the eleventh century, when the whole of the Eastern Provinces were raised into a separate principality by the founder of the Sena family." Now Bábu Rajendra admits that "Mahi Pála exercised full sovereignty in the province to the north of the Padmá. The vast sheet of water in Dinájpur, which still bears his name, the Mahi Pála Dighi, is a proof positive on this point." He also notes that " several local names, such as Mahigang, Mahinagar, Mahi-pur, Mahi-Santosh, Nayanagar, &c., also bear remains of the names of former Pála kings."

In these extracts Bábu Rajendra fully admits all that I have claimed for the Pála kings ; and I fail to see how his erroneous date of the Lakshmana *Sena* era has "upset" my date of the Pála kings, when he adopts the period of A.D. 1015 to 1040 for Mahi Pála, which had already been published by me.

But there is still one more point connected with the Sena kings, on which I venture to differ with the learned Bábu. He is of opinion that " the Senas were Kshatriyas of the lunar race, and not Vaidyas, as they are supposed to have been by the people of the present day." He founds this opinion on " the positive declaration of two inscriptions, and that of a work, the Dána Ságara, written by Ballála himself." He also quotes the Tarpandighi inscription, in which the Senas are called " kings of the race of *Aushádhinátha* (or the moon)." But as *Aushádhinátha* means a " physician," or the "lord of drugs," as well as the "moon" or "lord of herbs," I am inclined to accept the universal opinion of the people in pre-ference to the doubtful language of flattering inscriptions.

---

[1] Archæological Survey of India, Vol. III., p. 134.

The opinion that the Senas were *Vaidyas* is not the supposition of the "people of the present day," but the positive
statement of Abul Fazl, whose information was derived from
the best authorities in the time of Akbar.   That Ballâla Sena
himself was willing to take advantage of the double meaning
attached to *Aushâdhinâtha,* and to trace his descent from
the *Chandravansis* instead of from the *Vaidyavansis,* is in
perfect accordance with weak human nature, and I confess
that I am inclined rather to accept the general belief of the
people, which has been handed down for centuries, than the
doubtful language of royal panegyrists.

The genealogy of the Sena Rajas has already been given
from the three inscriptions of Deopâra, Tarpandighi, and Ba-
karganj.   From these we learn that the family were staunch
Brahmanists, the principal object of their worship being
Vishnu.   Their direct descent is traced from Sâmanta Sena,
the grandfather of Ballâla Sena, before whom mention is made
of only one name, Vira Sena, as óne of Sâmanta's.   Now just
as we have seen in the case of Gopâla, the progenitor of the
Pâla Rajas, who is also called by the synonymous names of
Bhupâla and Lokpâla, so I believe that *Vira Sena* may have
been also known as *Sura Sena.* This prince I would identify
with king Sûra Sena who married the princess Bhoga Devi,
the sister of Ansu Varmma, Raja of Nepâl, who was the contemporary of Hwen Thsang, and of whom Pandit Bhagwân
Lâl Indraji has published inscriptions, dated in A.D. 645 and
651.   In No. 7 of these Nepâl records the son of Sura and
Bhoga Devi is named Bhoga Varmma, while in another
record (No. 15) he is said to be the son of " the great Aditya
Sena, the illustrious lord of Magadha."   Hence it seems
probable that the latter Sena Rajas of Bengal were the
direct descendants of Aditya Sena Deva, the great king of
Magadha.

From these inscriptions, therefore, we learn that Aditya
Sena Deva was a contemporary of Ansu Varmma, whose date
is known as comprising the years 637 and 651 A.D.   This
date is confirmed by an inscription of Aditya Sena himself,
which was found by Mr. Beglar at Shâhpur near Bihâr in

Magadha[1].   This record is dated in Samvat 55, which being referred to the era of Sri Harsha, beginning in A.D. 607=1, gives A.D. 661.   Aditya Sena was, therefore, certainly reigning in the middle of the seventh century, A.D.   Now Babu Rajendra Lâl has already suggested that Vira Sena and Sura Sena were only *aliases* of the name of *Adisur*, the traditional progenitor of the Sena Rajas.   If these identifications could be established, we should obtain a fixed date for one of the chief events in the history of Bengal, in the settlement of the Kanaujiya Brahmans by Adisur.

In the Nepâl inscriptions just quoted, I find Bhoga Varman described as " the crest jewel of the illustrious *Varmans* of the valorous *Maukhari* race." His father therefore must have been a *Maukhari*, and so also must have been Yaso Varmma, who gave his name to Yaso Varmapura, about A.D. 730 to 750. Purnna Varmma, king of Magadha in 735, whom Hwen Thsang calls a descendant of Asoka, should also have been a Maukhari, judging from his name and the country over which he ruled.   Who then were the *Maukharis ?* The name of Varma suggests a Kshatriya origin but no descendant of Asoka could have been a Kshatriya.   On the other hand I find that *Graha Varman*, the son of Avanti Varma *Maukhari*, was the husband of Râjya Sri, the sister of Harsha Varddhana of Kanauj.   Now the king of Kanauj is called a *Fei-she*, or Vaisya, by Hwen Thsang, which would accord exactly with the Kayastha or Vaidya caste of the Senas of Bengal, but not with his relationship to *Silâditya*, the Kshatriya king of Malwa.   If Harsha Varddhana was really related to Silâditya, the caste name of *Fei-shi* must represent a Bais Rajput, and not a *Vaisya*.   In two previous reports I have already brought to notice a king of Western Magadha named *Santi-Varma* (now read as Isâna), who must have reigned some time during the sixth century[1], while Kumara Gupta II ruled in Eastern Magadha.   Dâmodara Gupta, the successor

---

[1] See Plate XI, No. 1. Pandit Bhagwan Lal reads the figures as 88, but they appear to me to be 55, each being the Bengali 5.

[1] Archæological Survey of India, Vol. III, p. 136; and IX, 27, where I have given a coin of this king.

of Kumára, is said to have encountered "at the battle of *Maushari*, the fierce army of the western Hunas," while the next king Mahásena Gupta obtained a victory over Sri Varmma[1]. From these notices of the Varmmas I gather that the name of *Maushari* is certainly the same as that of *Mau-khari*, as the *sh* is constantly pronounced as *kh*.

Some other Varmmas connected with Magadha are mentioned in the inscriptions of the Barábar and Nágarjuni caves. These names are Yajnya Varmma, Sardula Varmma, and Ananta Varmma. These princes must have been contemporary with the earlier Guptas.

Another king of the *Maukhari* race, named Kshetra Varmma, is mentioned by Bána, the minister of Harsha Varddhana, as having been cut off by assassins. There is no clue to his date, but he must have preceded Purnna Varmma, who was the contemporary of Harsha Varddhana.

Another family of five *Varmmas* of the *Maukhari* race is recorded on the Asirgarh Seal. As two of them intermarried with the Guptas, they also must be placed before Purnna Varmma. It is not, however, certain that they belonged to the reigning family of Magadha, although their connection with the Guptas is strongly in favour of it. Their genealogy is as follows[2]:—

> Hari Varmma married Jaya Swámini.
> Aditya Varmma married Harshá Gupta.
> Iswara Varmma married Umá Gupta.
> Isána Varmma married Harshini.
> Sarvva Varmma, the Maukhari.

The tribal name of Maukhari, which is quite clear in both engravings, puzzled both Mill and Wilson. The latter read it as Hovari. The first three kings are styled simply Mahárája, but the last two have the title of Mahárájádhirája. As this addition of title almost certainly denotes an increase of power, I think that Isána Varmma must have been contemporary with the later Gupta princes of the Aphsar inscription.

---

[1] Bengal Asiatic Society's Journal, XXXV, p. 273.

[2] Royal Asiatic Society's Journal, Vol. III, p. 378; and Bengal Asiatic Society's Journal, Vol. V, p. 482.

The names of the *Maukhari* princes, as derived from all the different sources just quoted, may be arranged tentatively as follows, side by side, with the later Gupta kings of the Aphsar and Barnârak inscriptions :—

A.D.	R. Magadha. Guptas.		W. Magadha. Maukharis.
475	Krishna Gupta.		Hari Varmma.
500	Harsha Gupta.		Aditya Varmma.[1]
525	Jivita Gupta I.		Iswara Varmma.
550	Kumâra Gupta, contemporary of		Isâna Varmma.
575	Dâmodara Gupta.		Sarvva Varmma.
600	Mahasena Gupta, contemporary of		Sri Varmma.
625	Mâdhava Gupta.	630	Purnna Varmma.
650	Aditya Sena Deva.		
675	Deva Gupta.	675	Bhoga Varmma.
700	Vishnu Gupta.		
725	Savitri Gupta.	730	Yaso Varmma.

The dates given above depend on the ascertained period of Aditya Sena Deva, and as each reign of the Gupta dynasty is also a generation, I have allowed 25 years to each.

The date of Yaso Varmma also is known from the *Raja Tarangini*.

Purnna Varmma's date is taken from the Chinese pilgrim Hwen Thsang, and that of Bhoga Varmma from the Nepalese inscriptions published by Pandit Bhagwân Lâl Indraji.

From the number of instances which I have quoted, it seems that the family name of the *Maukhari* tribe continued to be Varmma for many centuries. But if the Varmmas of Magadha were *Maukharis*, as they certainly would appear to have been, then Purnna Varmma, the descendant of Asoka, must have been a *Maukhari* or *Maushari*, which would thus become only a variant form of *Maurya ;* and in fact *Mauriya* would be a legitimate contraction of *Maukhariya*.

After Aditya Sena's great-grandson Savitri Gupta, we have no names of any paramount sovereigns until the time of Gopâla, the founder of the Pâla dynasty. From this total absence of all records of the rulers for nearly a century, I think that a severe struggle between Brahminism and Buddhism may have followed the death of Harsha Vardhana in A.D. 648, and that the latter, though at first unsuccessful,

[1] Aditya Varmma married Harshâ Guptâ, who was most probably a daughter of his contemporary of Eastern Magadha, Harsha Gupta.

during the rule of Aditya Sena and his immediate successors ultimately triumphed under Gopála in A.D. 813, and became the dominant religion of Magadha down to the time of the Muhammadan conquest.

The following lists show the genealogy of the Sena Rajas as recorded in their inscriptions, compared with the names preserved by Abul Fazl in the Ain Akbari:—

A.D.	Deopara Inscription.	Tarpandighi Inscription.	Bákarganj Inscription.	Ain Akbari.
650	Vira Sena, from whom descended—			
975	Samanta Sena.			
1000	Hemanta Sena.	Hemanta Sena.		
1025	Vijaya Sena.	Vijaya Sena.	Vijaya Sena.	Sukha Sena.
1050		Ballála Sena.	Ballála Sena.	Ballála Sena.
1076		Lakshmana Sena.	Lakshmana Sena.	Lakshmana Sena.
1106[1]				Mádhava Sena.
1108			Kesava Sena.	Kesava Sena.
1118	Lakhmaniya reigned 80 years [Tabakát-i-Nasiri].			
1198	Conquest of Bengal by Bakhtiár Khalji.			

For this chronology we have three fixed dates: 1st, in the death of Lakshmana Sena, A.D. 1106, and the establishment of the era named after him; 2nd and 3rd, in the accession and defeat of Lakhmaniya by Bakhtiár Khalji. I have accepted the probable date of the defeat as given by Blochmann in A.D. 1198, from which, deducting 80 years for the length of Lakhmaniya's reign, as stated by Minháj, we get 1118 for the date of his birth and accession, according to the romantic story told by the Muhammadan historian. I am the more willing to accept this long reign, as it harmonizes with the real date of Lakshmana Sena, who died in A.D. 1106. The only doubtful point, as it seems to me, is whether Minháj intended 80 lunar or 80 solar years. If the former, the actual reign of Lakhmaniya will be reduced to 78 solar years, and his accession brought down to A.D. 1120.

When Lakhmaniya fled from Nadiya he is said to have sought refuge in Bikrampur, where his descendants reigned

[1] As A.D. 1107 was the first year after the expiry of Lakshmana's reign, his death must have taken place in A.D. 1106.

for four generations, of whom the last was conquered by
the Muhammadans. Târânâth says that they were tributary to the Turushka kings, and that their race became ex-
tinct with Prati Sena. One hundred years later Bengal came
under the rule of a powerful king named Chagala Raja, whose
rule is said to have extended as far as Tili (Delhi?). He
died 160 years before A.D. 1608, or A.D. 1448 ; and if he
began to reign in 1400, the close of the Sena dynasty must
have taken place in A.D. 1300, which agrees very well indeed
with the period obtained by working downwards from Lakhmaniya, as four generations would just cover one hundred
years from A.D. 1201.

The Muhammadan rulers of Bengal.

The period of Muhammadan rule in Bengal is one of the
least known and most confused portions of Indian history. Of
late years, however, much has been done by Messrs. Thomas
and Blochmann towards fixing the chronology on a firmer
basis. The former working with the coins and the latter with
the inscriptions have shown that the dates assigned to many
of the kings are erroneous, and in some cases to the extent
of several years. I have added several valuable inscriptions
to the collection which I formerly made over to Blochmann,
amongst which there is a very important record of Jalâluddin
Masaud Jâni, dated in A.H. 647, or just 9 years previous to
the date hitherto accepted for his appointment to the Government of Bengal. As the history of this period is almost
wholly derived from the contemporary record of Minhâjus
Sirâj, I do not doubt the accuracy of the date given by him
in the Tabakât-i-Nasiri of A.H. 656; but I think that Masaud
Jâni must have held the Government for a short time, at least
at an earlier date, including the year 647 A.H., when the inscription was set up on the Gangârâmpur Masjid. His connection with Bengal most probably began at a still earlier
period, when his father Alâuddin Jâni accompanied Nasiruddin Mahmud, the son of Iltitmish, in his expedition against
Ghiâsuddin Iwaz, the ruler of Bengal ; and afterwards became Governor of Lakhnauti from A.H. 627 to 631. He

was succeeded by Izzuddin Tughril, of whom an inscription now exists in Bihâr, dated in A.H. 640.

Blochmann divides the Muhammadan period of the history of Bengal into five parts:

1. The "Initial period," or the reigns of the Governors of Lakhnauti appointed by the Delhi sovereigns from the conquest of Bengal by Muhammad Bakhtiyâr Khilji, A.D. 739 to 1338.

2. The period of the independent kings of Bengal from A. D. 1338 to 1538.

3. The period of the kings of Sher Shâh's family, and their Afghân successors, from A.D. 1538 to 1576.

4. The Mughal period, from A.D. 1576 to 1740.

5. The Nawâbi period, from the accession of Alivirdi Khân in A.D. 1740 to the transfer of Bengal to the East India Company.

As the history of Bengal is sufficiently well known from the time of Sher Shâh's conquest, I will confine my remarks to the first two periods of the governors and the independent kings.

Governors of Bengal.

A. H.	A. D.	
598	1201	Muhammad Bakhtiâr Khalji.
602	1205	Izzuddin Muhammad Shiran.
605	1208	Alauddin Ali Mardân.
608	1211	Husâmuddin Iwaz, became independent as Ghiâsuddin Iwaz.
624	1227	Nâsiruddin, eldest son of Iltitmish.
626	1229	Alauddin Daulat Shah [Ikhtiyaruddin Balka].
627	1230	Alauddin Jâni.
631	1234	Saifuddin Aibak.
...	...	Izzuddin Tughril Tughan Khan, inscrip. 640.
642	1244	Kamruddin Timûr Khan.
644	1246	Ikhtyâruddin Tughril Khan [Sultan Mughisuddin.] Jalaluddin Masaud Jâni, inscrip. 647.
656	1258	———— re-appointed.
657	1259	Izzuddin Balban.
664	1265	Muhammad Arsalân Tatâr Khan.
678	1279	Tughril, Sultan Mughisuddin.
681	1282	Nâsiruddin Mahmud, second son of Balban.

On the death of Balban in A.H. 685, or A.D. 1286, his son Bughra Khân, or Nasiruddin Mahmud, gave up the king-

dom of Delhi and became the first independent king of
Bengal, who was acknowledged at Delhi. Husámuddin Iwaz
had declared his independence some seventy years earlier, but
he was not acknowledged by the Delhi king, who was too
busily employed in other quarters to give any attention to
Bengal. Towards the end of his reign, however, he sent a
large army under the command of his eldest son, Násiruddin
Mahmud, who occupied Lakhnauti ; and afterwards defeated
and captured Iwaz, who was at once put to death. All the
great roads and embankments in Barendra are attributed to
this rebel chief, who seems to have been a vigorous and popular ruler. Several of his coins have been published by
Mr. Thomas. On some he acknowledges his allegiance to
Iltitmish, while on others he omits his Suzerain's name altogether, and boldly assumes the title of Sultán. These coins
are dated in A.H. 616 and 617, or A.D. 1219—1220. On his
later coins bearing the date of A.H. 620 he takes the still
loftier title of Sultán-ussulátin. Two years later Iltitmish
invaded Bengal at the head of a large force, and compelled
the rebel chief to acknowledge his sovereignty by placing
the name of the Delhi Emperor on his coins. A specimen
of these coins has been published by Mr. Thomas, along with
others, dated in 623 and 624. In the latter year Ghiásuddin
was captured and put to death, and the province of Bengal
was again attached to the Delhi Empire.

Ikhtiyáruddin Yuzbak Tughril, who was made Governor
of Bengal in A.H. 644, shortly afterwards rebelled, and
assumed the title of Mughisuddin. He is said to have been
killed in a disastrous expedition into Kámrup.

The Zubdat-ul-Tawárikh also says that he assumed the
title of Sultán Mughis-uddin, to which the Tárikh-i-Firuz
Sháhi adds that he ruled over Lakhnauti for 26 years, that
is from A.H. 644 to 670, when he was killed near Sunárgaon.
It seems scarcely possible that these two Mughis-uddin
Tughrils, each of whom rebelled and took the title of Sultán,
could have been different persons. I think, therefore, that
Minháj's account of Tughril's death in Kámrup must have
been only a report, which he noted at the time, and after-

wards forgot to correct. It seems probable that Jalál-uddin Masaud Jáni, on hearing of Tughril's defeat in Kámrup, must have set himself up as governor of Lakhnauti, as his inscription, which I have given in my account of Gaur, is clearly dated in A. H. 647, no less than nine years before the date on which Minháj states that the kingdom of Lakhnauti was conferred upon him. I think that this statement must refer to a re-appointment, and that between the date of the Gangárámpur inscription in A.H. 647 and A.H. 656, when he was appointed governor of Lakhnauti, he must have been expelled by Tughril.

In 657 Izzuddin Balban succeeded to Masaud Jáni, but very soon afterwards he was killed by Mahmud Arslán Tátár Khán. Of his fate nothing is known; but at the time of Balban's accession in A.H. 664, A.D. 1265, Tughril was in possession of Lakhnauti, and was confirmed in the appointment by the new emperor. For fifteen or sixteen years he remained faithful, but in A.D. 1280, when the Emperor and his sons were kept on the western frontier by repeated irruption of Mughals, Tughril rebelled. "He assumed royal insignia, and took the title of Mughis-uddin, which title was used in the *Khutba*, and on his coins. He was compelled to fly from Lakhnauti on the approach of Balban, and was shortly afterwards killed in the neighbourhood of Sunárgaon. During my tour in Barinda in 1879-80, I was informed that a large number of his coins, bearing the title of Sultán Mughis-uddin Tughril, had been found near Rahanpur, at the confluence of the Purnabhába and Mahánanda Rivers. I offered to give ten rupees for a single coin of Mughis-ud-din, but I could neither obtain one, nor get an impression of one. I have no reason, however, to doubt the accuracy of my informant's story, as he was quite able to read the inscriptions on the coins, and had actually seen some of them. It was from him that I received the first information about the Gangárámpur inscription of Jalál-ud-din Masaud Jáni."

In recording this rebellion Zia-ud-din Barani says—

"Shrewd and knowing people had given to Lakhnauti the name

¹ Initial coinage of Bengal—Journal of Bengal Asiatic Society XI.I, 1354.

of Bulghâkpur (the city of strife), for since the time when Sultâr Mu'izzuddin Muhammad Sâm conquered Delhi, every governor that had been sent from thence to Lakhnauti took advantage of the distance, and of the difficulties of the road, to rebel. If they did not rebel themselves, others rebelled against them, and killed them, and seized the country. The people of this country had for many long years evinced a disposition to revolt, and the disaffected and evil disposed among them generally succeeded in alienating the loyalty of the governors."

On the death of Tughril, the Emperor appointed his son Bughrâ Khân to the governorship of the Eastern Provinces and on the death of his father, he became the first independent king of Bengal under the title of Nâsir-uddin Mâhmud[1].

The Kings of Bengal.

A. H.	A. D.	Kings.	Coins A. H.	Inscrip. A. H.	Mints.
685	1286	Nâseruddin Mahmud .	...	...	
691	1291	Ruknuddin Kai Kaus .	691—695	697	Lakhnauti.
702	1302	Shamsuddin Firoz . .	702—722	709—715	Ditto.
718	1318	Shihâbud din Bughra II. .	718	...	Ditto.
711	1311	Ghiâsuddin Bahadur .	711	...	Ditto.
723	1323	Nâseruddin [under Tughlak]	...	...	723 to 726.
733	1332	Muhammad bin Tughlak .	733	...	Lakhnauti.
739	1338	Fakhruddin Mubarak .	739—750	...	Sunargaon.
742	1341	Alâuddin Ali . .	742—746	...	Firuzabad.
751	1350	Ikhtiyaruddin Ghazi .	753	...	Sunârgaon.
740	1339	Shamsuddin Ilias .	740—758	...	
759	1358	Abul Mujahid Sikandar .	750—792	765—770	
792	1390	Ghiâsuddin Azem .	772—812	...	Firuzabad.
814	1411	Saifuddin Hamzah [Raja Kans.]	814	...	
814	1411	Shâhibuddin Bayazid .	814?—816	...	Firuzabad.
818	1415	Jalaluddin Muhammad .	818—831	...	
835	1431	Shamsuddin Ahmad .	836	...	
843	1439	Naseruddin Mahmud .	846—848	859—863	Khalifabad.
864	1459	Ruknuddin Barhak .	873—879	865—868	
879	1474	Shamsuddin Yusuf .	883 & 884	882—885	Shamsabad.
886	1481	Jalâluddin Fateh .	886	886—892	Fatehabad
893	1488	Shahzâdeh Bârbek .	...	...	
893	1488	Saifuddin Firuz .	893	...	
896	1490	Nâseruddin Mahmud II .	...	896	
896	1490	Shamsuddin Muzaffar .	896	898	
899	1493	Alauddin Husain .	899—926	903—925	
925	1529	Nâseruddin Nusrat .	922—933	929—937	
938	1531	Alauddin Firoz .	939	939	Fatehabad.
939	1532	Ghiâsuddin Mahmud III .	939—943	941	Husenabad.
944	1537	Conquest by Sher Shah .			

[1] Elliot's Muhammadan Historians of India, by Dowson,—III., 112.

In the first part of this list, the dates of the Balbani kings, or descendants of Balban, from Nasiruddin Mahmud to Ikh-tiyaruddin Ghâzi, call for no remarks, as they have been established by coins and inscriptions.   But from the time of Iliâs Shah the dates of most of the kings are wrongly given in all the historians.   Many of these errors have been pointed out by Messrs. Thomas and Blochmann.   But there is one particularly dark period of nearly 100 years from A.H. 770 or A.D. 1368, the date of the great Adina Masjid built by Sikandar, down to the death of Nâsiruddin Mahmud I in A. H. 863, or A.D. 1459, of which we do not possess a single inscription. The reign of Sikandar himself is fairly illustrated by his coins from which we learn that he was still living in A.H. 792, or A.D. 1390, just 23 years after the date given by Ferishta for his death in A.H. 769. But the chronology of his son Ghias-uddin Azam is still more erroneous, ·as the date assigned for his death is A.H. 775, or just 37 years prior to the date of his latest coin, or 39 or 40 years earlier than the actual date of his death, as recorded by the Chinese ambassadors.

When Sir E. Clive Bayley published his coin of Ghiâsud-din Azam, dated in 812, he took it to be a " posthumous coin struck by some one else for special reasons in the name of Ghiasuddin[1]."   And this conclusion was natural enough, seeing that Blochmann had read the date of his son Hamza's coin as 804, and that of Bayazid as 812 or A.D. 1409. But the evidence which I can now adduce shows most conclusively that Azam Shah was alive in A.D. 1408 and 1409, when he sent embassies to China, and that he died in 1411 or 1412, when he was succeeded by his son Saifuddin.

In the Chinese annals translated by Pauthier[2], it is recorded that "in A.D. 1408, the king of *Pang-kola* (or Bengal), named *Ai-ya-sse-ting* (or Ghiâs-uddin), sent an ambassador to offer tribute" (that is, *presents*) consisting of the produce of the country.   These presents included horses and saddles, gold and silver ornaments, and " drinking vessels

---

[1] Proceedings for August 1874, Asiatic Society of Bengal, XLIII, 158.
[2] Journal Asiatique, December 1839, p. 453.

of white porcelain with azure flowers," and many other
things. The mention of glazed ware drinking vessels is
interesting, as it shows that the art of glazing earthenware
must have reached a much higher standard in the time of
Ghiâs-uddin Azam than would be inferred from the existing
glazed tiles of his father's Masjid at Hazrat Pandua.

In A.D. 1409, or A.H. 812, a second embassy was sent
from Bengal with a suite of two hundred and thirty persons.
In A.D. 1412 or A.H. 815, the Chinese ambassadors on
their way to India met the Indian envoys bringing the usual
presents. From them the Chinese ambassadors learned that
king Ghiâs-uddin was dead, and had been succeeded by his
son *Sai-fe-ting*, or Saif-uddin (Hamza). Another Bengal
embassy was sent in 1414; and in 1415 or A. H. 818, the
Chinese emperor sent an envoy to Bengal with presents,
which were received by the king and queen and the minis-
ters. On this occasion the Chinese envoy was " the illustrious
prince Tsi-chao." No other embassies to China are mentioned until A.D. 1438 and 1439.

In A.H. 818 Jalâl-uddin Muhammad had already ascended the throne as we learn from his coins, and, therefore,
the king and queen noted in the annals must be Jalâl-uddin
and his wife.

The minute accuracy of some of these Chinese notices
shows that they were made from actual observation and not
from mere hearsay. Thus they describe the silver money as
being called *tang-kia* (in Sanskrit *tangka*), which was the
actual name of the large silver coins until the time of Sher
Shâh who introduced the word *rûpi*. They give also the
weight and size of the *tangka*, the former being 2 *thsian*
plus 8 *fan* or 163·24 grains, and the latter 1 *tsun* or 1·41 inch.
Now the coins of Azam, as well as those of his father
Sikandar, and of his son Saif-uddin Hamza, measure from
1·2 to 1·3 inch, and weigh from 162 to 166 grains. It is
also said that there were coins of less value, but so far as
I know not a single specimen of these smaller coins has yet
been found.

According to the Chinese account quoted above, Ghiás-uddin Azam must have died in A.D. 1411, or A. H. 814, when he was succeeded by his son Saif-uddin Hamza. Only two coins of this prince have yet been found, of which one is in the possession of the Bengal Asiatic Society. The date of this coin is incomplete, the unit only having been read by Blochmann as *arba* = 4; and he accordingly fixed the date as A.H. 804. But I think that the letters following *arba* may be read as *wa ashr*, making the whole 14, or A.H. 814. The date of 804 would not, however, be impossible, as Hamza may have received the royal title from his father during his lifetime, just as Azam himself had received it from his father Sikandar long before his death. But there is a coin of Báyazid, which Blochmann assigns to the year 812, and which, if correctly read, would show that Raja Kans had already set up the puppet king Shihábuddin Báyazid at least two years before the death of Azam Shah. And this is not at all impossible, for if the length of rule of 7 years assigned to Raja Kans be correct, then the date of his as-sumption of power must be placed 7 years before 818, the earliest date on the coins of his son Jaláluddin Muhammad. I should however rather prefer to read the date on Báyazid's coin as 814, as the unit figure is very indistinct on the Asiatic Society's coin. On two other coins the date is clearly 816. The author of the Riyáz says that according to some writers the successor of Hamza was not his son, but an adopted son, and that his name was Shiháb-ud-din. Any how he reigned 3 years 4 months and 6 days[1]. Adopting this length of reign the accession of Shihábuddin Báyazid would fall in 814 or 815 A.H.

All the traditions of the country are likewise in favour of the later date assigned to Raja Kans and his son Jaláluddin. Thus both father and son, according to the Riyáz, were con-temporaries of Nur Kutb Alam, A.H. 800 to 851, and of Ibráhim Sharki of Jaunpur, A.H. 804 to 844. The Hindu name of Jalál is said to have been *Jadu*, or *Jaimal*, or

---

[1] Blochmann Bengal Asiatic Society's Journal, XLII, 259.

Chaitmal, according to various readings. Now there is a curious statement made by Târânâth, which would appear to refer to this prince both as to time and place. According to him there was a powerful king of Bengal named *Chagala Râja,* who extended his rule as far as *Tili,* or Delhi. As he died in A.D. 1448, his reign must have begun about 1400'or 1410, so that it just covers the whole period of the reign of Jalâluddin, or Chaitmal.

Jalâluddin is said to have ruled for 17 years, and as there is a coin of his son dated in 836, while his own earliest coin is dated 818, we may assign 835 as the probable date of his death. To Ahmed Shâh the histories assign a reign of 16 or 18 years, which must be reduced to 6 or 8, as there are coins of his successor Nâser-ud-din Mahmud I. dated in 846. Adopting 8 years as the true length of Ahmed's reign, Mahmud would have come to the throne in A.H. 843. His reign is variously stated at 27 or 32 years; for which I would substitute 21 years placing his death in 864 A.H. We have an inscription of his son and successor Rukn-ud-din Bârbak, dated in Safar the second month of 865, while the latest inscription of Mahmud himself is dated on the 28th day of Zilhaja 863, or just one day before the end of the year. To Bârbak the histories assign a reign of 16 or 17 years. Accepting the first of these numbers, the date of his death will fall in A.H. 880, which must be close upon the true date, as one of his coins is dated in 879, while the earliest inscription of his son Yusuf is dated in A.H. 882. The latest known date of this prince is 885, while we have both coins and inscriptions of his uncle Fateh Shâh dated in 886. But according to the histories Yusuf reigned 7½ years, which would place his accession in 879. Perhaps the 16 years of Bârbak may be only a round number for 15½ years, which would thus accord with the year 879, which date I have adopted in the list of kings. Fateh Shâh is also said to have reigned 7½ years, which would place his death in 93. of which very year we have a coin of his successor Saif-ud-din Firoz. This last king reigned for 3 years and was followed by Nâser-ud-din Mahmud II. of whom there is an inscription at Hazrat Pandua dated in 896 A.H. Mahmud was displaced by Shams-ud-din Muzaffar in the same year as shown by his inscription at Devikot. A second inscription dated on 17th Ramzân 898 shows that the length of reign of 3½ years assigned to him is most probably correct. This would place his death in 899, of which very year we have coins of his successor Alâ-ud-din Husen. Of this king both coins and inscriptions are very numerous. Of the former I have seen a gold coin dated in A.H. 907 and weighing 821·25 grains, or exactly five gold mohars. I have also heard of a ten gold mohar piece of the same prince. His inscriptions range up to 925, of which year there are also coins of his son Nâser-ud-din Nusrat. As the histories give this prince a reign of either 13 or 16 years, while there are coins of him dated in 922 and 924, before the death of his father, I would reckon the longer period of 16 years from 822 and the shorter period from 825, both of which would place his death in 938 A.H., and that of his father in 925. The date of 938 is supported by the Kalma inscription of Nusrat's successor Alâ-ud-din Firoz, which is dated in 939 A.H. His coins also are dated in the same year. But his reign must have been a very short one, some say only three months, as there is a coin of his successor Nâser-ud-din Mahmud III dated in the same year 939. There is an inscription of this prince at Gaur bearing the date of 941, but the murder of his predecessor Firoz afforded a pretext for the interference of Sher Shâh, who in 944 A.H., or A.D. 1537-38, invaded Bengal and drove Mahmud from his capital to seek refuge with the Emperor Humâyun. The Eastern Provinces were then placed under an Imperial governor, and Bengal once more became a dependency of the Empire of Delhi.

APPENDIX.

From the " Pioneer " of 17th August 1882.

THE HOT SPRINGS OF TUTTILA PANEE.

(FROM A CORRESPONDENT.)

IN the heart of the Monghyr district there are many places of interest, hitherto seldom, if ever, visited by Europeans. One of these is a weird-looking spot, situated amidst low rocky hills, where rise the hot springs of Tuttila Panee. These springs we had long determined to see, and in the early dawn of a day in February we started on our journey. We were a party of three Europeans and a long following of natives, pleased as children at the chance of seeing a spot little visited, even by themselves, owing to their fear of wild beasts.

Leaving the village of Hazari, with its beautiful cultivation and lovely crops of wheat and poppy in full bloom, we followed the high road to Kurruckpore for some distance, and then turned off towards the north. A narrow cart track led through low jungle, between great masses of quartz, passing huge ant-hills of red earth of a size not often seen. The road soon narrowed to a footpath, and the jungle grew more dense. Young Sukwa trees forced their way up through thorny bushes. Wild dates, alternated with the bastard plum, all thorns and little fruit, and the prickly cactus, hooked the unwary traveller as he scrambled over the rough ground. Ere long shallow ravines began to cross our path, and many a slip or slide brought one or other of our party to a sudden stop ; not to speak of pauses made to listen for the stealthy step of tiger or leopard—a meeting with either or both having been prophesied. Nothing was heard, however, but the cry of the partridge, the cooing of the wood pigeon, or, occasionally, the ghostly note of the great rock-owl, as, startled by the sound of human voices, he winged his way on his heavy pinions over our heads.

We had threaded our way through the jungles for some miles, when suddenly we came on a small clearing. It contained a Santal village and a few ill-cultivated fields. The villagers were sad to see— ill-fed, ragged, and dirty to a degree, and unhealthy, doubtless from bad and insufficient food. The Santals are usually a healthy, happy people, full of life and spirits. The inhabitants of this poor village afford a painful contrast to their more prosperous brethren.

It took us but a short time to cross the whole extent of this small village, and then we plunged again into the jungle. Proceeding forwards for a mile or two, we came unexpectedly on the signs of an age and a people long passed away. Half buried in the ground lay great heaps of well-made and well-burnt bricks of the same size and kind which lie in mounds on the sites of the ruined Forts of Hassanpore and Silivre, and here a shadow of a legend remains—a very uncommon thing in the Monghyr district, where tradition seems dead —of a great temple which once existed on the spot, whose god has fled, and of a king, who reigned over the land, whose name was Bheem Singh. Leaving, reluctantly, the suggestive heaps behind, we plodded on through scrub and briers, through deep ditches and water, till suddenly we came on a lovely stretch of green sward, ending unexpectedly on the edge of precipitous banks, between which ran as lovely a river as ever prompted a painter's pencil or poet's verse. The clear stream ran between steep banks, over which hung a wealth of tropical foliage, between whose branches the sun poured rays which coloured the deep clear waters with lines of crimson and blue. Great rocks here and there intercepted the stream, round which the water swished with a low rushing sound, refreshing to the ear, and then stole on, hiding its bright waters between the sheltered banks. We crossed the stream, ascended the opposite side, and continued our journey towards a low range of rocky hills in a valley amongst which, at length, we found the object of our travels—the hot springs of Tuttila Panee.

Very strange was the scene. The space enclosed within these dreary unclothed hills was cracked and rifted in every direction, and from numberless fissures crept out small streams of boiling water, so hot indeed that, even after being exposed to the cool air for many minutes, one could not bear a hand in it. Wherever one looked the water was bursting forth. From the sides of the hills, from cracks in the ground, from under loose stones, it made its way till, collecting in one large stream, the waters rippled quietly away, sending up great clouds of steam, which floated up and filled the valley like a cauldron.

Within twenty yards of the largest of these hot springs lies, under the shadow of a few fine trees, *an ice cool pool of clear water*, supplied by a spring which bubbles up from the bosom of the earth. Floating on its surface are small star-shaped, white water-lilies, with a yellow centre, and overhanging the low banks, lovely ferns, which mirror themselves on the bosom of this fairy lake. This, the only verdant spot at all near, with its cool waters, was a mystery to all, considering the steam, and heat, and barrenness that prevailed everywhere else. The water here was pure and sweet; as was also the water of the springs, when cooled, resembling in taste that of the famous Seta Khond, near Monghyr.

By a slight circuit, on leaving the hot springs, we reached the Bheem Bund, supposed to be an embankment raised by the king Bheem Singh. This embankment is evidently natural, caused by the force of a torrent which has torn away the earth, leaving a giant wall of rock standing on one side of the stream, and a rugged bank of earth and fallen stones on the other side, above which rise forest trees of splendid growth. The termination of the wall, rounded like a tower, ending in a deep pool, rises high and clear against the sky, its sides beautifully coloured by time and the oxides of iron. The end of the tower discloses the semblance of a door *deep sunk* in the rock, the sill of which touches the surface of the deep still pool; and a wondrous story of a secret passage leading down from a castle, which was supposed to have existed above, is told by the natives, but of which no sign exists. Sweeping round the edge of the pool rise well-wooded banks, shadowed by great trees, and no sweeter spot could be imagined than this, in which lie all the elements of sylvan beauty.

We scrambled out of our beautiful valley, being called on *en route* to notice a great perpendicular slab of stone which, bedded in a bank, sounded hollow when struck. In bygone days, when men were holier, and the gods better loved the earth, this slab was an open door, at which stood ever ready brass vessels of food to which every one was welcome on one condition, that the vessels should be replaced as soon as the food was eaten. On an evil day one of the vessels was stolen, and from that time the food disappeared and the rocky door closed for ever.

We regained the level plains, and reached a Ghatwal village, still more startlingly miserable-looking than the Santal one before mentioned; for, in addition to dirt and starvation, leprosy prevailed to a frightful extent. Leprosy in every degree, from the incipient thickening of the lobes of the ears and flesh of the forehead, till it arrived at the awful stage when the fingers and toes dropped off. The sick and the well seemed all to live together. The disease was so common that no particular notice seemed to be taken of it.

Huge mounds of slag were scattered about in every direction, which showed that smelting of iron had been carried on to some extent at some distant time by a people who had departed. The Ghatwals appear to exist on the products of the few poor fields granted to them in bygone times, on condition of their guarding the passes of the hills, and assisting travellers on their journeys through them, and protecting them from the attacks of wild beasts, the imprints of whose feet we saw surrounding a small pool of water not far off.   The sun was by this time high up in the heavens, but before leaving this place we were once more called on to view, not far off, a deep hole in the ground, lately dug.   We were told that the zemindar of this place, who is himself a descendant of that Kamdar Khan who was once a powerful ruler in Khurruckpore, had found in his family papers a record of a great buried treasure.   After long study of these records the zemindar had decided that a level space of rocky ground, surrounded by jungle, was, without doubt, the place where the treasure lay hid.   Hither he came with his picks and shovels, and laboured long, finding nothing, however, to repay him for his labour and his pains.

We soon regained the track by which we had entered the jungle, and, travelling on in sun and shade, we reached, ere long, our temporary home beneath the beautiful tope of mango and tamarind trees, where our tents were pitched, pleased to have accomplished the end we had long had in view—a visit to the hot springs of Tuttila Panee.

INDEX.

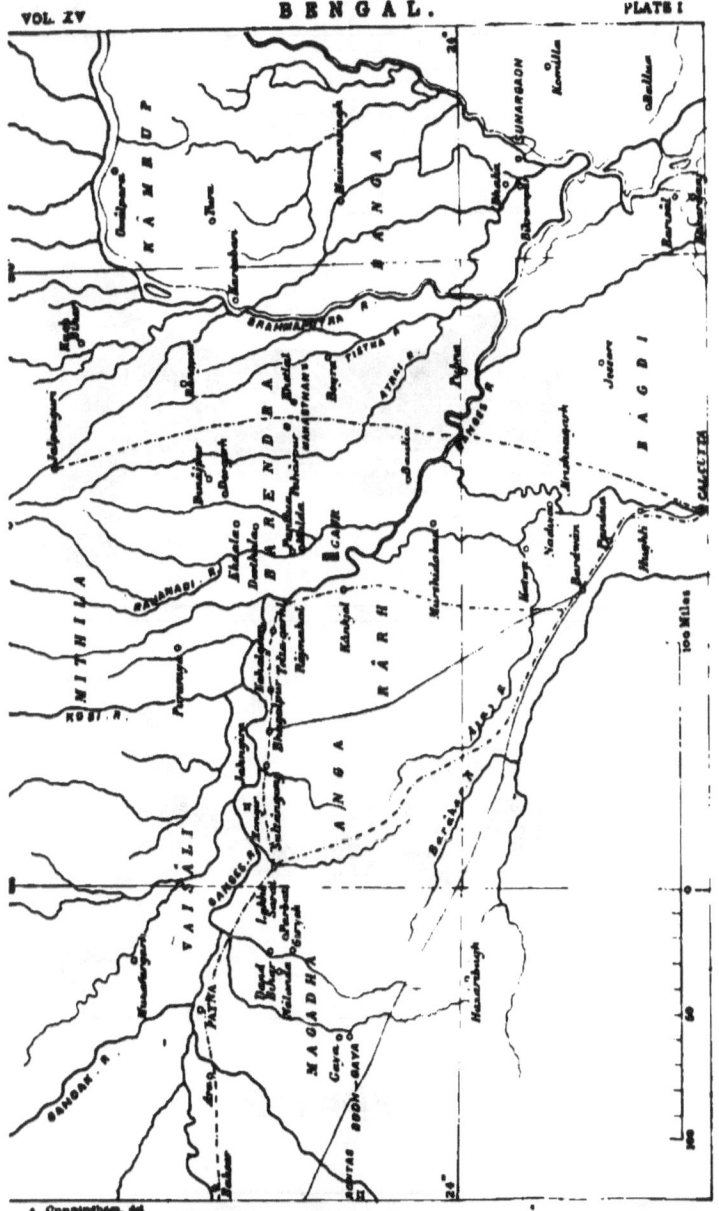

A Cunningham, del.

Lithographed at the Surveyor General's Office, Calcutta. September 1882.

ᛋᛉᛂᚤᚢᛈᚸᛏ

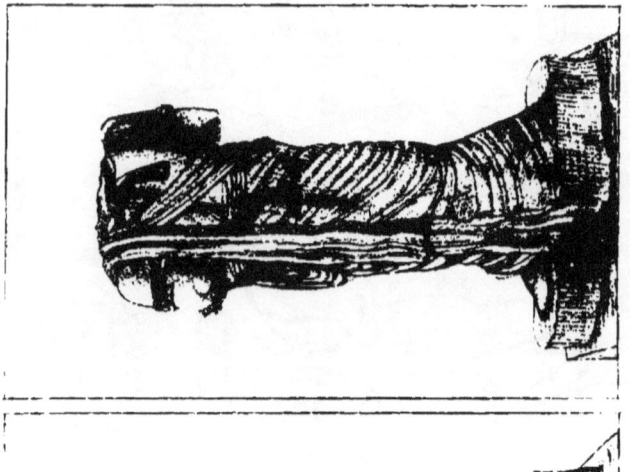

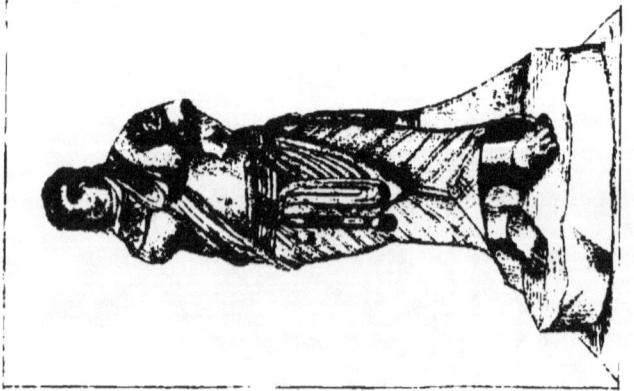

ᚤᛉᛏᚢᚦᚴᚢᛏ

. B. W. Garrick. del

Lithographed at the Surveyor General's Office, Calcutta, September 1883.

SEALS FOUND IN THE GANGES.

PANCH - PAHARI.

STONE STOOLS.

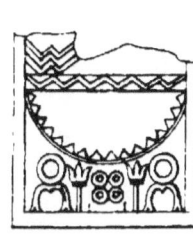 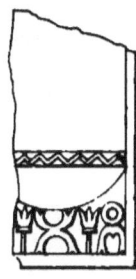 

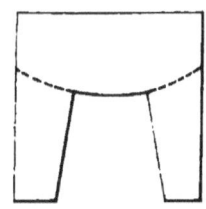 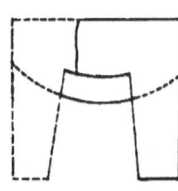

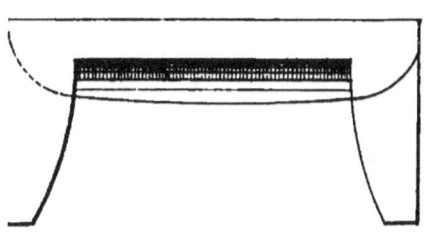 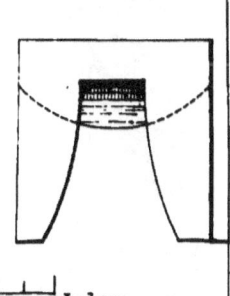

L. Cunningham, del.

Lithographed at the Surveyor General's Office, Calcutta, September 1882.

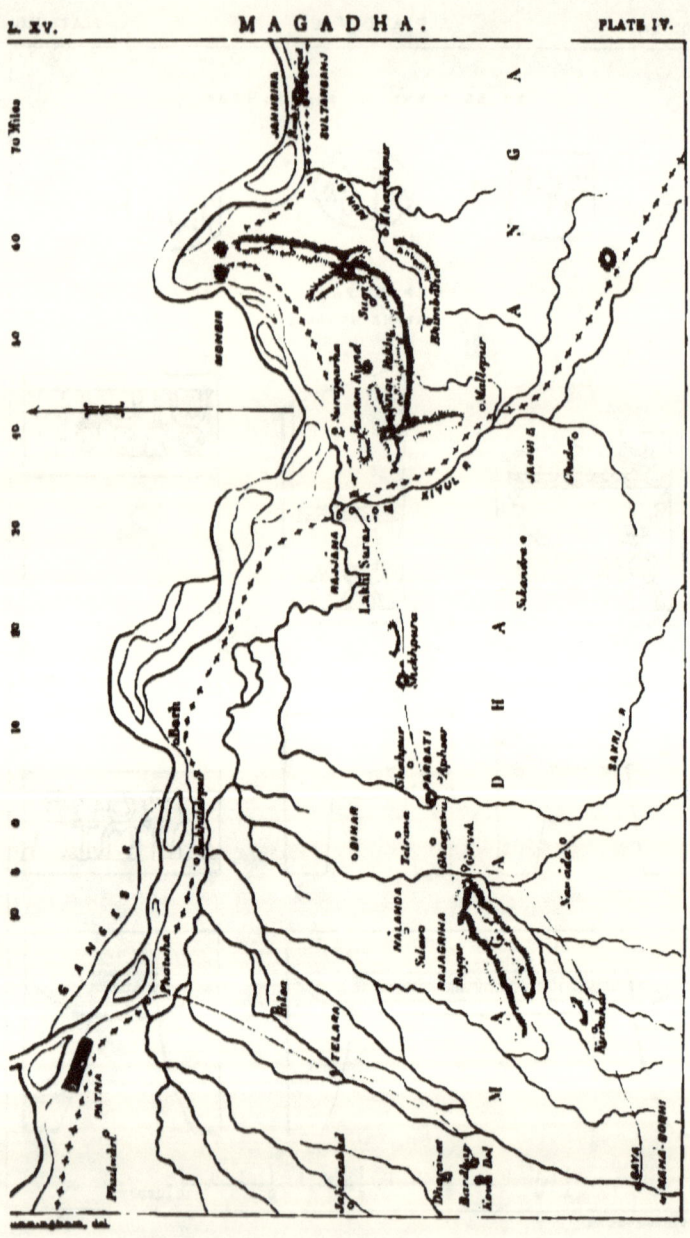

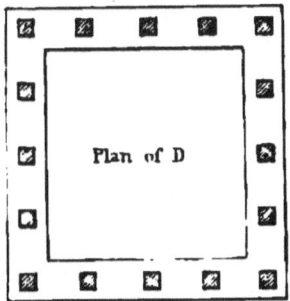

Plan of D

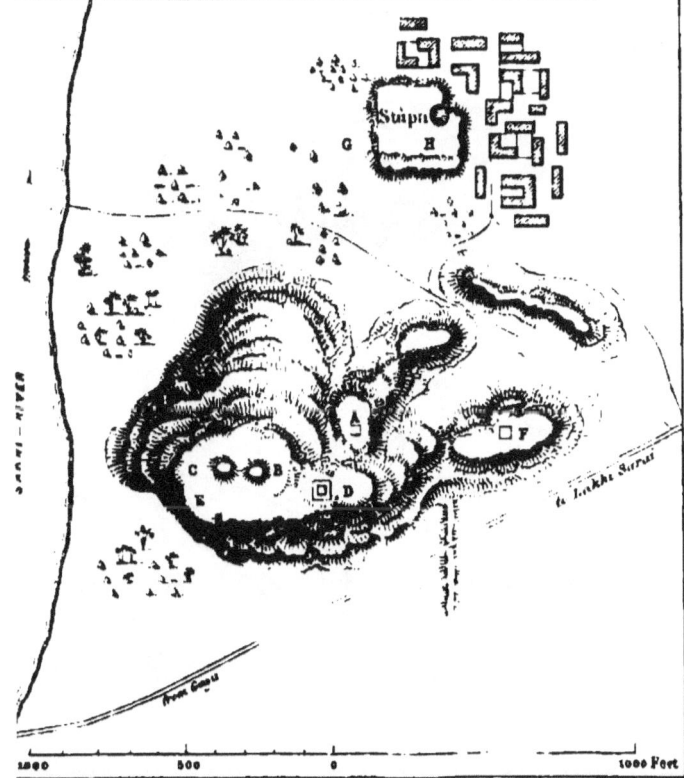

Cunningham, del.

Lithographed at the Surveyor General's Office, Calcutta. September 1872.

LUMP OF UNBAKED CLAY.

1

2

CLAY SEAL.   LAC SEAL.

3   4

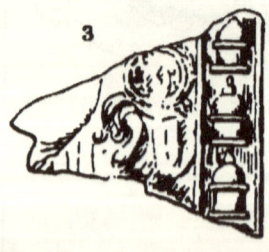
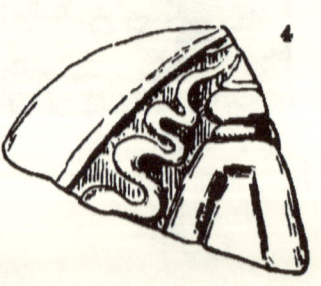

Cunningham, del.

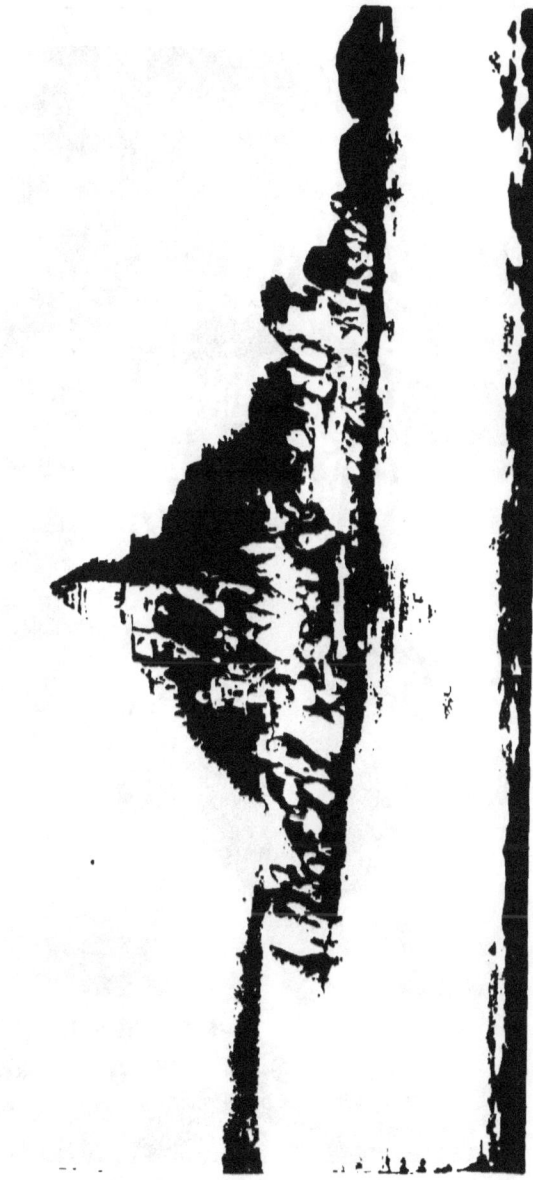

in y J D B r Reb ored at the Surveyor Genera   e   h

Photographed by J. D. Beglar

Lithographed at the Surveyor General's Office, Calcutta. November 1875.

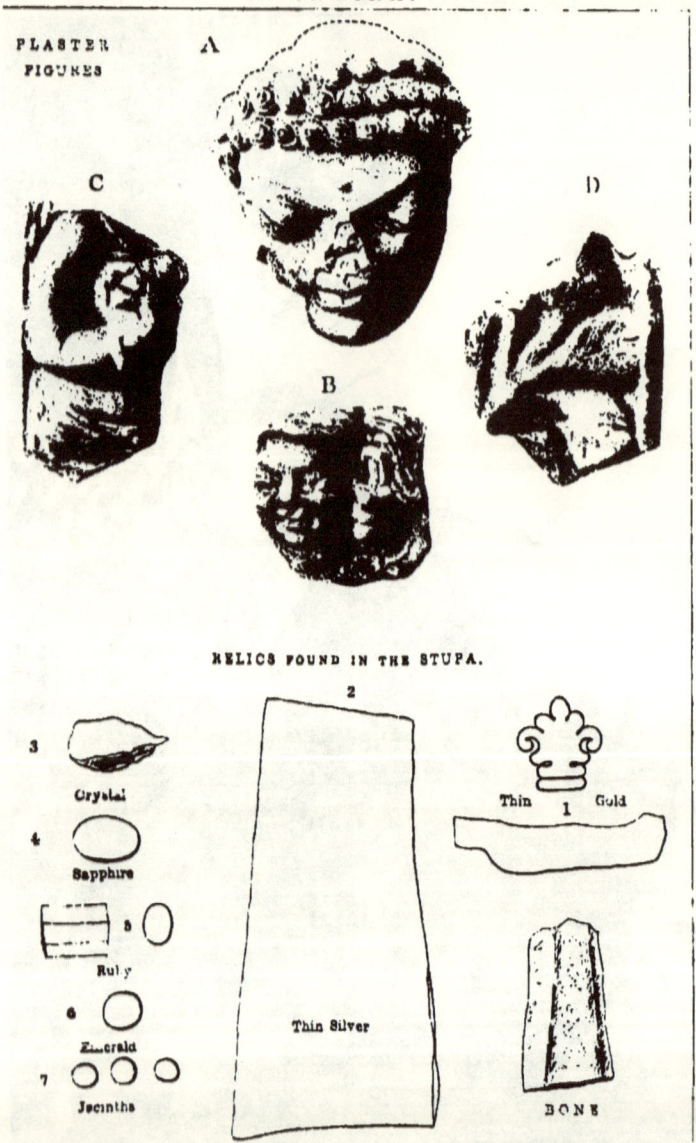

PLASTER FIGURES

A

C

D

B

RELICS FOUND IN THE STUPA.

2

3
Crystal

4
Sapphire

5
Ruby

6
Emerald

7
Jacintha

Thin Silver

Thin 1 Gold

BONE

A Cunningham. del

Lithographed at the Surveyor General's Office, Calcutta, November 1879.

SHAHPUR STATUE OF SURYA.

AHNGIRA MASJID ROCK.

2

3   **4**

5 - JAHNGIRA ROCK.

NGI - RISHI 6 - TEMPLE.

7 - PEDESTAL.

AHALGAON.

Rock-cut Temple.

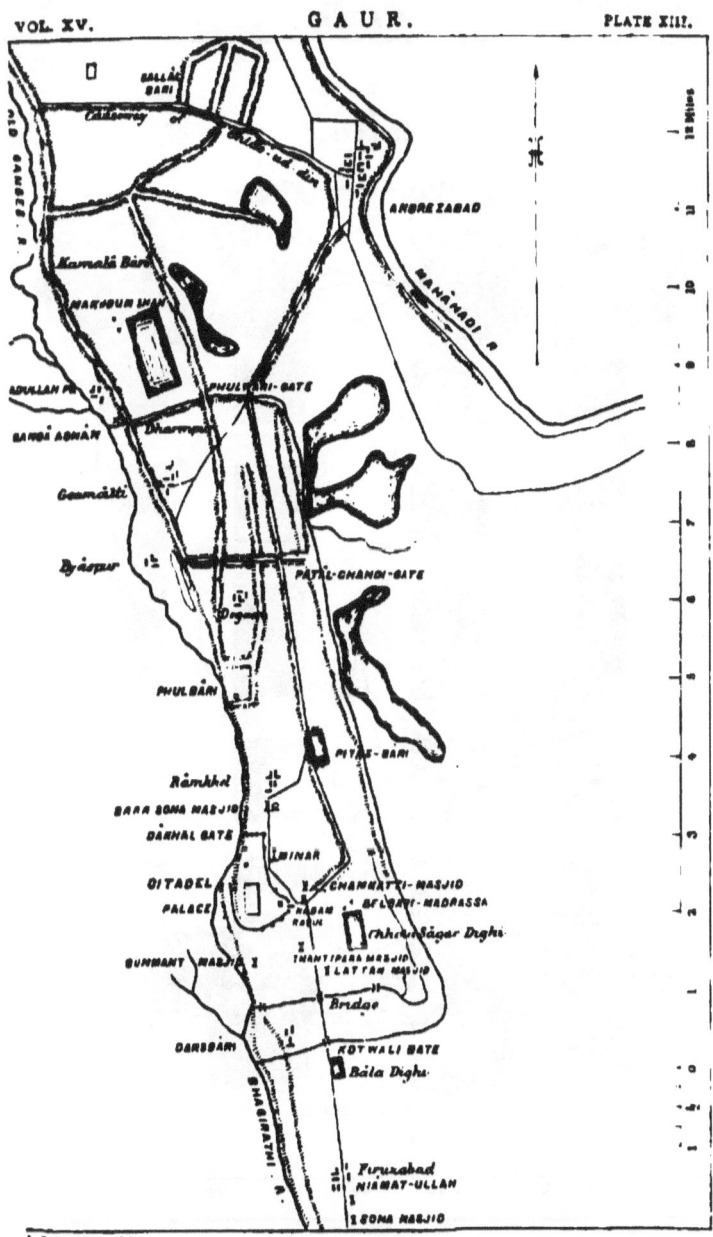

A Cunningham, del.

Lithographed at the Surveyor General's Office, Calcutta September 1882.

DAKHAL — GATE
OF
CITADEL

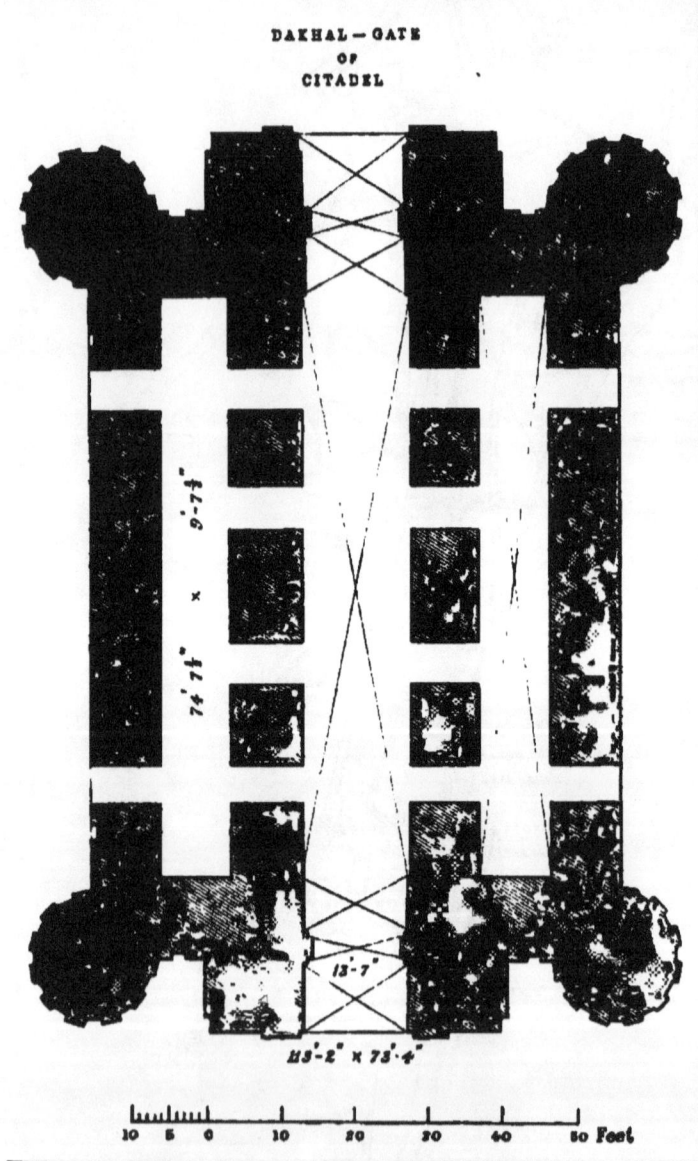

10 5 0   10   20   30   40   50 Feet

A. Cunningham, del.

Lithographed at the Surveyor General's Office Calcutta September 1880

BARA SONA MASJID.

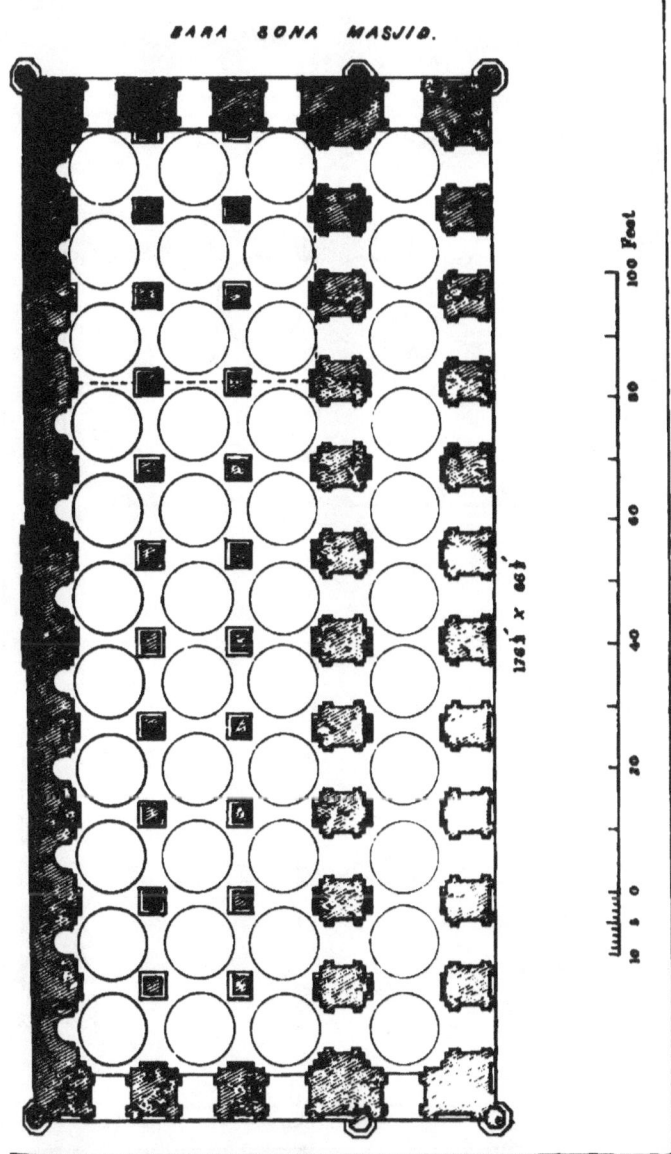

100 Feet

176½' x 66½'

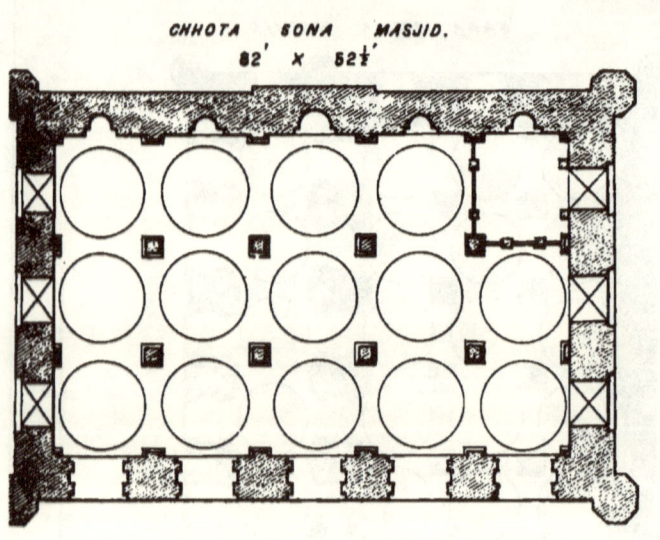

CHHOTA SONA MASJID.
82' × 52½'

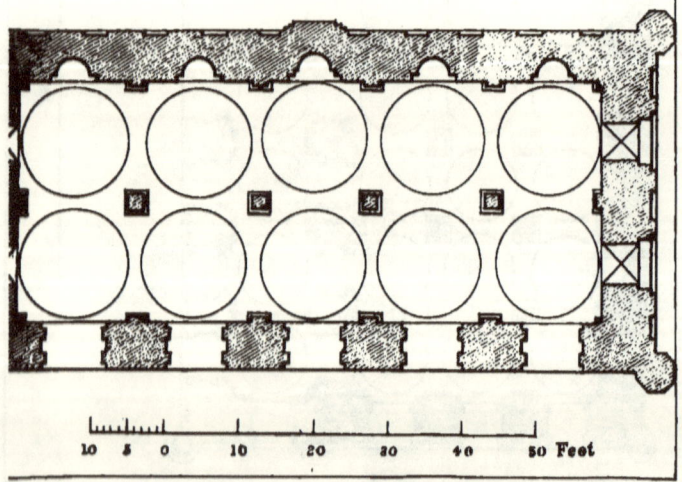

THÂNTIPÂRA MASJID.
91' × 43½'

10 5 0   10   20   30   40   50 Feet

sasa, del.

Lithographed at the Surveyor General's Office, Calcutta, September 1888.

THÂNTIPARA MASJID.

EKLAKHI TOMB - HAZRAT PANDUA.

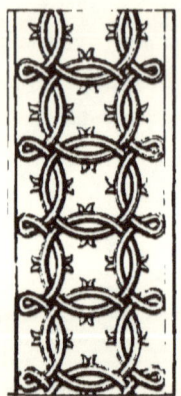 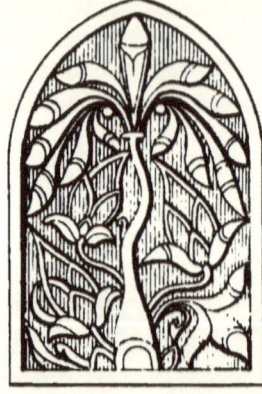 

THÂNTIPARA - MASJID.

A Cunningham, del.

Lithographed at the Surveyor General's Office, Calcutta, September 1882.

CHAMKATTA MASJID.
50'-4" × 34'-10"

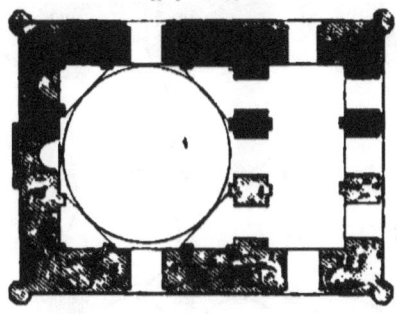

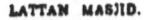

LATTAN MASJID.
74½' × 51'

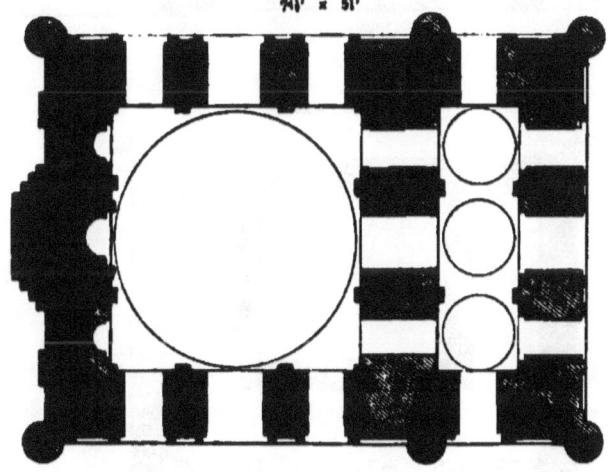

10   5   0   10   20   30   40   50 Feet

A. Cunningham, del.

Lithographed at the Surveyor General's Office Calcutta, September 1892

GÜNMANT MASJID
140'-9" × 53'-3½

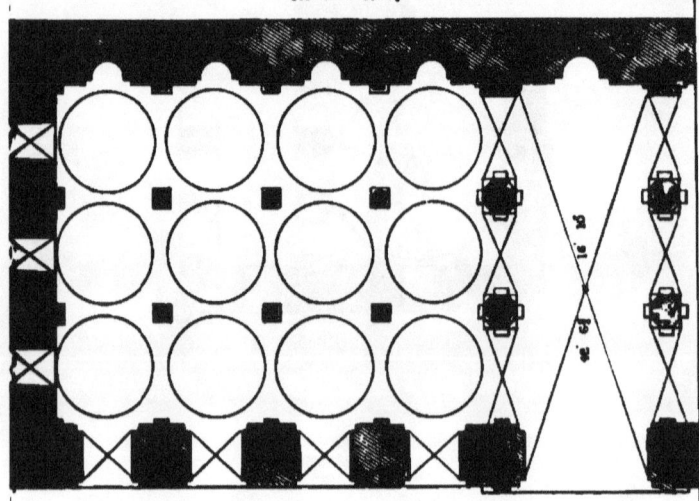

KADAM RASUL MASJID.
63'-3" × 43'-9"

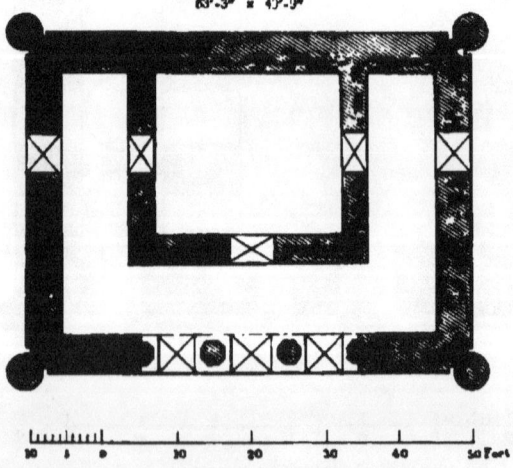

ILTITMISH — A.H. — 630.

GHIÂS-UD-DIN AZAM — A.D. 792—911.

MAHMUD. I — A.H. — 863.

INSCRIPTION
OF
JALAL-UD-DIN MASAUD JANI.
A.H. - 647 = A.D. - 1249.

Photo by J. Craddck

Lithographed at the Surveyor General's Office Calcutta September 1882

INSCRIPTION

OF

YÚSUF SHAH.

A.H. 884.

w by J Craddock.

Lithographed at the Surveyor General's Office Calcutta September 1872

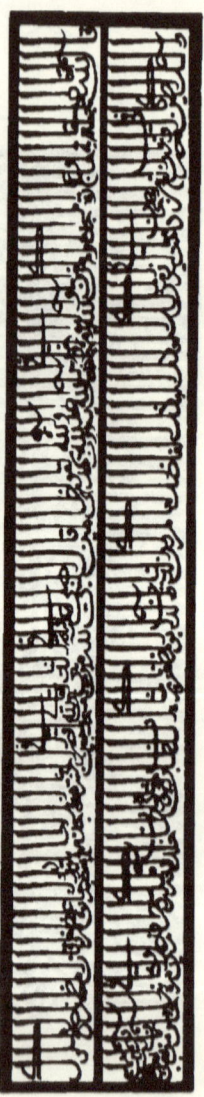

Photographs by J. Craddock.

Lithographed at the Surveyor General's Office, Calcutta, September 1898.

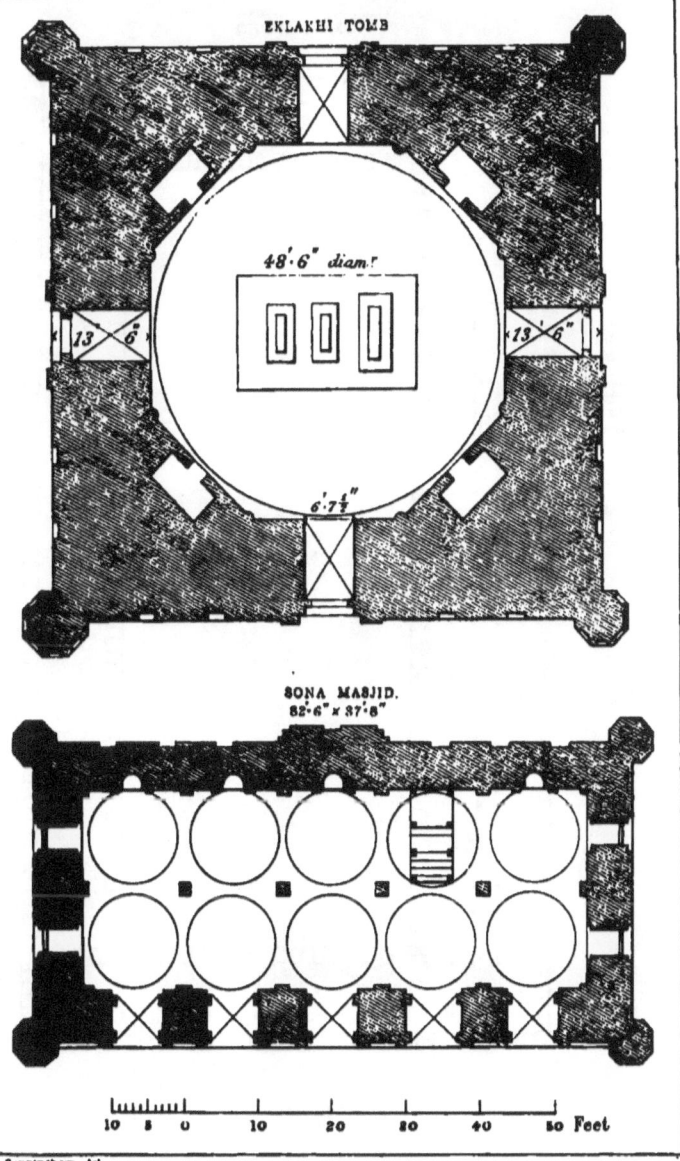

EKLAKHI TOMB

48′·6″ diam.ʳ

13′ 6″   13′ 6″

6′·7¼″

SONA MASJID.
82′·6″ × 37′·8″

10 5 0   10   20   30   40   50 Feet

. Cunningham, del.

Lithographed at the Surveyor General's Office, Calcutta, September 1882.

JÂMI MASJID

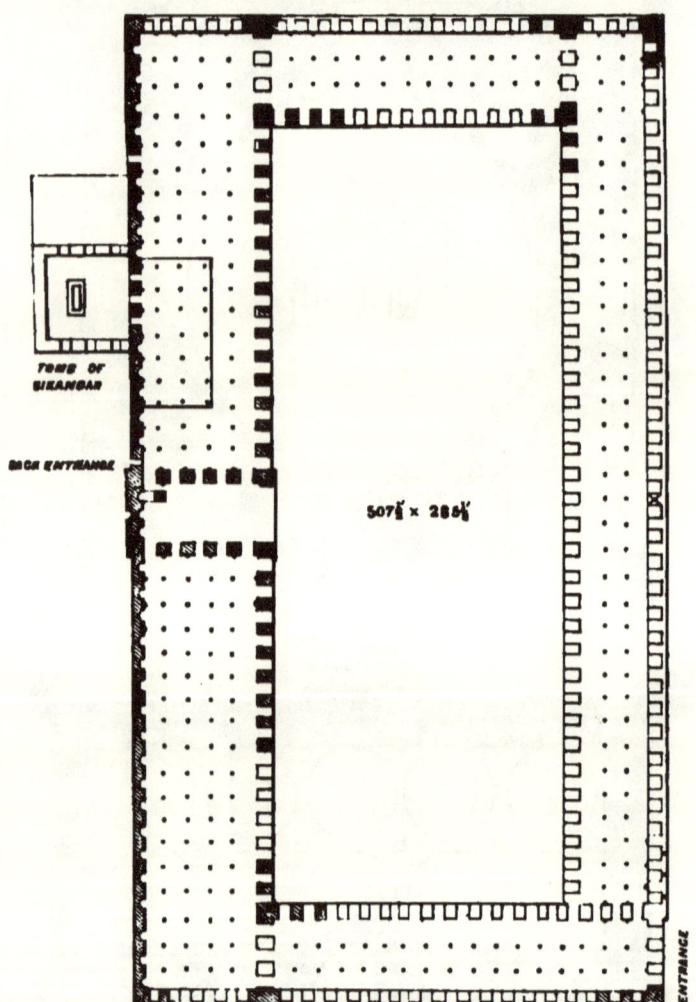

507⅝ × 285½'

TOMB OF SIKANDAR

BACK ENTRANCE

ENTRANCE

CARVED BRICKS.
EKLAKHI TOMB.

VISHNU.

18 inches × 7¼ inches.

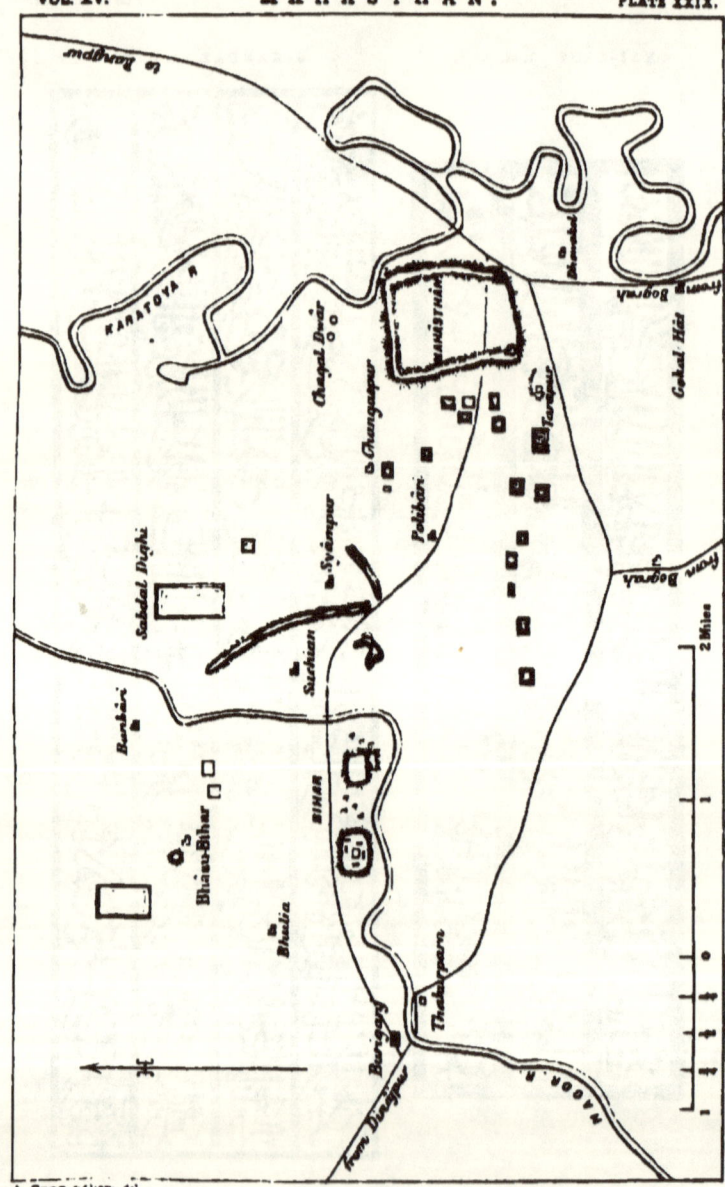

A. Cunningham. del

Lithographed at the Surveyor General's Office, Calcutta. September 1882.

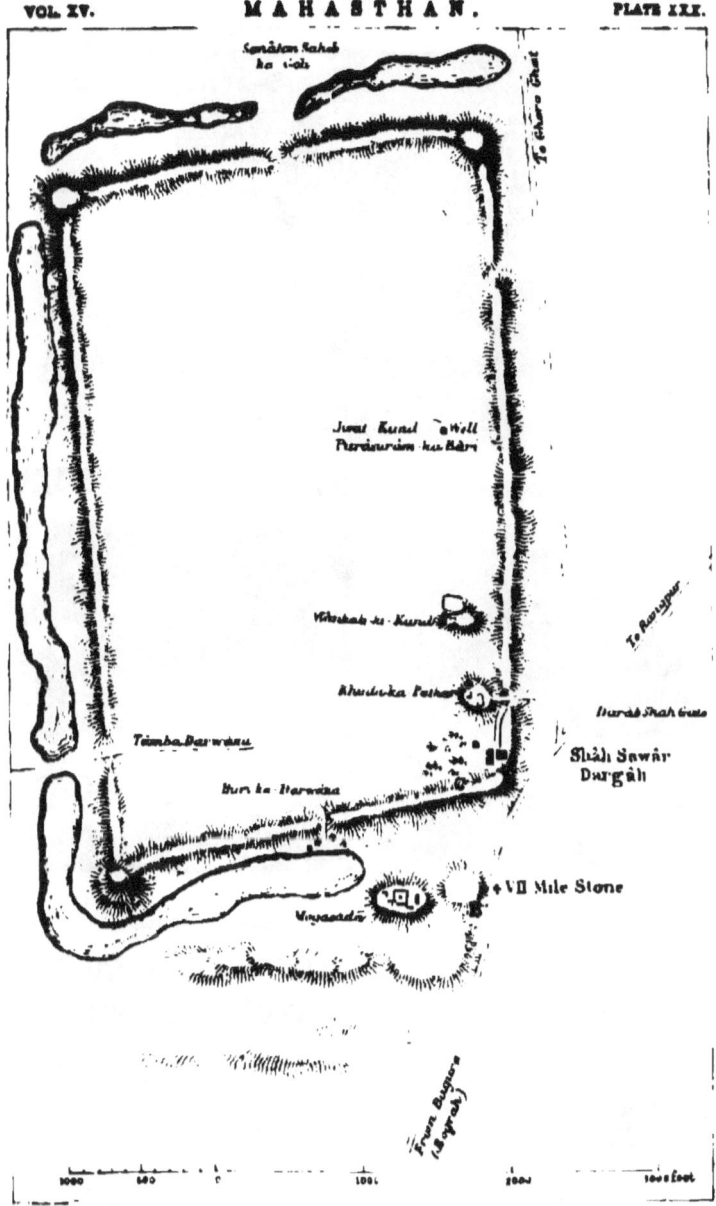

A. Cunningham, Sol.

Lithographed at the Surveyor General's Office Calcutta, September 1882.

Bracket

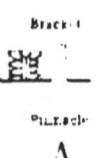

Pinnacle

under side

Eaves

5"   5"

Pinnacle

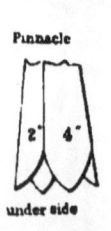

2"   4"

under side

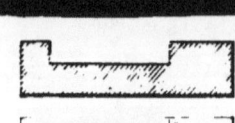

On Door-jambs of Darg'éh.

শ্রীল বর্ধিনুদাসস্ক ॥

শ্রীল বর্ধিনুদাসস্ক ॥

on Base of Statue.

বয়হার ॥

CARVED BRICKS.

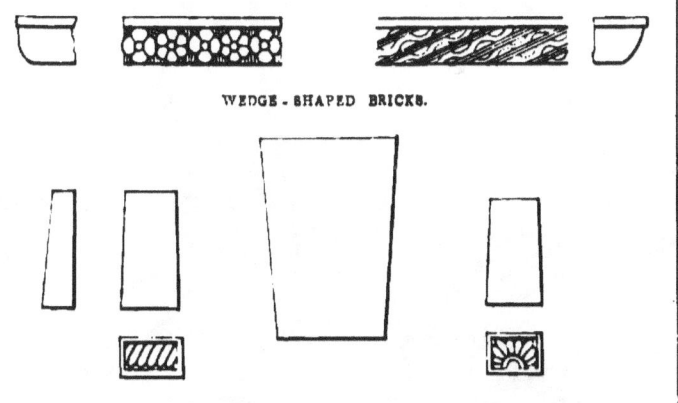

WEDGE - SHAPED BRICKS.

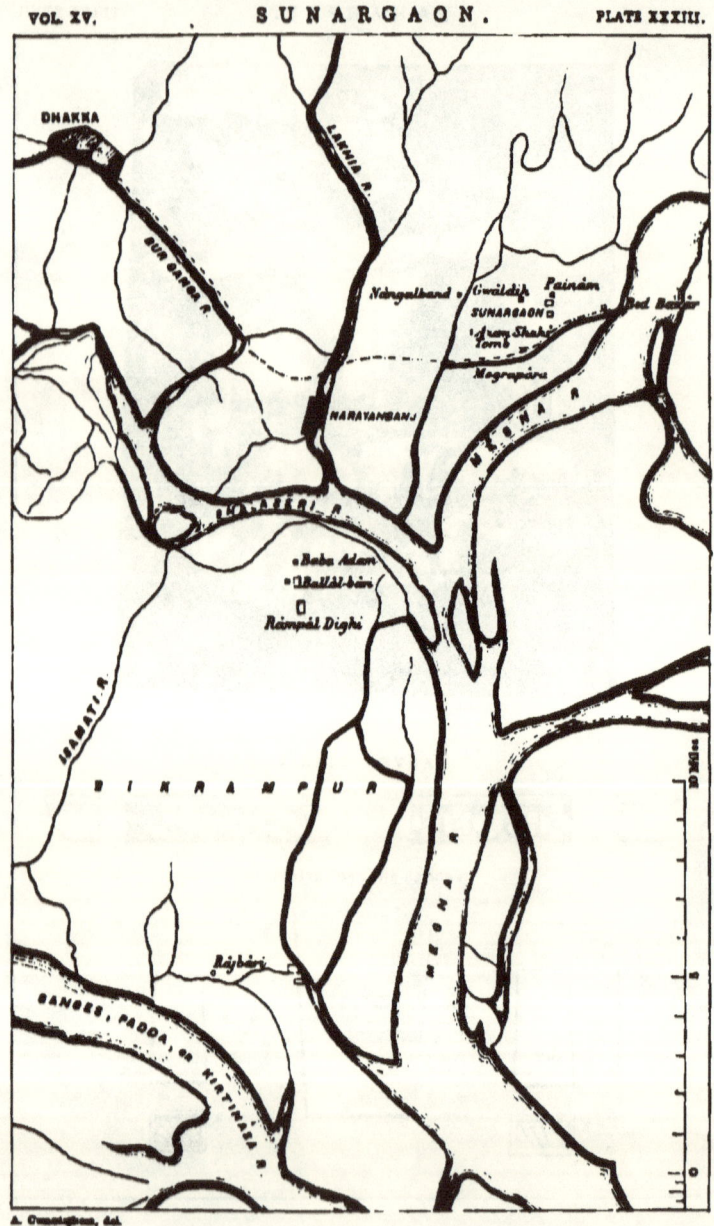

A. Cunningham, del.

Lithographed at the Surveyor General's Office, Calcutta, September 1879.

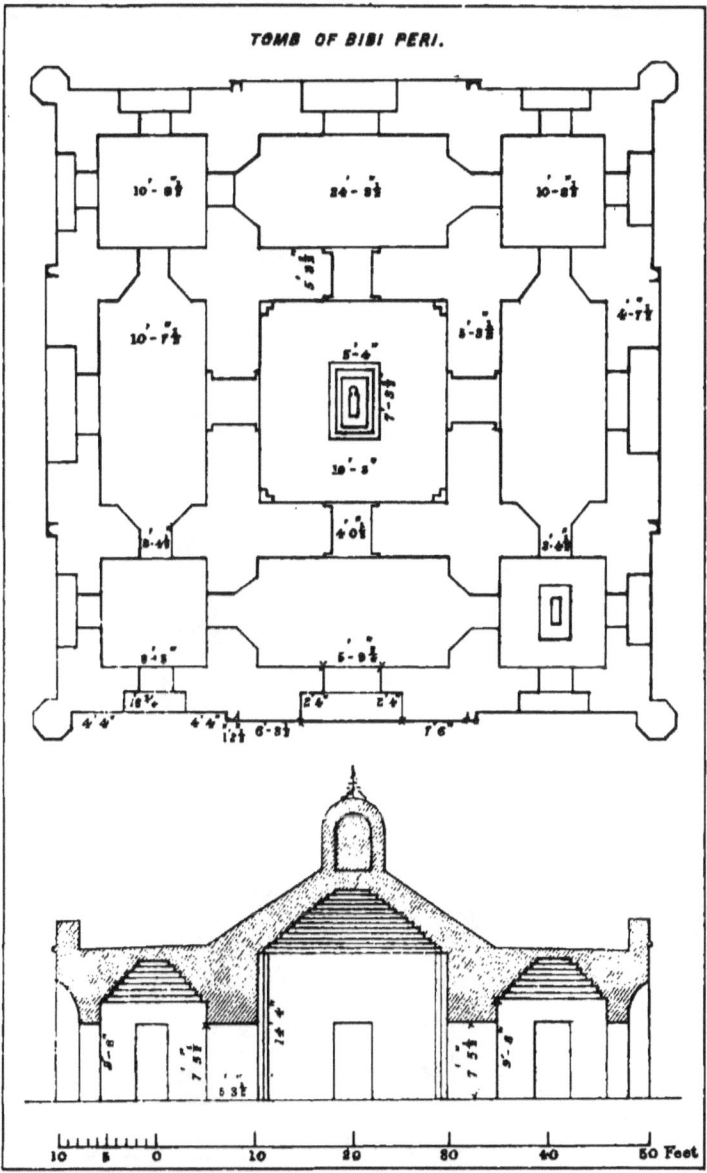

TOMB OF BIBI PERI.

A. Cunningham, del.

Lithographed at the Surveyor General's Office, Calcutta. September 1882.

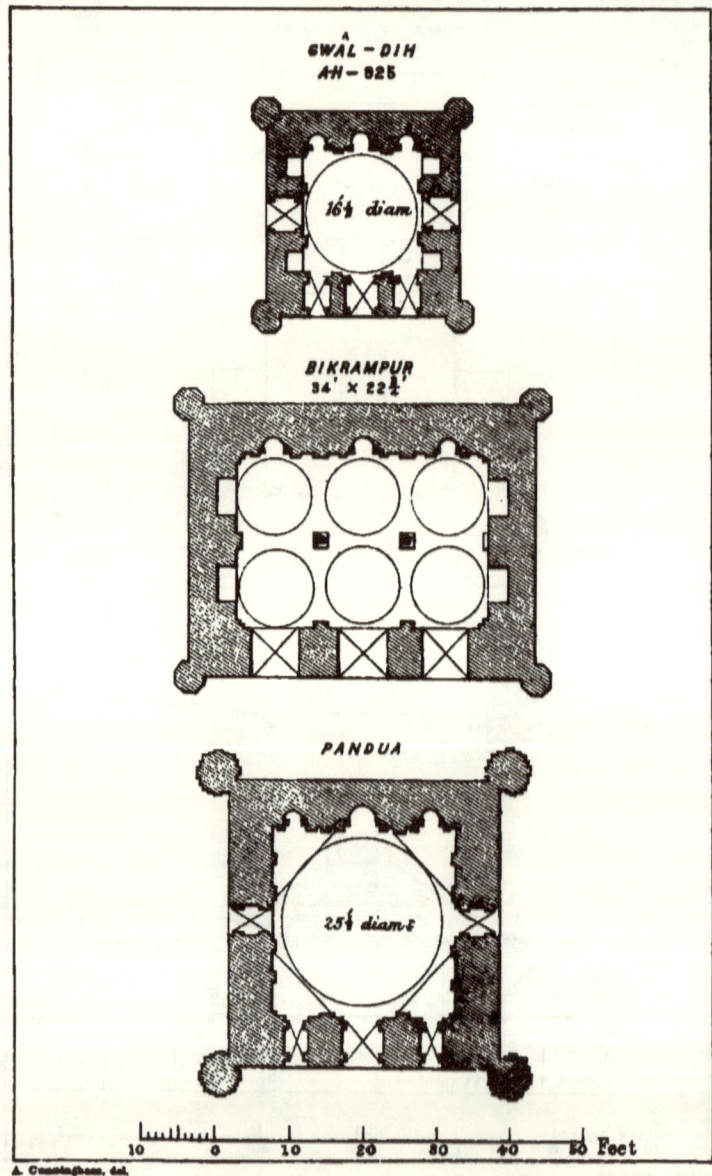

A
GWAL – DIH
AH – 925

16½ diam

BIKRAMPUR
34' × 22½'

PANDUA

25½ diam=ᵗ

10   0   10   20   30   40   50 Feet

A. Cunningham, del.

Lithographed at the Surveyor General's Office, Calcutta, September 1882.